DISTRICT
NURSE

DISTRICT NURSE

by
Lucy Agnes Hancock

DISTRICT NURSE

To

Florence and Lida

BECAUSE THEY LOVE MY STORIES

CHAPTER ONE

I THINK YOU'RE a very foolish and stubborn girl, Deborah," Mrs. Hackett said as she prepared to bid her daughter goodbye. "And why you should wish to keep on messing around with a lot of poor foreign children is a mystery to me. I can't think how you got that way in the first place. Even though your grandfather Bradley was a surgeon, surely that fact is no reason for devoting your life to nursing. Come on, darling. Christmas is over and you did your full duty by every sick child in your district. The worst three months of winter are still to come. I'll stay another day. Let's get away from this bitter northern climate. We'll have fun down south and you may meet the right man—one often does, you know. I always say Florida is the most romantic spot in the world, and I should know."

"Yes, you should know, Mother," Deborah answered, a smile curving her lips. "I think you're the youngest, most fascinating woman I know and I don't wonder men fall in love with you. But, darling, your last two marriages weren't very successful, now were they? I wish you would be careful——"

"If they weren't successful, was that my fault? I'm sure I had no idea Henry was hopelessly lazy when I married him. I assure you he took good care to keep it well hidden. And as for Sam Hackett—well, the less said about him, the better. I can't understand your——"

"Mother," Deborah protested, "the only thing I blame you for is being so lovely that men lose their heads over you." She put her arms about her mother and hugged her. "Only do be careful this time, darling. I would come with you only it would do no good, you know. You always do just exactly as you please. But promise me you'll watch your step and not rush into anything you'll be sorry for later."

Mrs. Bradley-Burt-Hackett looked up at her tall young daughter and her wide blue eyes darkened for a moment. "Sometimes I think there must be a mistake—that you're the mother and I the daughter," she complained. "Really, Deborah, I'm sure I never worried about you. I never filled your ears with warnings not to do this or that."

"There was no occasion, darling," Deborah reminded her. "You see, I'm like Father entirely sane, not too attractive and——"

"You could be attractive if you would only spend a little time on yourself."

"Oh, no, Mother. I lack what it takes—also I'm afraid I lack the inclination. I think they're about ready to start, darling." She pulled her mother into her strong young arms again and kissed her. "Have a grand time, precious, and——"

"Do be careful!" her mother mimicked and made an appealing little grimace as she hurried toward the waiting plane. "Now don't wait, Deb," she called over her shoulder. "It's terribly bad luck to watch a departure, you know. 'Bye, honey!"

Deborah waited until she saw her mother disappear inside then turned and walked swiftly to where she had parked her car. The plane was coming alive and she turned the little car and started to leave the airport, her eyes still on the pulsing monster crouched ready to soar aloft. There was a sudden wild yell, a ripping sound and her little coupé swerved halfway round. The taxi stopped and the driver began a tirade against women drivers. Deborah stared coldly at him.

"Want a ten acre lot to turn around in?" the man demanded sarcastically. "Women drivers!"

The occupant of the taxi had stepped to the ground, a bag and brief case in one hand, his hat under his arm.

"Never mind the fireworks," he said sharply, as he handed the driver a bill. Then he took a step toward Deborah and held out a card. "Send the bill to me," he murmured. "I'm sorry—my fault. I'll see you again," and he was running toward the plane.

The taxi driver stared open-mouthed at the bill in his hand and Deborah brought him sharply back to earth.

"I have a good mind to report you for reckless driving, Mat Chico," she said firmly.

He looked at her, his eyes still glazed. "Did you see what that guy gave me?" he asked, holding it out for her inspection. It was a twenty-dollar bill.

"Probably he meant you to pay for the damage to my car," Deborah told him. "You certainly gave that fender a permanent wave all right. It belongs to the City you know so you'd better see what you can do and at once. I can't drive a car looking like that, Mat."

Mat growled something unintelligible and began working on the crumpled fender. "I can fix her all right, Miss Bradley," he promised. "It won't cost you a cent."

"I'm sure it won't," Deborah assured him. "You see, it wasn't my fault at all. You were driving at a sinful rate and might have killed me."

"But the guy hadda get that plane, Miss Bradley. He's gotta be in Florida by Thursday. He'll be in South America prob'ly by night or he acted as if he would. Twenty bucks, Miss Bradley! What that won't do for Angela an' me! Oh boy!"

The droning of the plane was dying away. Deborah shaded her eyes and stared after it.

"Oh, I hope she'll be sensible this time," she worried as the plane dwindled to a mere dot above the horizon of tree tops. "Maybe I should have gone, but what good would it have done? Anyway, she'll need every cent of that money—bless her!"

"There!" Mat said, straightening his back with a groan. "Pretty good, ain't it?"

"No. It's terrible! It won't do at all, Mat," she said firmly as she viewed the result of his work on the fender. "I'll follow you to the first garage and we'll both stay right there until that fender is fixed right, understand?"

"Now, Miss Bradley, you know I gotta get on the job. I work on a schedule an'——" began Mat, his voice taking on a whine intended to evoke pity. It did nothing of the sort, however.

"You'll either stay and see this fender is fixed properly, or I'm going to your boss and tell him you're not fit to drive one of his taxicabs. Which is it to be, Mat?"

"Aw, you wouldn't do that, Miss Bradley," Mat pleaded, his velvety black eyes forlorn. "You know I'm a swell driver an' I didn't mean to ram you—it was that you——"

"Oh, no you don't, Mat," Deborah interrupted quickly. "You can't blame it on me. Why, even your fare acknowledged it was your fault."

"The dirty double-crosser!" Mat cried angrily. "He told me to drive like hell, didn't he?"

"All right, Mat, and he paid you well for doing it, but I'm sure he didn't want you to smash the fender of an innocent bystander."

"Honest, I didn't do it a-purpose, Miss Bradley, an' —oh, aw right. Let's get goin'. I know Tony Germani's place here at the Forks an' we'll get yer fender fixed. Okay?"

"Okay. Lead on, Macduff," Deborah ordered and pressed the starter.

It cost two dollars to straighten the fender and she watched Mat pay for it with dimes and nickels and pennies counted into Tony's greasy palm. She wondered what he was going to do with that twenty dollars the stranger had given him—by mistake, she had no doubt. Well, it would serve the man right if he found himself financially embarrassed before he reached his destination. There was no sense in being so careless with money.

"Thanks, Mat," Deborah smiled, when Tony pocketed his pay and kicked her nearest tire experimentally. "There's air enough," she told him, "and I don't need gas or oil just now. If I do when I'm out this way, I'll stop. You did a very good job on that fender."

Tony beamed toothily on her. "Fine? First class," he said proudly. "You come soon—Tony give service—first class!"

Deborah followed Mat's taxi for the first mile and a half then turned into a side road and sped toward town. She had one or two places to visit before going back to the Center and the first was the Polycletus family where there were two victims of the recent infantile paralysis flare-up. She parked her car in front of the big frame tenement on Fernald Street and a swarm of youngsters were instantly on the running board.

"Give us a ride, Miss Bradley," they shouted. She shook her head, frowning severely, but they only grinned at her. They weren't afraid of her frowns. Didn't she bring them fruit and ice cream when they were sick, and toys at Christmas?

"Hello, Nurse!" an older girl called from a nearby basement. "Const cried all night last night an' now he's

yellin' somethin' fierce. Mis' P'letus 'most killed Ma fer
'phonin' Doc; but he was out anyways. An' she won't
let anyone in there. Bet you can't get in either. She's a
devil when she's mad. Ma says she guesses he ain't long
fer this world. Ain't it awful, Miss Bradley?" The girl
seemed not to have breathed between sentences and repeated the news with morbid relish.

Deborah slipped from her car, taking the key with
her, and hurried up the five flights to the top floor apartment of the Polycletus family. The place was clean
enough but pitifully meager. Mrs. Polycletus, still re-
taining traces of her girlish beauty in spite of her hard
life, stood at the door of the dark little bedroom from
which came long-drawn sighs and moans of pain. Her
hands were clenched and her face looked belligerent. A
boy of about four lay on a folded quilt on the living
room floor, his hands moving restlessly as he tried to cap-
ture a sunbeam that slanted palely through the one window. Deborah bent over him for a minute and spoke.

"Hello, there, Philip!" She smiled and he smiled back
at her, his cheeks dimpling. She caught one of his hands
in hers and he tugged hard in an effort to pull himself to
a sitting position. Deborah caught her breath at the look
of bewilderment in his eyes when he found his efforts vain.
She rose hastily and hurried into the bedroom.

Const was seven—a beautiful boy before he was
stricken, but now twisted and helpless. His fever was high
and he was raving in delirium. Deborah paled at sight of
the child and turned an accusing face to his mother.

"Why wasn't Doctor Brown sent for? This is terrible!
Oh, how could you?" Then, more calmly and with the
firmness she had found from experience brought results,
she said: "We must get him to the hospital at once, Mrs.
Polycletus. There's not a moment to lose. Run out and
telephone now—tell Mr. Fenerro at the corner—he'll do
it. Mercy Hospital and tell them I ordered it. Mercy
Hospital and hurry. I'll stay right here—only hurry—
hurry!"

Cowed by the girl's crisp, authoritative manner, the
boy's mother hurried away and it was not long until the
siren of the ambulance drew neighbors to the street and
sent youngsters scurrying into doorways. Little Const

Polycletus was taken away and the neighbors shook their heads fatalistically. Const would never come back alive!

Deborah lingered. Mrs. Polycletus was stoically calm. The more emotional neighbors wept and moaned and called upon Heaven and the saints to witness their grief. Only Deborah realized how intense and bitter was the mother's silent suffering. She sat on the floor beside Philip, his hand in hers, his wide blue eyes searching her face. Since his illness, Philip talked but little.

"I'm sure Philip will recover in time, Mrs. Polycletus," Deborah told her gently. "His attack was milder and he is getting stronger. I could feel it when he tried to pull himself upright. We must get him to the Reconstruction Hospital as soon as possible. He will respond very quickly, I'm sure."

"You would take both my sons from me?" the mother muttered accusingly. "Their father will not have it."

"He will when he understands, I'm sure," Deborah soothed. "How much better that Philip should be where he can have the best of care, the newest treatment and be watched every minute of the day and night. Some day Philip will be strong and well like other boys."

"I watch him, too. You say Philip will be well some day? Const—my firstborn?"

Deborah shook her head sadly. "I don't know. We can only hope, Mrs. Polycletus. Wonderful things have been done and at the hospital they know what is best for him. Keep up your courage and trust us, for you may be sure we are doing all we can."

She made her way carefully along the narrow halls and down the rickety stairs. One never knew what might be lurking there—anything from a bedraggled kitten to an equally bedraggled child. Why on earth didn't the city do something about this wretched place? Everyone knew it was a fire-trap. It had been condemned years ago and yet every tiny flat was crowded. As soon as one family moved out there was another moving in. The city fathers would wait until something terrible happened; then they would hold up their hands in horror and shake their heads over the strange ways of Providence. Politics! Bah!

She shooed the swarm of youngsters from the running boards of her car and drove away. The children waved and shouted after her and she raised her hand in acknowledgment. Her heart was heavy. It was so hard to help some of these people—so hard to make them understand she was their friend.

There was one more place at which she must stop—off on the Flats—the colored section. Her mother constantly complained that Deborah had the worst district in town. Why couldn't they have assigned her to the South Side which was at least entirely white and almost wholly American. But Deborah didn't mind. In fact, she liked her people and most of them adored her. Now she drove to the last place on the Flats road. It was scarcely more than a shack. Unpainted, the small yard rubbish-strewn with a lean hound and a billygoat tethered one on either side of the sagging porch.

"Now how do they expect me to enter that door?" Deborah asked herself as she stopped at the curb. The hound bayed and sniffed the air. The goat turned a wicked eye in her direction and shook his head menacingly. As Deborah sounded her horn the front door opened. A huge negress peered nearsightedly toward the road.

"Hello, Mrs. Knight!" Deborah called. "I want to come in but don't dare with those ferocious beasts of yours guarding the front door. Call them off, will you please?"

Throwing her gingham apron about her shoulders, Mrs. Knight waddled to the gate that swung forlornly on one rusty hinge.

"I'll take care o' you, Nurse," she chuckled throatily. "They don't dast to do any o' their monkeyshines with me. Law, child, you ain't got enough meat on yer bones fer either Billy or Alexander to bother with." She shepherded the girl before her into the house while dog and goat completely ignored their progress.

"How's Cissy, today, Mrs. Knight?" Deborah asked, drawing off her gloves and discreetly putting them in her bag.

"I don't know, Nurse. She ate little dinner this noon an' said it tasted good, but she still cries such a lot! I declare it 'bout breaks my heart. An' they ain't nothin' to her. Jest skin an' bones."

"That doesn't mean much," Deborah told her. "You know they say a lean horse for a long race—it's her inertia and loss of appetite we've got to fight and that sweating and nervousness. Have you been to the clinic lately?"

"Yes'm, jest day before yest-dy. She ain't got th' T.B., Nurse, an' she ain't sweatin' so bad either. It's her age, I guess, an' I guess they thought they wasn't much th' matter with her. Doc didn't think they was any special danger——"

"Any immediate danger, you mean. Is she awake now?"

"I'll see, but first I want to tell you somethin'."

"All right. Go ahead."

"D'you know, Nurse, I been a-thinkin'. Cissy ain't been jest right ever since that good-fer-nothin' Tad Jackson lit out. I don't know if they was sweethearts exactly, but I know Cissy thought a pile o' Tad. Her pa did, too. I been a-wonderin' lately if that might have somethin' to do with it."

"But Cissy's not sixteen, Mrs. Knight. She ought to be in school."

"School!" scoffed Cissy's mother. "That's been th' trouble with her—her nose in a book every minute she could—night an' day, when she oughtta be out workin' in th' garden or playin' with th' neighbors' young'uns. I don't hold with so much schoolin'. It was her pa's idee her goin' t' High School."

"Has Mr. Knight come home yet?"

"No, he ain't, an' I don't care if he never comes home," his wife said vindictively. "He's no 'count. Cis an' I get 'long better without him clutterin' up th' place. But d'you think mebbe Cis's pinin' fer that Tad Jackson?"

"What became of him? Why did he go? Can you get in touch with him? You might try." Deborah didn't believe that disappointment in love caused girls to pine away nowadays, but Cissy Knight was sentimental like most of her race. Deborah knew girls married very young down here on the Flats—perhaps Tad's departure was a contributory cause.

14

"Oh, he's prob'ly over to his mother's in Corinth. She's one o' these here hen women–always cluckin' fer her brood o' roosters t' come home." Mrs. Knight chuckled at her own wit. "She gets money from a rich fam'ly she worked fer once an' lives like a queen; owns her own house an' has a cow an' chickens an' a garden. Tad says it's a swell place. I ain't seen it." She said the last as if she took it all with a large pinch of salt and would have to be shown.

"Corinth? Just where in Corinth?" Deborah asked. "I go over there once or twice a week and I might look him up," she offered.

"Would you do that, Miss Bradley?" Mrs. Knight beamed. "You sure are a mighty sweet girl an' I hope you have lots o' luck yerself. It's a mile out Clay Street after you pass th' city limits. A yella house with blue shutters. Fresh painted. You can find it—easy. Now come in an' see Cissy."

They entered the tiny bedroom—little more than a closet. Deborah watched the light breathing of the girl on the bed.

She was a pretty child, with clear olive skin and better features than her mother possessed. Her hair was short and lay in moist ringlets close to her well-shaped head. Her hands were slender, well kept. She was thin — very thin and she sighed in her sleep. Deborah gently took her wrist in her hand. Her pulse was weak—her hand hot and dry. Not much chance for her here in this low marshy section, she knew. Perhaps Tad was the answer—Tad and the country beyond Corinth with his mother.

She motioned Mrs. Knight from the room. "We'll see if it is Tad," she said and left quickly before Mrs. Knight could insist upon her staying for supper, quite forgetting the hound and the goat until she reached her car. Cissy's mother waved from the doorway while Deborah backed and turned her car to speed back to town and the Health Center to make her daily report.

It was when she was removing her coat at her desk that the card given her by the stranger at the airport fell to the floor. She picked it up and read:

Oliver Cromwell Turner, the author! She tried to re-

15

call just how he looked. Not at all her idea of a writer. Tall and lean and dark-eyed; teeth very white; hair reddish brown, thick and curly. She laughed to herself.

"I had no idea he made such an impression on me," she scoffed. "Probably I've mixed him up with someone else. I don't believe I should recognize him if he were to walk in here this minute."

CHAPTER TWO

DEBORAH BRADLEY shared an apartment with Alice Morgan, secretary to "We-Sell-The-Earth-Michaels." Alice was a writer on the side and often pounded her typewriter far into the night—nights when Deborah wished she was back in Farmington where nothing disturbed the quiet except the occasional barking of the dog next door. But she and Alice were congenial so she bore with the discomfort and slept until the last possible minute in the morning. Often she had to drag Alice from bed so that she could reach her office by nine o'clock.

It was Deb's job to get breakfast each morning although the original plan had been turn and turn about. But Alice was no cook and Deborah rather enjoyed it. Their breakfasts were usually light, except on Sundays and holidays when Deborah sometimes made muffins or waffles and even broiled ham or sausages. But on most mornings the meal consisted of orange juice or grapefruit, toast and coffee. This morning she had everything on the small gate-legged table when Alice came from her shower still in pajamas and bathrobe.

"Brrr!" she shivered as she sipped her orange juice. "It must be cold this morning. Did you look?"

"Only ten above," Deborah told her, pouring the coffee. "That's not cold. If you mind that, what will you do when we have real winter weather, say twenty below and a blizzard to boot?"

"You do think of the coziest things!" shivered Alice.

"Trouble with you is, you don't get enough sleep," the other remarked. "What time did Paul leave last night? Has he no home that he keeps laboring women up until dawn?"

"It was only a little after one when he left." Alice buttered a piece of toast with a lavish hand. "Did you hear us at the refrigerator? And what became of the remains of that chicken we had Sunday?"

"You ate it last night for dinner—don't you remember we had it creamed on baked potatoes? What did you find? I hope you didn't eat the ham."

"No. We had bread and jam and milk. I wasn't

17

going to do any cooking at that hour. Anyway, we ate nearly all the bread."

"I know you did," Deborah muttered, pulling out the toaster plug. "This is every smitch of bread in the place. We'll have to get some so don't forget to order it this morning."

"I wish you'd do the ordering, Deb," the other complained. "I always forget something. You can do it from your office just as well as I can."

"But I don't have a minute then," Deborah told her. "No, I'll order before I leave. We'll make out the list and I'll put in the order early. Everything can be left in the milk cupboard except the meat and one of us will have to bring that when we come home at night."

"Why don't we go out to dinner nights, Deb? I don't think it would cost much more and there would be no dishes to wash afterward."

"Now you listen to me, Alice Morgan," Deborah said severely. "We can't afford to buy our dinners and I don't want to anyway. We have this apartment and we're going to make use of it. I don't mind cooking the meals and even ordering supplies but I think you should be willing to wash the dishes and make your own bed. That's certainly little enough to ask of you. If you remember when we began this thing—everything was to be fifty-fifty. You were to keep house one week and I the next and how long did it last?"

"But darling, you're such a grand cook——" began Alice, her voice ingratiating.

"She can bake a cherry pie in the twinkling of an eye—
She's a young thing and she has left her mother,"

she sang.

"That's not the point. I work just as hard as you do. I pay half of everything and yet you expect me to do all the work. No, sir, I'm not going to do it. If I take care of the cooking—you can take care of the clearing up. Well?"

"Of course, Simon Legree, I'll ruin my hands in soapy dishwater and I'll make my own bed, but please don't expect me to wave any banners while I'm doing it. I hate housework!" Alice tipped the percolator for the last drop of coffee and sighed. "I wish I had another piece of toast. Isn't there a cooky about the place, Deb?"

"I don't think so. There isn't any bread—you ate it. Anyway, you've had a good breakfast—all you ever eat. Stack the dishes in the pan and cover them, Alice. You won't be able to do them this morning but you'll have to wash them before dinner or you'll inveigle me into helping you. I know you, my girl, and I'm not going to do it. I'll stop in at the grocer's and pick out some things and explain we want our order sent on the three o'clock delivery."

"Oh, all right. You ought to be a matron in some orphan asylum, Deborah Bradley. System—schedule—that's all you think about."

"I have to work on a schedule," Deborah said coolly. "If I didn't I could never accomplish what is planned for me each day. That's your whole trouble, Alice. You have no system—you do everything haphazard and you get all balled up."

Alice stood in her pajamas, hands on hips and contemplated the girl opposite. "How old are you, Miss Bradley? Don't tell me you're only twenty-three! And never brag that you're a year younger than I am—nobody will ever believe it. You sound like the old lady who lived in a shoe. Forget it, Deb! Time's a-wastin' and your beauty and youth are laid on the altar of duty. Here we've been in this apartment eight months and you haven't had a single man caller. I don't count the doctors who come to ask about some case or to drag you off to some clinic or emergency. What's the matter with you—aside from your schedule? Unbend! Do a bit of flirting and let's see you act like a normal girl who has an object in life—having fun while laying her net for a good husband."

"Don't be vulgar, Alice," Deborah rebuked her calmly. "I've told you a hundred times that I'm not interested in men. You knew it when we took this apartment."

"I heard you say so but I didn't believe it, Deb. Why, you're lovely when you forget to look businesslike and efficient, and when you're not wearing that atrocious uniform. Why don't they let you wear white like any self-respecting nurse should, instead of that dingy blue?"

"How long would a white uniform remain white in

19

some of the places I have to go?" Deborah asked sarcastically.

"Then why don't you change your job to one where you can dress the part? You look like an angel in white, Deb, with that chic little bit of organdy perched on your curls. Have you no honest pride, gal?"

Deb wrinkled her nose at her.

"It's nearly eight-thirty, Alice. You'll never get to work if you don't hurry," she said, and reached in the closet for her rough cloth coat and plain blue felt hat. "Goodbye! See you tonight and don't forget what I said. Wash dishes?" she called as she left.

"And you see that you bring home the bacon, darling," Alice shouted after her.

There were several special calls listed on her desk-pad when Deborah reached the Center some half hour later. She had stopped at a grocery store with an order to be delivered that afternoon. Later she would get a steak and perhaps something for a salad. Why couldn't Alice help more? She supposed she was easy to do so much but she enjoyed having a home where she could relax after the day's work. A room wasn't enough. She wanted her own kitchen in which to experiment with flour, eggs and baking powder: a living room with books and magazines and her work basket on the table. With comfortable chairs, a desk of her own and perhaps a plant or two. Yes, definitely, a living room: even with Paul Hendricks lounging there for an hour or two, three times a week, it was much better than living in just one room. And yet she couldn't swing it alone.

The mail arrived and she found a letter from her mother. She slit the envelope unfolding the closely written sheets of gray paper. Outside the snow lay thick on tree and ground. The roads would be slippery this morning. She must see about chains. Back to her mother's letter. The Florida weather was delightful. She had already met many charming people. Her room in the hotel was much better than the one she had had last winter. There were not so many real young people here as usual but quite a number of unattached men. Wouldn't Deborah reconsider and come down? They could manage quite well if they lived carefully and who knew but she might find a suitable husband? It was certain she never would while she was working in the slums as she was now doing.

She had gone bathing with some of her friends but as Deb knew she didn't care particularly for the water. But she had to go in occasionally if only to prove she was still young enough to enjoy such things and to demonstrate that her figure really was as youthful as it appeared. One thing was certain, she had no intention of spending her life playing bridge with a lot of stupid old women who were quite satisfied to remain on the shelf. No, indeed, she was much too young for that. After all, forty wasn't old—she had married very young.

Deborah smiled as she read on. Her mother insisted she had been a mere child when she married Richard Bradley but Deborah knew that she had been twenty. Her mother was nearly forty-five, but if it made her feel younger and happier to insist she was only forty, why let her be forty for as long as she wished. Only she must not try to make her daughter younger than she was. Deborah had no desire to be thought a child. She was a woman earning her own living and she gloried in the fact.

Deborah wondered if she might not have been different if her mother had been less irresponsible. From her earliest memory she had thought of her mother as a girl—lovely and vivacious. Her father had always petted and spoiled her. Between them, they had done a thorough job of it and when her father had died soon after her twelfth birthday, Deborah kept up the illusion. Her mother had to be protected at all costs. There was not a great deal of money. Richard Bradley had left a trust fund to be shared equally by his wife and daughter. He had wanted Deborah to go to college when she had graduated from the local High School. But it cost a great deal to live and the girl knew it was impossible. So although her mother shuddered at the idea of her daughter becoming a nurse, Deborah pointed out the advantages to them both.

By that time, Sylvia Bradley was again active in the social life of the little community and complained bitterly that her share of the estate was pitifully small—certainly not large enough to keep her in the style to which

21

she had become accustomed. Deborah was a quiet, serious girl and required but little. She wanted her mother to be happy—that seemed to her the most important thing in life—her mother's happiness. It wasn't hard to convince her mother that if she were allowed to enter a hospital training school, her expenses would be negligible and there would then be ample for her mother to live where and how she pleased.

Sylvia Bradley was not a cruel mother—simply a foolish and rather selfish one. She gave her consent and, at a little past seventeen, Deborah had entered the Mercy Hospital in Medford and later taken up public health work. She had been at it for three years.

Doctor Alec Brown came over to her.

"The Polycletus boy died this morning, Bradley," he said somberly. "He hadn't a chance from the first and in a way it's a blessing he didn't linger any longer." He sighed. "There seems to be no hope of the parents letting the younger boy go to Ithaca. I argued and pled with them last night but they are like granite. Now they act as if the older boy was murdered."

"I know, but I haven't given up hope yet, Doctor Brown," Deborah told him. "Phil is such a darling! It will be a crime if he doesn't have his chance. I'll stop in there this morning."

"You'll find them very bitter, I'm afraid," the doctor said. "Like so many of them down there, they seem to hold us responsible, yet God knows we sweat blood over that boy—day and night. But it was no use. They insisted on taking the boy home with them. Oh, we advised against it, but I guess it means something to them —having the funeral from his home. You can't make them see."

"I know," Deborah said again.

She did know. It was an uphill fight, sometimes a losing fight, to try to make these people understand they were their friends—trying to help them to a broader, better, healthier life. So often they considered them enemies—experimenters. She thought of them as her children —to be treated gently and kindly but with firmness. Sometimes she felt they loved and trusted her: then something would happen—like the Const Polycletus case—

and she sensed their hostility. She was sorry for Alec Brown this morning. She knew that the death of a child always hurt him as nothing else could. Now he looked at her, his dark eyes reminding her of a spaniel she once had.

"Try to make them realize we did our best," he pleaded. "It wasn't the polio—directly—Bradley. It was the intestinal obstruction. Perhaps if we had had him sooner—try to make them see that. You can if anyone can."

"I will, Doctor." She picked up her bag and turned to leave the room. She had nearly reached the door when he called to her.

"Doing anything tonight?" He spoke hurriedly, then before she had time to answer, he urged; "Have dinner with me and see a show. I need it and I bet you do, too. I never see you anywhere I go. Don't you have any social life at all? You take your work too seriously. Come on out with me for a while tonight."

Deborah hesitated. She didn't particularly care for doctors and had never encouraged their attentions. Now, however, she wondered if it wouldn't be the kind thing to do. Alec Brown looked utterly fagged and she knew he was miserable over losing Const Polycletus.

"Thank you, that will be grand!" she smiled up at him.

"Fine! I'll be around to your place at seven or a little after, then. We'll have ourselves a time."

As Deborah sent her coupé into the traffic of Green Street, she wondered just why she had let herself in for this affair tonight. She had never been out with Alec Brown. It was reported that Cynthia Marvin, the girl to whom he had been engaged, had jilted him, then repented too late. She haunted the Hospital where he was on the staff and the Center, but never seemed to have much luck in contacting him. She was one of the town's wealthiest girls—an ash blond of rather amazing beauty but little if any brains. Deborah wondered what would happen if they came upon her during their wanderings tonight. Well, she didn't care. Alec Brown was nothing to her.

She stopped at the Polycletus place and was met by a stoney-faced mother.

"Const died," she accused.

Deborah could only murmur pityingly, "Yes. Const died. Maybe it is better so if he was never to be well and strong again. But it was this new sickness that killed him, Mrs. Polycletus. This intestinal infection—it had gone too far. How is Philip?"

"No. No. Philip, he stay with us. If you take him, he die, too."

"No," Deborah said positively. "Philip will not die. He will be well and strong and able to run and jump like other boys. It is his only chance, Mrs. Polycletus. Won't you trust me?"

"No. No. I trust no one. You take my oldest born and he died," she muttered in a singsong wail, swaying back and forth in a passion of grief.

"May I see Const?" the girl asked.

She was led to the dark little bedroom and looked down at the dead face. Quiet, peaceful, almost happy, the boy had regained much of his beauty. Deborah's eyes filled with sudden tears. Oh, why couldn't his mother see that it was better for him this way? She saw no signs of the father nor of Philip. She wondered where the younger son was.

"Philip is where you will not find him," Mrs. Polycletus, apparently reading her thoughts, said as Deborah turned to leave. "You shall not take our only son."

"I'm sorry," Deborah said as she reached the door. "But it is the only way."

All the things she was trying to do for these people seemed utterly futile. Ignorant, stubborn, they refused to move forward one inch. Poor helpless little Philip, doomed to lie on his back all his life because of the blindness of his parents.

She continued her rounds. Two pneumonia cases had developed overnight, one for hospitalization, the other mild. Several cases of colds and flu, two of whooping cough and one of measles. She passed Doctor Brown on the stairs of one tenement and he asked;

"What luck?" She shook her head and hurried on.

She gave four baths, changed several dressings, tried a new formula on a wailing baby, watching while he reached hungrily for his warm bottle and, at last, slept. She had

had difficulty getting away. Little Marcio had kept the family and boarders awake for two nights and days now and the parents were vociferous in their gratitude, eager to bestow largess on their benefactress. Doc Hamilton liked sour wine and Deborah always turned it over to him, so she accepted the generous bottles and fled while Marcio's mother burrowed in a dark corner of the kitchen for cakes.

She stopped for a minute to visit an old woman, stricken with palsy but cheerful in the face of direst poverty, trying desperately to help her daughter-in-law with the housework. She called briefly on a middle-aged man who had lost both legs in the mill but who was learning to pull himself about on a homemade cart. Her spirits lifted—she was helping some of them—they loved her and looked forward to her visits.

She ate her late luncheon with one of the other nurses from the Center and started out on the second half of her list. More colds. She visited a woman who had suffered two strokes and was patiently awaiting the third—positive it would come and be the last in spite of anything doctor or nurse could say to the contrary. She saw twin boys rosy and healthy in the midst of filth. She attended a christening where she was given the complimentary degree of honorary godmother to her seventeenth baby. She had left a silver dollar for his bank account. She often wondered how many of those silver dollars actually went into a bank. But it was a little thing for her to do and brought inordinate pleasure to the proud parents.

Five o'clock found her ready to call it a day and she turned the little car toward the Center with a sigh of relief. It had been a particularly hectic day. Back in her mind still lurked the worry about Philip Polycletus. But perhaps if she kept at the parents, they would weaken, especially after the funeral was over.

CHAPTER THREE

So YOU'RE TAKING my advice, Deb?" Alice grinned when her friend told her of her engagement for the evening. "Did you bring the meat and lettuce for the salad? Oh, I see you did. Always running true to form. I somehow wish you'd forgotten them."

"Lamb chops and endive, my dear," Deborah said, depositing a large paper bag on the table. "Do you want me to cook your dinner or can you do it yourself, helpless?"

"Don't be mean, Deb. Of course I can cook a chop and I'm not especially keen about endive so I'll pass that up. Just a chop and a roll and a cup of coffee. I'm eager to get on with my story. When is your Big Moment coming?"

"Don't call him my Big Moment, Alice. It's Doctor Brown and I'm simply doing an act of charity. The man's jittery over the death of one of his little patients and needs to relax and forget it. I'm being the means to that end or contributory to it."

"Oh, ye-ah? Well, see that you're an attractive contrib, my dear. Let me give you the once over before you leave. I don't trust you. Run and take your bath and I'll go over your glad-rags." Deborah laughed and went to hang up her hat and coat.

An hour later when Doctor Brown reached their apartment, Deb was about ready. She had hesitated over wearing the blue lace as a little extreme but Alice insisted. It was a charming frock—one her mother had maneuvered her into buying on their last trip to New York, and was vastly becoming. The dusty blue of the gown brought out unexpected blue lights in her gray eyes and intensified the whiteness of her skin.

"Heavens, Deb!" Alice exclaimed as she spread her own fur wrap over the back of a chair. "You're positively devastating in that outfit! Why on earth don't you go out more? Now don't you dare refuse my evening wrap. You would look nice wearing a plain cloth coat over that creation! Why don't you buy yourself a fur coat—a real one? Do you know, Deb, sometimes I wonder if you're tight."

"Tight!" Deborah scoffed. "On what?"

"Oh, I know your salary isn't especially princely," conceded Alice, "but we live simply, at least you do. I bet you squander your money on the derelicts you nurse. It isn't enough that you spend your time and health on them—you have to waste your salary on them, too. Did anyone ever tell you what a sap you are, Deborah Bradley?"

"Yes. My mother often tells me I'm a fool; but, you see, I like doing what I'm doing. It isn't a sacrifice or a disagreeable duty either. It's my job and I love it."

"Sez you," her friend retorted. "I don't believe you. You've told yourself that fairy tale so many times that you think you're convinced but in your heart you're not, you know. You're young—you're lovely. It isn't natural for you to be happy in the environment in which you spend most of your waking hours. I don't want to be a Jeremiah, my dear, but I'm frank to tell you I'm looking for a complete turnabout. Some day you're going to get such a revulsion that you'll throw up the entire sponge. I hope I'm within call when the time comes."

"Well," Deborah laughed, "you certainly do like to hang plenty of crepe, don't you? But why do you suppose I chose Public Health in the first place if I didn't expect to stick to it?"

"Oh, you probably had some fantastical notion of healing all the wounds and sore spots in our fair city. You'll find out some day that it isn't a cure but a preventive—an immunizing—that's needed."

"Yes?" Deborah asked. "And just now can that be done?"

"Now we're getting into politics, darling, and you know I'm rabid when it comes to politics, especially city politics," Alice told her. "My boss is trying to interest this city in slum clearance and, believe me, he's having a tough time of it."

The bell rang and she went to release the catch. Doctor Brown entered the little apartment. He had been here only once or twice before but appeared to feel quite at home. He and Alice visited while Deborah lingered for a moment in her room. When she appeared before him he smiled approvingly at her.

They were still at dinner in the Mauve Room of the

Cosmopolitan when Cynthia Marvin entered with a party of young people. She saw Alec with Deborah and stopped in her tracks, then, with a little rush and cry of delight, came over to their table. Alec stood to receive her, his eyes cold, his lips unsmiling.

"Darling!" Interested diners, looking up, smiled and whispered. "I've tried so hard to see you! Come over to our table. You know them all—the gang." Her glance swept Deborah appraisingly. "Bring your friend if you like."

Alec introduced the girls but neither was cordial, Deborah because she disliked all that Cynthia Marvin represented in the world and Cynthia because Deborah was with Alec.

"I'm sorry, Cyn," Alec said quietly. "Miss Bradley and I are taking in Pygmalion and must be going almost at once."

"But so are we! Can't we get together afterward and go some place to dance?" she persisted pleadingly.

"I think not. You see both Deb and I are working folk and have to be in bed decently early. Glad to have seen you, Cynthia. Say hello to the others for me."

"Oh, Alec!" The girl's face was almost indecent in its open adoration. Deborah turned away. She felt ashamed for her. "Won't you come to see me? Please, dear. I want you to——"

"Of course," Doctor Brown said. Deborah knew he was embarrassed and unhappy. "But you know I'm a busy man—doctors have little time for social calls."

"I know," the girl's voice was humble, "but you'll come? You promise? Soon?"

"I'll try, but——" He turned to Deborah who felt sorry for him. "We really must be going, Deborah," he said. "We don't want to miss that first act. Goodbye, Cynthia. Remember me to your mother." He lifted Deborah's wrap, held it for her then hurried her from the room. As he reached the door he swore softly.

"Sorry that had to happen," he muttered as they found his car and prepared to leave.

"It's perfectly all right. I quite understand."

"I was a fool to ever get mixed up with that brainless crowd in the first place," he complained bitterly.

"Miss Marvin is very lovely," Deborah murmured.

"And completely selfish and empty-headed," the man said.

"She's young and no doubt spoiled," Deborah excused. "Too much money."

"And too little discipline," he added grimly. "But let's forget her. Do you know this is the first time you've been out with me on what we used to call a 'bat'? Why is that?"

"Well," Deborah explained demurely, "one reason I can think of is that I've not been invited before, but perhaps the most important is—I don't go out nights very often because I'm usually pretty tired and need rest and sleep."

"But all work and no play, you know, makes Jill just as dull as it does Jack."

"That may be, Doctor," Deborah said, "but I've no desire to shine socially. I don't care the least bit for society. I like and enjoy my work."

"So do I, but I find it helps me to get out among people and forget my work for a while. I think I'm a better doctor for it. Why not try it oftener, Deborah—do you mind my calling you that?"

"Why no—if you like. It's my name, you know," Deborah smiled.

"Well, how about doing this again soon?"

"Not too soon," she stipulated.

It was nearly two when she opened the door of the apartment and she knew that she had never been quite so tired before in her whole life. They had gone back to the Cosmopolitan after the play, and danced. It had been fun but now Deborah experienced a feeling of reaction and let-down. She knew it was going to be hard for her to get up in the morning. Alice was still at her typewriter, heavy-eyed and weary. She turned as the door opened.

"Well, how was it? How do you like night life in our gay metropolis, Deb?" she asked, yawning and stretching wearily.

29

"All right if one doesn't do it too often," her friend replied. "I don't see how some girls stand it. I'm dead on my feet."

"Was Doc as bad as that? You poor kid!"

"Oh, Alec was all right. It's just that I'm no butterfly, Alice. Once in a while this may be fun but not for a steady thing. I'm going to bed. Seven o'clock comes altogether too soon to be wasting any more time. You better follow suit, my dear, or I'll have to use violence in getting you up."

For some time after she was in bed, Deborah lay staring upwards at a spot, which wavered as the wind tossed the bare branches of the elm tree outside her window. Here she was, only twenty-three and worn out from a one night date. It wasn't normal. She didn't think she had been dull. In fact, she had sparkled in a way that had surprised her. It had been fun. Alec was right: she must plan to go out oftener but just now the important thing was to get to sleep, but sleep was slow in coming.

She thought of her mother and wondered why they were so different. Her mother adored society—thrived on night life and hectic living. Deborah felt that she must be a throwback to some Puritan ancestor, for she knew she would never be satisfied to live as her mother lived. She had to have an object in life—some worth-while goal. That is why she had chosen nursing, and later Public Health Work. "Brave living," Doctor Hamilton had preached to his staff. "Brave living for the duration of the war on disease, ignorance and superstition." It all sounded very noble and wonderful but just now she was dead tired.

She sat up and breathed deeply of the clear cold air sweeping in from her open window. Inhale deeply—slow-ly. Exhale—slow-ly. She lay down and drew the blankets closely about her and drifted off into the heavy sleep of complete exhaustion. Her last conscious thought was that she must buy that pink housecoat Cissy Knight longed for. Cissy and Tad were having a wedding in two days and she had promised to stop in tomorrow and see her trousseau—why, that was today! She had seen just the one Cissy wanted at Parker's department store and it looked just Cissy's size, too. "Poor Cissy!" Deborah murmured sleepily, and yet the girl had bloomed like a damask rose under the benign influence of requited love. Unconsciously she breathed a prayer the love would last, for if it did not, Cissy would fade and die like all roses did.

CHAPTER FOUR

I FEEL THAT at last there is some chance of happiness for me, Deborah," her mother wrote in the letter Deborah received late in February. "Mr. Tremaine is a charming man—a gentleman, Debby—a retired army officer—very English and a little lame. He was injured during the war. He tells me he has a small estate in Devon and showed me pictures of the place and of the surrounding country. Oh, darling, it is all so lovely—you don't know! Now don't ask me if it is all true, you suspicious girl! I took care to investigate thorougbly and it is all quite true. He is not rich, but quite comfortable so that if I yield to his really importunate desires and marry him, I shall be able to turn your father's entire estate over to you and you can leave that horrible nursing job and live in a manner befitting your birth and station.

"Darling, I insist on your coming down to St. Petersburg at once, for I want you to know Arthur. I'm sure you will like each other. He is so thoughtful, Deborah! Wire me when you will arrive so that I can arrange accommodations for you."

Deborah sighed. Another marriage for her mother! This Tremaine sounded better than the others and yet how was one to know? She ought to go down. But how could she? Medford was peppered with influenza and colds and it seemed to her that the North Side was especially bad. She only hoped she would be able to keep well. Last night she had felt grippy and ready to drop, but a hot bath and a good night's sleep had done wonders for her and while tired from the constant drain on her strength, she felt quite able to go on this morning. Old Doctor Hamilton came into the room.

"How are things over your way, Bradley?" he asked, eyeing her closely. "Tough, isn't it?"

"Pretty tough, Doctor, but I'm hoping the worst is over. If only we have several days of dry, cold weather now, I'm sure things will look brighter. It's these sudden changes that have been so hard on people whose resistance is low."

"Weather man says 'clear and cold' so I guess you'll get your wish all right. You look sort of peaked yourself, this morning. I think I'll prescribe for you, young lady. Can't have having you sick, you know."

"Oh, I'm all right, Doctor—only a little tired," Deborah told him. But she took the envelope he handed her and put it in her bag.

"Those are for you, remember. See that you take them and eat decent meals at proper times. Sleep, too, plenty of sleep." He patted her shoulder and rushed away. Deborah smiled as her glance followed him. He was a great one to give advice to be careful. The man took absolutely no care of himself. He was untiring, the hardest worker on the Board.

She must write her mother and tell her she wouldn't be able to make the trip until later—perhaps the end of March. But now she must get on her job.

In and out of airless, crowded apartments she went, preaching the gospel of cleanliness, cheerfulness and hope. Often the word fell on deaf ears but she kept everlastingly at it. She was welcomed by most but some scowled upon her as a "buttinsky," a trouble-maker, snooping into private affairs for no good purpose.

Today the air was crisp with a cloudless sky overhead and hard whiteness underfoot. Deborah felt strong to combat every evil.

Alice and Paul had quarreled and Paul had gone to Chicago on business. Alice had sold her first short story and was in a crazy mood. She had wanted to give up her job, to devote all her time to writing. Paul told her she was a nut to think that one acceptance made her a writer and Deborah advised her to do nothing foolish. Her job was good and writing was a precarious way to earn a living —especially when the writer was unknown as Alice was. For days Alice spoke but seldom and then with cool disdain. But she kept her job and was working on another story.

They both missed Paul. He was lively and good fun, helping with dinner, sometimes bringing in little luxuries for dessert. He would sit perfectly quiet for hours, his mind on his work and his eyes on the fire, while Alice rattled away at her typewriter as Deborah mended stockings or wrote letters. For the past week Deborah had been too worn out to do anything. After dinner she had gone to bed, sometimes to lie awake for hours planning and worrying although she knew it was wrong and detrimental both to her health and efficiency.

But today was a little better. The air was invigorating. Snow was thick and white over the countryside, covering unsightly debris and giving a fairy touch to the world. Roads were packed hard on main thoroughfares and, with chains on her little coupé, Deborah made good time. Morning passed. She ate lunch in a tiny hole-in-the-wall off the Boulevard. It was a good lunch and she lingered over a second cup of coffee. There had been improvement all along the line and she felt this must be one of her lucky days. She would stop at the Polycletus apartment to see how they fared and try again to induce them to let Philip go to Ithaca. Maybe today she would succeed.

She paid her check and pulled on her heavy gloves. At the door breathing deeply the invigorating cold she crossed to the curb where her car stood. If things went as well this afternoon as they had this morning, she would be through early and would have time to write her mother before going home. She turned into Fernald Street and heard, above the noise of traffic, the sirens of the fire trucks and caught glimpses of people running toward the far end of the street. She parked her car and she, too, ran. Oh, she hoped it wasn't that old fire-trap! It housed forty or fifty families. People poured from tenements on both sides. She was caught up in the crowd and rushed forward. The fire trucks turned the corner and jarred to a stop not far from the end of the street. Deborah ran on and into the building. There were so many children here and several old people. Just last week she had again reported this building to the Center as unsafe. Up the stairs she raced, fighting her way through downcoming crowds. Old Mrs. Martin was bedridden on the fifth floor in front of the Polycletus flat, and with her were two children both ill with measles. She must get to them. So many mothers in this district went out to work. Worked by the day, scrubbing, washing, anything that would add to the family finances. She hoped Mrs. Polycletus had heard the fire sirens and had carried Philip to safety: but she knew there was no one to help old Mrs. Martin. She must get

34

to her. Smoke began to seep through a door on the third floor. Her breath came hard. She paused to allow a man carrying a girl wrapped in a blanket to pass.

"You can't go no farther, Nurse," he told her. "It's on this floor—over there beyond that wall in Luini's kitchen. I told the old fool he'd burn us all out some day and now he's done it." The last was shouted as he turned a corner in the hall. Deborah was already halfway up the next flight. Someone screamed in terror. Feet pounded behind her. The smoke was smothering now but she was near the top. A man yelled just behind her.

"You fool! What d'you think you're doin'? Stop, I say!"

Deborah turned a corner and raced on to the Martin apartment. She tried the door—locked. She ran down the hall to the kitchen door and through into the tiny, smoky front room. The two youngsters were standing at a window watching the scene below apparently unaware of their danger. The grandmother, propped up on pillows in the bed, screamed at them to tell her what it was; then ordered them back to bed. A fireman was behind Deborah.

"She's helpless," the girl cried. "You take her and I'll get the children."

"Souse a towel and wrap it round your head. Cover your nose and mouth," he ordered. "We've got to move." He picked up the old woman, bedding and all and turned toward the door. "Can you manage? Thank God, here's Mac—give her a hand, will you?"

Deborah gave the boys over to Mac and ran down the hall.

"Where in hell you goin', sister?" Mac shouted.

"I'll be all right," Deborah answered and disappeared into the Polycletus flat. The place seemed deserted and she breathed a sigh of relief. She turned back to the hall and stopped as a faint choking call reached her. It seemed to come from the tiny room off the kitchen where the occupants of similar apartments kept their fuel. The call came again, faint and strangled. She flung open the door. There lay Philip Polycletus in his crib—gasping for breath. The smoke was much worse in here.

Deborah caught him up and raced to the door through

35

which smoke now poured in dense, suffocating billows. Cries and screams and smothered curses came up to her. The hall and stairs were thick with smoke and the faint ominous crackling she had heard when she left the Martin flat was now more pronounced. Down one flight and through the hall—endless it seemed to her. Philip clung to her neck, his nose and mouth buried in the towel— no longer wet—with which she had swathed her head. Her lungs ached; she could scarcely see; her feet were leaden and Philip weighed a ton. Another flight and above her a glow showed through the black smoke. A shout went up from the crowd outside.

The roof! Deborah prayed as she ran. She felt hot searing air on her forehead and her eyes refused to open but she struggled on and then, just as she felt she could go no farther, someone snatched the child from her aching arms—strong hands lifted her and she sank down into a blackness from which she now had no desire to escape.

Followed days and nights of darkness and pain for her. Once or twice she drifted back to see her mother bending over her and once a strange man took her hand in his and murmured something pityingly. But for the most part she was entirely unaware of her surroundings. And then one morning, weeks later, she awoke to the persistent calling of a robin outside her window. She opened her eyes and stared around. Why, she was in the hospital! And that was Marian Holton sitting there writing something on a chart! It was daylight and that was a bird. How did she get here? What had happened? She closed her eyes and tried to think back. The fire! She was trying to get Philip Polycletus to safety!

"Tell me, Holton," she began and was amazed at the weakness of her voice. The startled nurse came over to the bed.

"Don't talk, Bradley," she said softly and her eyes were soft and shining as if with unshed tears. "You're too weak to exert yourself the least bit. What a time you've had and what a scare you gave us! But, darling, we're all so proud of you!"

"Proud? Of me?" Deborah asked wonderingly. "Why?"

"Why? When you're stronger we'll show you what Medford thinks of you and more particularly the nursing profession, my dear. Wait until you see all the flowers from your admiring public, Bradley. I wish we could have kept the first ones that came."

"Philip?" Deborah murmured, too tired to follow the other's conversation.

"Oh, he's fine—thanks to you. He's here in the hospital temporarily. There was quite a row at first but Hamilton talked to his parents like a Dutch uncle. The idea of leaving that child while his fool mother went over to Mill Street to iron for someone—at least that's the story. But the child's going to Ithaca all right—thanks again to you." She had slipped a thermometer under Deborah's tongue and now drew it out. "Mm," she murmured complacently, "we're quite normal this morning, young lady. How about breakfast? Hungry?"

"Starved!" Deborah smiled faintly. "What happened to me?"

"Oh, you merely had double pneumonia, darling, plus a complete collapse. It's a Miracle you weren't killed but it was superb! The fire department has made you an honorary member and there's a big handsome brute they call Mac who's been haunting the place ever since you were brought here."

"Mac? I remember Mac-he carried the Martin boys, and swore at me because—— How long have I been ill, Holton?"

"Five weeks—nearer six. Gosh, darling, I'm glad you're better. And I'm proud as a peacock they put me on your case. It's an honor, Bradley. Now it's only six but I'm going down and get you something to drink. You can have your breakfast later—that's a laugh, but we'll fix up something. Orange juice, eh?" She paused at the door. "Don't go passing out on me while I'm gone."

"I won't," Deborah promised and meant it. She felt like new only very, very weak. Her hands were like claws as they lay on the white spread. She wished she had a mirror, for she knew she must look terrible. She was glad Philip was to have his chance. He was such a darling! Her mother? Had her mother really come back, or had she dreamed it? It would be too bad to spoil her pleasure. The robin began his insistent calling again. How she loved the song of the first robin! Later they became quite a nuisance and some mornings when she wanted to sleep late, she felt like wringing their necks. But now it was heavenly. The clean white curtains swayed in the soft spring breeze and Deborah felt a little throb of happiness stir within her.

She wondered if everyone in the tenement had been saved. If she could only have gotten there sooner! She knew just who were ill—too ill to walk. She knew which of the tenants would be absent during the day and which families had old people. She could have done so much more if she could have reached the place sooner.

Holton returned with the glass of orange juice and held the glass tube while Deborah sipped slowly. It tasted good—refreshing to her parched throat. Before her thirst was satisfied, the tube was withdrawn.

"That's enough for now, darling," Holton said regretfully.

"I know," Deborah smiled. "I was thirsty." She slept almost at once and awoke to see her mother and a strange man sitting beside her.

"Mother!" she whispered and her mother went down on her knees beside the bed and kissed her.

"Darling!" she wept. "Why won't you take care of yourself? I have been so terribly frightened, but you're better now? Tell me you are going to be all right."

"Of course, silly," Deborah said. "I feel fine—except that I'm weak. Is this——" she began.

"My husband, dear. Your new papa. Arthur was so anxious to stay and help if he was needed that we decided to marry at once. And just as soon as possible we are going to take you to England with us. The ocean trip will do you worlds of good."

Deborah said nothing. With abnormally large gray eyes in which a challenge lurked she looked at the strange man. "You better be good to Mother," they said plainly and the man seemed to sense her thoughts. "If you're not, you'll answer to me."

Arthur Tremaine returned her gaze with one equally sober.

"I shall take good care of your mother, dear girl," he said and Deborah liked his voice. "We hope you will make your home with us and give up this ghastly nursing business."

Miss Anderson, the superintendent, entered with Doctor Hamilton and the callers were hustled out. Miss Bradley was to be kept very quiet for the next few days and all visits were limited to fifteen minutes. Sorry, but Mr. and Mrs. Tremaine could come in again after lunch if they liked.

Deborah was surprised to see tears in the eyes of the stern superintendent while Doctor Hamilton found it impossible to do more than press her hand and bluster that she had been a foolish, headstrong, glorious idiot, dammit! And he blew his nose in a way that was far from delicate or polite. The House Physician bustled in to pat her hand. The others melted away. Stanton, the day nurse, brought in flowers and more flowers until the room was a bower of spring blossoms.

During the day, nurses drifted in and out, saying little or nothing but smiling mistily at her.

"They've been doing that for five weeks, Bradley," Stanton told her and Deborah's heart swelled with gratitude that they loved her.

After lunch Alice Morgan came in and brought her a beautiful bed jacket.

"You didn't possess such a thing, you poor dope," her housemate told her. "I suppose you thought you were immune, didn't you? Well, this is one time you were mistaken, Miss Bradley. And have I been on the busy end of a telephone these weeks you've been lying here in blissful peace and quiet! And did you know that you were signally honored with a call from Oliver Cromwell Turner, the novelist, some four weeks ago? That is, our apartment was. I did the interviewing. The man's an ill-mannered brute. He was fine as long as I was answering questions about your heroism but when I tried to get a few pointers from him about writing, he shut up like a clam and just bolted out the door. I always liked his stuff but I wouldn't read another book of his if he was given the Nobel prize. What a frost! I was warned not to stay more than fifteen minutes and not to let you talk so I'm running along. Paul will be in tomorrow and he sent his love."

"Then you and——"

"Oh, everything's lovely, darling, and the goose, meaning me, hangs high." She held out her left hand. "It's new, you see, so I'm saving on gloves. It's the queerest thing how warm a diamond engagement ring can keep one!" she laughed happily. "Like it?"

"Love it!" Deborah told her. "I'm so glad you've made up. You and Paul were really made for each other."

Deborah improved rapidly. When she was able to sit up, her mother again broached the subject of living in England and now Deborah told her that she couldn't do it.

"I wouldn't be happy there, Mother," she explained thoughtfully. "I'm an American and I shall live and die here."

"Well, you almost died here," her mother reminded her.

"But I didn't, you know. Of course you must live in your husband's home and I'm sure you will be happy there. I like Mr. Tremaine, Mother. He's charming and I know he'll be good to you."

Her mother beamed. "Isn't he a darling, Deb? He admires you, too, but can't understand how you can possibly be my daughter. I explained that I married when a mere child. That's one thing about this country he dislikes—such youthful marriages." Her eyes twinkled for a moment then she said softly; "You won't tell him that you're over twenty, will you, darling? And you don't look even that, right now."

"But Mother, why is it necessary to lie about such trivial things? What difference does it make——"

"Arthur admires my youth, Deborah. He's proud of my figure and my complexion. He is sixty and is so grateful that a young and beautiful girl like me should be willing to marry him. It won't hurt you to let me keep my secret and especially if you're over here."

"All right, darling, if it makes you feel better. I don't mind," Deborah said, relieved that the matter of her future residence was settled.

"And Arthur suggests that your father's entire estate be turned over to you, Deborah. We shall see about it before we leave. And listen, darling, please, for my sake, give up nursing. Take a house or an apartment somewhere and live in a manner befitting your station. I shall not draw a contented breath until I know you have quit this terrible job."

"Maybe I shall, Mother," Deborah said slowly. "Somehow I feel now that I never want to see a sick person again as long as I live. The very thought of it makes me shudder. Perhaps it is only a phase of my illness, but I think I shall follow your suggestion, Mother, and go away somewhere and live an entirely different life. But don't you worry about me, darling. I'll get along splendidly and with all that money I shall be able to live like a queen."

Her mother sniffed disdainfully. "Oh, there's not enough for that, Deb. You can't be very regal on two thousand a year. I never could."

Two thousand a year! Deborah thought it was wealth. Her salary for the past three years had been twenty-five dollars a week and she had found it quite adequate. And she had worked hard, too, to earn it. Now to be receiving a check for one hundred seventy-five dollars every month for doing absolutely nothing sounded unbelievable to her.

CHAPTER FIVE

SYLVIA TREMAINE and her new husband sailed for England on the twenty-fifth of April and Deborah wept a little when they bade her goodbye. And though she felt happier about her mother than she had since her father's death, she experienced a feeling of loneliness, too. She had so few relatives and none nearer than Wisconsin. It would be another two weeks before she was able to leave the hospital and she shuddered at the thought of going back to the North Side.

It was Mrs. Holcomb, the night superintendent, who discovered her aversion to continuing her work in the Health Department.

"It's shock, Deborah," the older woman explained. "It may take months for you to get back again. Why not go right away and rest for six months or a year?"

"I'm ashamed, Mrs. Holcomb," Deborah said. "But I wish I could go some place where no one was ever sick or maimed or handicapped in any way. Where there wasn't a doctor or a nurse in the whole community and where I could forget there was such a thing as an underprivileged child. I'm sick to death of hospitals and nurses and doctors."

"Well," said the superintendent, dryly, "I guess you're thinking of Heaven, aren't you? 'There shall be no more death, neither sorrow nor crying, neither shall there be any more pain,' " she quoted.

"Oh, I don't expect to find such a place," Deborah replied, ashamed of her outburst. "But it would be heavenly if I could."

"The nearest thing to it that I know of is Harmony," Mrs. Holcomb said. "That's the healthiest place I ever heard of. It's a resort in a way, and yet nearly all the residents live there the year round except for traveling— going abroad or south and so on just on trips or to avoid the winter cold. I own a little place there—in fact, Polly Quick, a second cousin of mine who brought me up, lives there now—quite alone except for her dog. Five years ago I leased it to my nephew, Doctor Ball, and he hung out his shingle. Well, the boy nearly starved. Not a soul was ever sick. So he packed up and moved to

Chicago. Why, even the undertaker left the place years ago —nobody died. Yes, I guess Harmony's about the healthiest place in the state—the country, maybe. When anyone feels like being sick, he stays in Buford, thirty miles inland. There's a fine hospital there and dozens of doctors. Anyway, you never see one of the creatures in Harmony, at least that's the story. When I retire in about ten years from now, I'm going there to live."

"It sounds grand, Mrs. Holcomb." Deborah had been listening avidly. "Would you lease your place to me? And how about your cousin? Do you suppose she would stay on and keep house for me?"

"I bet she would," the superintendent said. "Polly's a grand cook and fussy as the dickens, but she knows her place, too. She's sixty-ish but wiry and can work like a horse. She's a devout Methodist and does a lot for the church. I'm sure you'll like her; everyone in Harmony does—she's helped more people out of trouble and tight spots than anyone I ever knew and is what she herself calls a 'natural nurse,' whatever that is. I'll write and ask her, if you want me to. It's high and dry and I'm sure you'd find yourself there as quickly as you would anywhere."

"That's settled then. Let me know when you hear and I shall plan on leaving just as soon as you know your cousin will take me. We can settle the terms of the lease then. You're a godsend to me, Mrs. Holcomb," Deborah said gratefully. "It's taken a load off my mind."

When Alice called again, Deborah told her of her plans for a long vacation and Alice shrieked with delight. "It's fate, darling!" she cried. "Paul and I are planning on being married early in June—oh, just a visit to the parson—absolutely quiet, you know—and I've been worrying about you and the apartment. Now I won't have to look for another place. Paul can come right there until you come back and everything will be grand. It's none of my business, Deb, but just what arrangements— financial, you know——" she began diffidently.

"Oh, Alice, I'm rich!" Deborah exclaimed. "You see my father left a trust fund for Mother and me and now that Mother has married a comparatively rich man,

43

I'm to have it all. Perhaps to some people it wouldn't be so much but it seems like wealth to me."

"I'm glad," Alice told her and meant it. She had felt more than a little guilty about telling Deborah she was going to move from the apartment, for she knew Deb couldn't swing it alone on the salary of a Public Health Nurse. Now everything was perfect. "I hope you aren't planning on blowing it all in on the poor, the maimed and the halt, you poor dope."

"I am not. I'm going to be selfish, Alice. I'm running away from the North Side—from all the poor and sick and underprivileged. I'm fed up. I feel that I never want to see a nurse's uniform again as long as I live—much less wear one. That fire did something to me—I don't know——"

"That fire did one thing, my dear," her friend told her. "The city is all het up over better housing. Down with slums! Up with model, fireproof apartments having courts for children to play in and with every room sunny! Sounds screwy to me but my boss said it's what he's been slaving for all his life. So you see, darling, your heroism brought about a reform all right. I think the city should erect a tablet or a statue to you—they would have if you had died——"

"I don't want any statue, Alice. It's reward enough that the Polycletuses are letting Philip go to a reconstruction hospital. I had about decided it was hopeless to try to convince them."

"Where are you going? What do you think you'll do, if anything? But of course you can choose your place of residence and your own kind of job now, can't you?"

"Did you ever hear of a town called Harmony, Alice?" Deborah asked.

"Mm-mm," Alice shook her head. "Sounds like a political rally to me. Where is this place, Deb?"

"On Penguin Lake—thirty miles from Buford. It's the very healthiest place in the world and I'm leasing a little house there and I want you and Paul to come visit me. Will you?" Deborah's gray eyes shone and there was a lovely flush on her thin cheeks.

"Surest thing you know, Debby. We'll come up for a week end or maybe for our vacation if we have a vacation. Paul says it will be hard going for a while, but he doesn't take into consideration the money I'm going to make from my writing. I've started a book now and think of what I'll make from that when it's done—and sold! Do you know, Deb, sometimes I get peeved with Paul—he takes my literary talent so lightly. But I'll show him! Some day he'll be proud of me."

"He's proud of you now, Alice," Deborah told her. "And I hope your book will be a best seller, but don't go haywire if it comes back a dozen times. I've heard they often do, you know."

"Mine won't," Alice said confidently.

Deborah drove her new sports roadster through the fresh spring countryside to Harmony with an eagerness such as she had not experienced in years. The new car was blue with leather upholstery of a lighter shade and in her blue-gray knitted suit, rough straw hat and warm woolly coat, she felt as different from a P. H. Nurse as if indeed she were another person. She was still much too thin and pale but felt sure that the change of scene and environment would be all that was needed to restore her to her normally perfect health.

She had said goodbye to her associates with mixed feelings. Doctor Brown was frankly distressed and yet Deborah felt sure he had no sentimental interest in her. She was just a safety valve. She had served as a protection from the onslaught of Cynthia Marvin. The other P. H. Nurses were sorry to see her go. They all liked Deborah even while standing a little in awe of her because of her indifference to flattery or male attentions. Doctor Hamilton tried to extract a promise from her to return to them in the fall. She had been his greatest success and he was sure he could not replace her immediately if at all.

As she left Medford behind and swung north into the early spring traffic, her spirits lifted. The oppression that had weighed on her heart for months disappeared. She hummed softly to herself as the little car skimmed over the concrete ribbon to freedom and a new happiness; for she felt that somewhere, somehow, happiness awaited her.

By mid-afternoon she was well on her way and found that she was healthily hungry. She would stop at the first likely place and order a light luncheon, for she had an idea Polly would have dinner ready when she reached Harmony. A smart wayside tearoom appeared as she topped a little hill. She drove in through the inviting rustic gate to a sizable pavilion in which some half dozen people sipped cool-looking drinks from tall glasses.

"A glass of iced tea with lemon, a leafy salad and plain bread and butter sandwiches, please," she told the pretty little waitress who came to her. She leaned back in her chair and glanced interestedly about. This place must be about forty-five or fifty miles from her destination. She would ask when her luncheon arrived.

Two men and three girls seated some distance away were watching her. One of the girls was insisting something was right. They stopped her waitress as she passed and questioned her but the girl shook her head and came on with Deborah's order. She set the tray down before Deborah and smiled shyly as she examined her more closely.

"Are you Miss Bradley?" she asked after a minute.

"Why—why, yes," Deborah said. "Why?"

"Nothing, only the people over near the pillar asked me if you were and I didn't know." The girl's eyes held awe and admiration as they met hers.

Deborah glanced over at the group and encountered five pairs of eyes fixed on her.

"But I don't know any of them—I'm quite sure I don't," she said frowning. "There must be some mistake—it must be another Miss Bradley. I'm a complete stranger in this part of the state."

The girl looked disappointed as she left her and stopped at the other table for a moment. Deborah heard one of the young men give a jeering laugh and cringed inwardly. She continued to frown as she ate her lunch. If she had nursed anywhere but in the worst section of Medford, she might have thought one of those people had perhaps at some time been a patient: but surely no one as smartly dressed as these five were had any least connection with or need of a Public Health Nurse. She finished her meal and stood up preparatory to leaving.

"I'm sure I'm right," she heard with positive distinctness as she left, and waited for the masculine jeer of disbelief.

"All your geese are swans, Jean," came the dissenter's voice. "She's probably gone into movies by this time. A little notoriety plus long eyelashes and a gal's made."

It wasn't until Deborah was miles away that the thought came that perhaps the story of the fire had made her a marked figure. Oh, she hoped not. She wanted to forget it. After all, she had done nothing more than any person would do under like conditions. She didn't feel in the least heroic. One of the nurses had asked her if she hadn't been scared and she had answered truthfully that she didn't think so. In fact, there hadn't been time to be scared. The girl had looked at her curiously, but it was the truth. It had all happened so quickly. She hoped the lurid newspaper stories wouldn't follow her here. She hated all that notoriety—it was cheap and common and she wanted none of it.

The day was glorious. From time to time now she caught glimpses of the lake. Cars with trailers attached passed her all going north. She was beginning to grow tired. Perhaps it would have been better if she had listened to Doctor Hamilton and broken her journey halfway. She had been climbing steadily for the past half hour and knew she must be nearing Harmony. She stopped while a herd of cows crossed the highway in deliberate leisure. She smiled at the small parade of ducks that waddled along the path beside the road in single file solemnly following the leader, a huge gray fellow with dark blue markings. The reflection of sun on the concrete hurt her eyes so she put on dark glasses. The clock on the dash said quarter of six. She felt dusty and sticky and yet the day had not been particularly warm—just pleasantly so. But she supposed she had not quite recovered from her illness. She wasn't as strong as she insisted she was.

The lake was in plain view now and she entered the outskirts of a small town. Yes—"HARMONY WELCOMES YOU" was there beside the road. Deborah was suddenly excited. She felt strangely at home and as if she had lived here before. The houses she passed had a

47

delightful, lived-in look and the yards were beautifully landscaped and cared for. She drove slowly. There were few people about. Evidently it was the dinner hour. The second corner after passing the traffic light, her directions said, then turn right. The third house on her right. Why, the place was charming! She drove onto the graveled drive between low hedges of clipped privet and up to the front of the house. A startlingly ugly English bulldog waddled off the porch and down the short walk to the car where he raised his head disclosing two long tusks upthrust against his crumpled black muzzle. Deborah opened the car door and held out her hand to him.

"Hello, there!" she greeted him. The animal gave her a look of haughty disdain, then turned back toward the porch. Deborah alighted and followed him. She hoped he had decided to be friendly for she adored dogs, especially bulls. She stepped carefully around him as he plopped down in the sun, and rang the bell. There was the sound of hurrying footsteps and a thin, white-haired woman in crisp pink gingham unhooked the screen door.

"Land sakes!" she cried. "You're early. That is, if you're Abbie's Deborah Bradley. You are, ain't you? Come right in. Where's your luggage? I'll get it. You trot right upstairs to your room. Abbie told me to make you lie down's soon as you come. Slip off your clothes, why don't you, and there's plenty of hot water so's you can take a bath if you like. I know girls like lots of baths nowadays. I'll have supper on the table in half an hour. Fried chicken, mashed potatoes, asparagus, fresh rolls and coffee, and I made some ice cream with angel food cake for desert. Pie ain't so good at night—leastways 'taint for me. Now you just make yourself right t'home. I'll bring up your bags and slip 'em inside your room. My, you do look sort o' washed out. But we'll soon have some roses in them cheeks. And say," as Deborah started up the stairs, "I can bring your supper up to you if you like. No trouble a-tall. I'm that glad to have someone to cook for besides myself, I don't know. The front room on your right—nice view there."

"I'll be all right, Mrs.—Mrs.—I only know you by the name of Polly," Deborah stammered. What was it Mrs. Holcomb had called her?

"Well, what's the matter with Polly? It's my name, ain't it? Sure. Call me Polly and more than likely I'll call you Debby before you been here many days. Miss Bradley's too stand-off-ish for me. When supper—I mean dinner's ready, I'll ring that there Chinese gong Abbie sets such store by. Heathenish, I call it, but she would hang it there. Listen. When you hear the sound of the gong," she struck it with the tiny wooden hammer, "it will be exactly supper—dinner time." Her voice became that of one of the well-known announcers of a popular radio station. Her face was expressionless, however, and Deborah decided that Polly had a sense of humor as well as an overworked tongue. Mrs. Holcomb had said she knew her place which no doubt meant she wouldn't intrude. Well, just at present Deborah felt she wanted solitude. Later, perhaps, she would enjoy Polly.

She found her room delightfully fresh and attractive. A huge canopied bed, a mammoth mahogany dresser and a very frilly, feminine dressing table reminded her of the pictures she and Alice had cut from magazines against the day when their dream houses should materialize. There was a rosy chintz-covered chaise longue near a wide awninged window from which one could lie and watch the ever changing color of Penguin Lake. The door opened and two bags thumped against the floor. Deborah turned quickly.

"Want anything else?" Polly whispered sibilantly, only her head inside the room.

"Not a thing, Polly. It's all lovely. I'm sure I shall adore it here. Thank you for bringing up my bags, but you shouldn't have, you know. I am not an invalid any longer."

"Oh, that's all right. It's good for my figger," she said as she disappeared.

Deborah bathed, slipped into a soft satin housecoat and stretched out on the chaise longue. The soft May breeze brushed her cheeks and she sighed in deep content. In the distance the lake lay shimmering in the late afternoon sun. Shadowy fingers of purple began to creep out from the shore. A small fleet of sailboats lay motionless in the little harbor almost as if painted on the dark blue of the lake. Outside the window a robin called

49

throatily and on the lawn two others tugged at an attractive piece of string. A long sleek cat crept stealthily through the hedge and Deborah leaned forward and hissed:

"Scat!" The sleek intruder, a front paw raised, lifted yellow eyes to the window and crouched low in the grass. But the robins had departed leaving the delectable piece of string for some more intrepid home builder.

How peaceful it all was! From below came faint sounds of activity. And that was fried chicken Polly was cooking. Deborah knew she had never before been quite so hungry. A faint scratching on her door startled her for a minute and she listened. It was repeated somewhat impatiently and she rose and looked into the hall. The huge bulldog lumbered in and settled himself close to the chaise longue.

"Is that dratted dog up there, Miss Bradley?" Polly called from the foot of the stairs.

"Yes, he just came up," Deborah explained. "I don't mind."

"Well, I do. He drags mud and dirt in. Come down here, you Kitchener. You hear me?"

Kitchener grunted and dropped his ugly head on his paws.

"Give him a shove, Debby," Polly urged. "He'll, stay there till doomsday if you don't. Such a beast! Here Kitchener! Come on and get a cook-y—dar-lin'," Polly crooned.

The dog raised his head and grinned for all the world as if he suspected Polly of spoofing, but he got ponderously to his feet and padded toward the door, looking back once or twice to see if Deborah meant to follow. The girl laughed aloud.

"All right," she said. "I'll come, too." And she followed the cumbersome body as it dropped from stair to stair with an accompanying grunt at every step. When he reached the lower hall he turned to wait until she joined him then led the way to the kitchen from which the delicious odors emanated.

"He's the funniest thing I've ever seen, Polly," Deb orah said as they entered the kitchen.

"He's an old fraud!" Polly declared, poking him with the toe of her slipper.

Kitchener grunted again and sniffed her ankle.

"Go 'long with you!" Polly ordered, then reached for a paper plate and placed a cooky on it. "He wouldn t hurt a fly," she explained, "but he's a grand watch dog just the same. He just has to look at a peddler or a bum and you can't see their heels for dust, they run so fast."

"He's probably too fat," Deborah said.

"That ain't fat—it's bone and muscle. Look!" She stooped and caught hold of his neck which lay in great folds. "See? You feel."

And Deborah saw that while Kitchener was well padded, he was indeed a huge monster of bone and muscle. She patted his ugly head. He grunted again and nuzzled her hand.

"I guess he likes you all right. They's some he don't and they find it pleasanter to keep their distance. You'll find a fresh towel over there on the reck—no knowing what's lit on him since he was washed this mornin'."

Yes, Deborah decided, Abbie was right. Polly was finicky, but she was sure she was going to like her.

CHAPTER SIX

DEBORAH FOUND HARMONY not quite all that its name implied. She was surprised to find very few children in her immediate neighborhood and those few scarcely children any longer. The people were friendly but Deborah wondered if perhaps they were inclined to be cliquy and snobbish. She found that the neighbor on her right had nothing to do with the one on her left. She wondered why until Polly told her that Mrs. Norman on her left had been a factory girl from over in Buford while Mrs. Thompson on the right was a Buford Junior Leaguer. Both were childless and Polly looked down her straight little nose at them both.

Both ladies called on Deborah and invited her to join their own particular bridge clubs. Deborah didn't care for bridge but promised to consider their invitations. She explained that she had been ill and must rest a great deal. She attended Polly's church on Sunday because it was near; but, being an Episcopalian, decided she would drive on to one of her own denomination the next Sunday. This she did and met several charming women besides the rector and his wife who, the day before, had received word from Mrs. Holcomb to look out for her. After that, it seemed as if she had little time to herself. And she found that she was taking to community life as easily as a duck takes to water.

She had been in Harmony several weeks. June was rioting over the countryside. The bathroom scales showed an alarming increase in weight and Deborah warned Polly to cut down on her desserts.

"You get out and play tennis, Debby," Polly ordered. "Swim and go out to the Country Club for some golf and go to a dance occasionally. What d'you want to be stickin' around with all these married women for—playin' bridge! 'Tain't accordin' to nature. And what's the matter with the young men in these parts? Why ain't they been around?"

Deborah laughed. "I'm not a man's girl, Polly," she said. "And I've not been invited to join the Country Club."

"I'll see about that," Polly declared firmly. "Not a man's girl, indeed! Fiddle-daddle!"

And see about it she did. Young Mrs. Barstow from up on the hill called one afternoon and bore Deborah off for tennis and tea at the Club. She was given a guest membership for the duration of her stay and later she met some of the young men home from college. After that her days became full and her evenings hectic.

It was during a dance at the Club that a tall young man was introduced to her who looked vaguely familiar. From his frown as he heard her name she wondered if he, too, had recognized her. But where? His name meant nothing to her. Jordan—Peter Jordan. She danced several times with him and at last he drew her through one of the wide French windows and down the steps to the shadowy lawn. They walked a little way along the grassy path to where a bench encircled a giant elm tree.

"Isn't this glorious?" Deborah murmured, her head against the tree, her eyes on the moonlit lake and pinpoints of light in the purple distance. Fireflies flitted in and out of the darker shadows; the mingled scent of roses and honeysuckle was almost unbearably sweet. Deborah's throat ached with the loveliness of it all. The man beside her was silent as if he, too, sensed the rare, poignant beauty of the night. Deborah sighed and he turned his head.

"That was a prodigious sigh, young lady," he said quizzically. "Do you know, you puzzle me, and I dislike puzzles. We have met before. I'm sure of it. But where? It's unthinkable that having met you I could ever forget. Your name is familiar, of course, because it's the same as the little nurse who was the heroine of a fire somewhere down state—Medford, wasn't it?"

"It was Medford, Mr. Jordan," Deborah answered, "and we have the same name—Deborah Mary Bradley. I seem to know you, too, but your name means nothing to me. I can't imagine where we could have met."

"Oh, Jordan! Peter!" someone called from the Clubhouse porch. "Telephone—long distance!" The man who came toward them through the soft June night was Jason Miller and Deborah recalled rather guiltily that she had the next dance with him and had forgotten about it.

Now he sat down beside her as Jordan rose. "Run along, big boy," he said. "I feel like staying right here for a while myself."

Jordan excused himself and started for the Clubhouse, calling over his shoulder;

"Stay right there, Miss Bradley—I'll see you again."

Deborah had heard Mr. Jordan call those same words over his shoulder before. Memory awakened. That was it—the man at the airport. But his name hadn't been Jordan. The card he had given her bore the name of Oliver Cromwell Turner—the famous novelist. Was he here incognito? She could not ask Jason if that were the case. And no one here knew her as the P. H. Nurse who had gotten into the papers. The pictures had been terrible and not at all like her so that she had been able to remain entirely unknown. Polly knew her merely as one of her cousin's patients with plenty of money who was recovering from a bout with pneumonia. All this went through her mind while they watched Peter Jordan mount the steps and disappear inside the Clubhouse.

"How do you like Pete, Deb?" Jason asked after a moment in which he contemplated the girl beside him with serious eyes.

"I don't know him," Deborah laughed. "So far he appears all right. Why? Has he a dark mysterious secret in his life or perhaps a wife hidden away somewhere in the background?"

She didn't know just why she asked such silly questions, but she was still puzzling about that name which the man must still have been using when he called at the apartment while she was in the hospital too ill to see anyone.

"His wife died several years ago," Jason told her. "He hasn't seemed to care much about women since although I assure you it hasn't been the fault of the females in this town. The rest of us have to take back seats when Pete favors Harmony with his presence. What has Peter Jordan got that I haven't, Deb? Tell me that."

"I'm sure I wouldn't know, Jason," Deborah answered. "I've just met the man. What does he do for a living, if anything?" she continued curiously.

"Oh, he's pretty well off as far as that goes," Jason

told her, "but I believe he's interested in some publishing house in New York. At least he's down there a good share of the time."

For a moment the tall form of Peter Jordan appeared silhouetted in the lighted doorway before he ran down the steps and strode toward them.

"Beat it, Jason!" he ordered pleasantly. "Miss Bradley and I are renewing an old friendship."

"Friendship, my eye!" Jason snorted youthfully. "You never laid eyes on each other until tonight. Quit your clowning, Peter. Anyway, you cheated me out of that last dance, and I've a good mind to——"

"Oh, be a good egg, Jason. Trot along. I'll see you again," he called after the departing young man.

"That's what I remember about you," Deborah said impulsively. " 'I'll see you again.' You said that to me once."

"I did?" He laughed ruefully. "I reckon I've said it to several million people. It's a tag."

"A graceful way of getting rid of people—of saying goodbye, I suppose."

"But where was it I said it to you, Miss Bradley?" he insisted. "I must have meant it in your case—see you again, I mean."

"Oh, no. You see, your cab driver rammed my car when I was leaving Medford airport one afternoon last winter. You gave Mat Chico a twenty-dollar bill and me your card but the name on it wasn't Jordan." She smiled and went on. "Have I discovered your secret, Mr. Turner?"

The man beside her slapped his knee. "I knew I had met you before besides recognizing your name. Then you are Deborah Mary Bradley, the Public Health Nurse who risked her life in that tenement fire, aren't you? I remember now. Your car had a red cross on the door and you had on some sort of uniform—anyway it was blue—dark blue coat, untrimmed, and your hat was—well—it was just a hat. So you're a nurse!"

"Shh!" Deborah warned him. "No one knows it here and anyway I'm not a nurse any longer. I came to Harmony because Mrs. Holcomb says no one ever gets sick here. I'm fed up with sick people. I never want to see another hospital as long as I live," she finished vehemently.

"I don't wonder," he murmured sympathetically. "It must have been a terrible experience——"

Deborah shuddered. "Please don't let's talk about it and please never mention it to anyone else, or I shall have to leave. I—I can't stand it."

"Of course I'll not mention it," he assured her.

"Perhaps I'm silly, but I can't seem to help it," the girl said then turned abruptly. "But why are you incognito?"

"I?" he asked. "But I'm not. I really am Jordan—Peter Jordan. What makes you think——"

"But the card you gave me had the name Oliver Cromwell Turner on it and when you called at the apartment for an interview with my housemate you gave the name of Oliver Cromwell Turner," Deborah explained.

"I call at your apartment? In Medford? But I didn't. I never was in Medford but once and then just for connection with the Florida plane. I lost the one at Corinth and nearly missed my appointment with Countess de Bienville in Miami." He looked puzzled then his face brightened. "Probably I had one of Turner's cards in my pocket and gave it to you by mistake. Did you send the bill for repairs to Turner?" He laughed joyously. "No wonder he called at your apartment. Probably wondered if someone was trying to blackmail him."

"I didn't send him any bill. Mat Chico paid for the repairs," Deborah told him. "I made him—out of the twenty dollars you gave him."

"Did I give him twenty dollars? I certainly must have been loony. Now you tell me a few things, Miss Deborah Mary Bradley," he began.

"I'd much rather you told me a few things," Deborah countered, demurely. "Just who is Oliver Cromwell Turner if not the famous novelist? Or are there two men by that name? That would be a little difficult to believe."

"Oh, he's the novelist all right if you mean the owner of the card I passed out to you. You see he's one of our writers."

"Your writers? But I thought his publishers were Crane, Fish and Company," Deborah said. "Their im print of a crane, standing on one leg with a fish in his mouth, has always intrigued me."

"I'm the Company," Peter Jordan said whimsically, "and I'm thankful there is nothing about me or my name they could include in that imprint. I've kidded Bill Fish about his precarious position for years. He doesn't give a hoot, though—thinks it's clever. Anyway, it's on a good many excellent books."

"You live a long way from your business, don't you?" Deborah remarked after a pause in which they listened to the tantalizing strains of the swing number the orchestra was playing.

"Oh, I run down occasionally, but the business doesn't really require my presence. Crane and Fish are both capable of running things. When they need me it's an easy matter to reach me. How do you like Harmony and is it doing for you all that you hoped it would?"

"I like it," Deborah said simply. "I'm quite happy here. And Polly and Lord Kitchener spoil me with their complete devotion. I adore them both."

"And the villagers? How do they react to your charm, youth and beauty?" he asked.

"The people I have met are lovely to me. Of course there must be dozens of young people I haven't met. I suppose July and August are the months when people flock back here and open their homes. I have been curious about the sort of people who probably live in one or two particularly attractive places. There's one high up on the cliff. A huge place. It must be wonderful up there. Do you know who lives there?"

Peter Jordan examined the candid eyes raised to his but found them quite devoid of guile. "A man by the name of Jordan lives there," he said dryly. "In fact, he built it for his bride."

"O–oh!" murmured Deborah, then quickly; "But it looks quite old." She was suddenly embarrassed.

"It is old. My great-grandfather built it in 1834. My grandfather, father and I were all born there. Now my mother and dad live in California near my sister and the house became mine when I married. My daughter and I live there now—at least I do—practically the year round."

"Your daughter? How old is she?" Deborah asked,

not that she wanted to know, particularly, but because she felt it was expected of her.

"Seven. Nancy was three years old when Marcia, my wife, died. She's at present staying with her grandmother and aunt near Boston. I'm not keen about her spending so much time away from home: but Davis, the famous child specialist, advised it for both their sakes. You see, Marcia was Eve's only sister and they look very much alike. Nancy would no doubt have suffered acutely except for Eve who has actually taken a mother's place. I just don't like the situation because Eve spoils the child. I suppose it's natural, but I can't think it's good for her. Then, too, it's a burden on Eve who is young and very beautiful, yet she insists upon Nancy spending the greater part of each year with her. When she's home with me, Eve runs over for week ends and we disagree constantly over the child. It worries me no end."

"But you're her father. Surely a seven-year-old girl ought to be with her parent or else in school, it seems to me," Deborah said.

"Oh, Nancy has a tutor. That's another thing upon which Eve and I disagree. I feel that a governess would be better for her at her age, but Eve insists that a tutor has a better influence and is less apt to coddle the child."

"So of course Nancy gets a tutor," Deborah said dryly. "I never heard of such a thing. A tutor for a seven-year old girl! Now if the child were a boy——"

"Oh, I know," Peter Jordan said ruefully. "You think I'm a jellyfish, don't you? Well, sometimes I think so, too, but you see——"

"But I don't see," Deborah said stiffly, "and it isn't at all necessary that I should see. It really isn't any of my business, only, as a woman, it seems to me perfectly ridiculous to employ a tutor for a small girl. And a motherless girl needs a certain amount of coddling as you call it. Although, no doubt, you supply all that is necessary for her well being and her aunt attends to the rest."

"But, you see, Nancy isn't an ordinary child, Miss Bradley, and Eve is far from an ordinary woman. She's —she's—well, she's Eve and——"

"I say, old man, this is too much of a good thing," Jason Miller complained. "What's the idea of monopolizing Deb all evening? She happens to be my date, you know. You stags give me a large pain. You barge in and ᵛsnatch our girls whenever you like——"

"Sorry, old chap," Peter murmured getting to his feet. "Miss Bradley and I have been comparing notes and talking over mutual acquaintances and didn't realize how quickly time passed. Forgive me. I'll see you again," he said and laughed somewhat wryly as he watched them move toward the Club.

"I thought you said you didn't know Pete," Jason said aggrievedly.

"I thought I didn't, but it seems I met him last winter," Deborah explained and wondered why she found it necessary.

"Do you know Eve Fowler, his sister-in-law? Now there's a gal! People say she'll land him yet. She's nuts over the chee-ild. Poor little tyke!"

"I promised this dance to someone," Deborah murmured.

"I claim this number, Deborah." Jason hurried her along the path and up the steps as the orchestra began. "Come on, it's the supper dance and I could do with something wet. How about you?"

Back under the elm tree Peter Jordan watched them disappear inside the brightly lighted Club. He had hesitated over coming here tonight but now he was glad he had made the effort. The girl at the airport had stayed in his mind during that plane trip to Miami—until the business of signing up the temperamental Countess de Bienville had driven everything else out. He had liked her clear gray eyes, her air of independence and the way she had stepped from her rammed car and faced his driver. It had all occurred in the twinkling of an eye so to speak: but she had registered as clearly as if his mind had been a camera set for instantaneous exposure. Queer how things happened. Queer, too, that they should meet again, here in Harmony.

CHAPTER SEVEN

PETER JORDAN appeared in time for lunch next day and
Deborah discovered that he was a special pet of Polly's.

"Polly's fed me when I was hungry, clothed me when I
was—well, practically naked, nursed me when I was sick
and once even visited me when I was in jail. Remember
that time, Polly, and how you brought me an apple turn-
over all gooey with brown sugar and cinnamon? Mmm!
Never have I tasted anything so delicious. I needed it,
too, to sort of fortify me for the lecture and laying on of
hands I endured when Dad got me home."

"You sure were the beatin'est, Peter," Polly said
affectionately.

"Beatin'est, Polly? I guess I got the worst of it although the other fellow did look pretty bad. But his
father didn't whale him. As I remember it, I was blamed
for the whole thing—leading Lester into temptation and
beating him up. I remember that when Dad heard from
the opposition, he bought me a new boat—a humdinger.
After that, the memory of that whaling lost its sting. By
the way, I met Lester Parker in New York one day last
spring. He's quite successful, too. Doing sports stuff for
the *Gazette*."

"Nasty little rat!" Polly declared vindictively. "But
comin' from the home he did 'tain't to be wondered at.
What you and Debby aimin' on doin' this afternoon?"

"I want her to see Cliff House, Polly. She said it sort
of intrigued her and I want her to see it at its best,"
Peter said, "before the family returns and—well—the
ghost——"

"Have you a ghost? Oh, I'm glad there's a ghost—I
adore ghosts!" Deborah cried. "Tweedie Manor, my
stepfather's home, has a ghost, Mother writes me. I think
that's the only thing that would induce me to spend the
winter in England. It seems she's a very charming ghost
and hums softly as she wanders through the halls from
midnight until one o'clock on February fifth of each year
and on special occasions when anything important is to
happen to one of the family. February fifth was the date
she was to have been married to her cousin, the youngest
son of an ancestor of my stepfather. He was killed in one

of the wars and she died of a broken heart when the news reached her. It's all very charming and romantic and Mother says the ghost was a very lovely girl in real life; her picture hangs in the great hall."

"Ghosts!" scoffed Polly. "I don't hold with any such foolishness. Tell me, has anybody ever seen this here ghost?"

"Oh, yes, of course, Polly," Deborah said. "It's a tradition in the Tremaine family. Just before a member of the family marries, the ghost always appears, that is, if she appears it is understood to be a satisfactory match. She sort of gives the affair her blessing, you see. Mother says that the very night before she and my stepfather were married in Medford here in the United States, Marianna Wentworth was seen strolling through the halls and humming her endless song. So his relatives were quite prepared for the news when it arrived in England. Why, Polly, ghosts are nourished and treasured in all the best families in England. They are proud of them."

"Fiddle-daddle!" Polly snorted. "I bet their ghosts can all be set down to something they et, or too much licker. I hear tell the English are pretty fond of their licker."

Peter laughed. "Have you no poetry in your soul, Polly? No imagination? Isn't there a drop of romantic blood in your veins?"

"No," Polly retorted stoutly. "I got good red American blood in my veins and plain common sense in my head. Ghosts, indeed!" and she left them.

"I'm afraid our ghost isn't the kind to thrill you, Deb," Peter said as they sped through Harmony and took the cliff road. "Mine is a rather somber one." The girl sensed bitterness in his voice. Then he shrugged as if to get rid of an uncomfortable burden and went on quickly;. "But we've got just about the finest view in these parts. I want you to see the garden, too. I think it's at its best right now. I've got an English gardener, Toby Wren, who can do anything with flowers. He's been with us now for fifteen years and I doubt if he will ever leave. He's just a little 'teched'—mad about the place. In fact, everyone at Cliff House has been with me for years excepting Johnny, the man-of-all-work. He's

61

Toby's nephew who has ideas of being a G-Man some day. They're all devoted to Cliff House."

"And to its master?" Deborah asked demurely.

"Oh, I guess they like me all right. I'm not a hard one to please and they do about as they like. The only thing I demand is loyalty. I'll have no divided service. If they work for me—what I say goes. We get along very well, except——" He stopped and his face saddened, but he went on;. "Feel the difference in the air? It's always cool up here. That's one of the reasons why the first Jordan built on this cliff."

The powerful car climbed the hill through thickly wooded land. Trees laced their branches overhead making a cool, green arcade. A low stone wall kept back the forest from encroaching on the highway, and wild grape and ivy twined over the gray mossy stones. Clumps of fern and streamers of myrtle hugged the base and Deborah knew that without doubt goldenrod, wild aster and Queen Anne's lace would appear later in the season. Through the trees an occasional glimpse of the lake appeared but for the most part nothing was to be seen but the soft cool green of trees. It wasn't a long ride and they soon reached Cliff House, standing serenely amid spruce and cedars and hardy maples. A long winding drive, bordered with closely clipped privet, led from the highway to the big stone house at the top of the cliff. Gay awnings shaded windows and wide porches and two red Irish setters raced down the drive to meet the car. Peter stopped and, one on either side, the dogs jumped on the running boards and rode to the house.

"That's an established custom," Peter told her. "Rommie and Remie ride with me but with no one else. They refuse to touch a car if I'm not in it. Otherwise it might prove embarrassing to callers.

"They're beauties, all right," Deborah said, dropping her hand on the head of the nearest dog. "How can you tell which is which? They look exactly alike to me."

"They are identical twins with but one tiny distinguishing mark. Remie has one white toe—you can see it when they get down. They are grand old fellows and are the only dogs on the place. Some day I'm going to have kennels like Grandfather had, but——" He paused and went on quickly. "Welcome to Cliff House, Deborah Mary Bradley! Like it?"

"Love it, Peter," Deborah murmured, her gray eyes taking in the beauty of the sprawling old house. "But isn't it huge, Peter? Aren't you lost in it?"

"No. Somehow it has never seemed too large—to me. Of course I am seldom alone here, and for another thing, it's home. Dad and Mother offered to come east and live with me after Marcia died, but I wouldn't let them. My sister has a big family of youngsters and the climate out there agrees with Dad better than this does. They come east once or twice a year—always for Christmas. Imagine leaving California in midwinter. But they come and are no doubt glad to get back there, too. As for me, I couldn't be pried loose from Cliff House."

"I don't wonder." Deborah was slightly awed by the charm and beauty of the place—the quiet, unobtrusive grandeur that only generations of wealth and gracious living can give. The wide hall was breath-taking with its paneled walls and ceiling: its beautiful staircase and rich furnishings.

"Great-grandfather traveled a great deal and most of the rugs and tapestry and a lot of the furnishings are trophies of his wanderings. There's the old boy up there. Looks a bit of a pirate, doesn't he? I imagine he wasn't averse to making a pretty close bargain at times, either. That's Great-grandmother next. On this side are Grandfather and Grandmother. Handsome pair, aren't they? Dad and Mother are in the drawing room. Let's go see them."

Deborah saw a lovely woman in the bridal finery of the nineties and a man so much like the Peter Jordan beside her that she gasped in astonishment. Peter laughed.

"That's a grand compliment, Deb," he told her. "I'm mighty proud to be thought like my father. He's one swell chap!"

"How lovely your mother is, Peter!" Deborah murmured.

"And she hasn't changed much either. It's hard to believe she has a grandson in military school and a granddaughter almost ready to enter college."

Deborah looked around for portraits of Peter and his

wife, but saw none. As if he read her wandering glance, Peter laughed shortly.

"Mother took my picture with her and Marcia's porttrait hangs in Nancy's bedroom. You'll see it when we go upstairs. But first we are going to have something cool to drink." He pressed a button and in a few minutes a maid appeared with a tray on which two frosty glasses and a brimming pitcher tinkled invitingly as she passed it to Deborah and the master of the house.

Deborah's eyes roamed the long, enchanting room took in the exquisite hangings, the soft oriental rugs and the priceless furniture. She had never been in such a place before and her heart beat fast, her eyes shone and her breath caught in admiration and delight. Her mother had written of the beauties of English homes she had visited, but surely nothing anywhere could surpass Cliff House.

"Peter Jordan," she murmured, excitement staining her cheeks a lovely pink, "you're a very lucky man—privileged to live in the midst of such exquisite beauty. It's almost more than one person is entitled to natural beauty outside and then this. How can you bear leaving it—even for a day?"

"Like it, Deb?" Peter asked again, and now his eyes glowed and the face, that in repose wore a somewhat tragic look, lightened.

"Oh, Peter, I adore it!" Deborah whispered, clasping her hands to her breast in childish delight. "I have never seen anything like it. Why doesn't Nancy——"

"Come." He stood up abruptly. "Let's see the rest of it and then I'll show you the garden. Toby Wren will be pleased if you take an interest in his roses. Some people come here with a complete knowledge of every single flower he has and poor Toby is disgruntled—he gets no chance to display his own unique views."

Deborah laughed and nodded understandingly. "A word to the wise, etc. I see. But as a matter of fact, while I love roses, I can't tell an American Beauty from the ordinary common garden variety except by the length of stem. I know one pays according to yardage when buying American Beauties."

"Received lots of American Beauties, I suppose,"

Peter said and his voice sounded like that of a small boy who had been beaten to his goal by some luckier youngster.

"Only to arrange them for some more fortunate female," Deborah smiled. "Nurses don't often receive flowers unless a grateful patient remembers her upon leaving the hospital. I don't think I ever had American Beauties given me—except once." She added that last with a touch of malice. Peter looked so relieved that she felt compelled to bother him a little. It was funny to see his face change. But she remembered that after the fire there had been quantities of flowers of all kinds and it was quite conceivable there were offerings of American Beauties among them—not for her, personally, but a tribute to the heroine of the fire.

"O-oh," he murmured. "I see." Deborah wondered just what it was he saw. "And what is your favorite flower?" he asked. "What particular kind was sent you —on special occasions?"

Deborah thought for a moment, a slim finger against her lower lip. "I don't know that I have a favorite. Daffodils in early spring; lilacs after rain: delphinium and iris in summer—I love their cool look—and chrysanthemums in the fall. Oh, and valley lilies and purple and white violets and—yes, narcissi. I don't care for gladioli nor for dahlias, can't explain why, I just don't, nor for zinnias."

"You haven't mentioned roses at all," Peter reminded her.

"But everyone loves roses—that's perfectly obvious."

They were standing in Nancy's sitting room. A charming room with long French windows opening onto a high, wide veranda overlooking Penguin Lake. Peter had indicated the child's bedroom and Deborah had glimpsed a typical nursery, perfectly sanitary and sparsely furnished except for the huge portrait above the fireplace, which completely dominated the room. Again it was a bride pictured there. A beautiful blond girl with wide blue eyes and full, petulant mouth, wearing a white satin gown, heavy with lace. The face was amazingly beautiful and yet there was something faintly repellent in it. Peter had walked to one of the open sitting room windows where he stood with his back to the nursery door.

"Proud and spoiled and willful," Deborah said to herself. "I wonder if you really loved your husband. What unhappy memories have you given him?"

The girl in the picture stared back at her as if resenting her intrusion and Deborah turned away a little shocked and puzzled at her feeling of dislike of Nancy's dead mother. She joined Peter at the window.

"This is the very nicest room in a house full of charming rooms," Deborah exclaimed watching a boat skimming across the lake, its sails white against a background of intense, vivid blue. "Imagine living with that view ever before one. A greeting upon awakening in the morning—a benediction before going to sleep at night!"

They went downstairs again and along brick walks between fragrant shrubs and sweet-smelling borders, to the rose garden. There they found Toby Wren in brown smock and khaki pants, his sandy hair on end and his blunt fingers stained with soil. He had the clearest, bluest eyes Deborah had ever seen and a wide mouth below a button of a nose that gave him the appearance of wearing a mask. He pulled a long forelock when Peter introduced him to Deborah and bobbed his head.

"Miss Bradley doesn't know one rose from another, Toby," Peter said ingratiatingly, "so do your stuff, man."

Toby beamed on her. "You're a lover of flowers, Miss. I can see that. Likely you never studied botany?" he asked hopefully.

"I may have studied it in my youth, Toby," Deborah said, wrinkling her nose childishly, "but I doubt if I ever got a passing grade in the subject. I know a daisy when I see it and I can tell a lily from a rose, but as to their own private or family names, I'm absolutely in the dark."

"The Lord be thanked for that, Miss! Some of these experts come in here and make me fair sick with their fancy Latin talk. I don't insult my flowers by callin' them any such heathenish gibberish. A rose has got feelin's and I give her a pretty name when I plant her. Now here's one I call 'The First Kiss': ain't she a pretty thing? Soft pink with just the faintest scent. This one's 'The Flirt'—yellow tipped but pink at heart. Here's

'The Widow'—pure white outside: but shading to dark red near the centre—when she's open. I don't care for her. This one's my favorite—white all the way through. 'Mother Love.' I named her after my own mother—dead these many years. Tell me which you like best, Miss," he urged.

"Oh, I don't know, they are all so lovely! Here, this one is beautiful—I think I like this one best." She had stopped beside a low bush upon which pale yellow buds were beginning to unfold their waxen petals.

Toby chuckled. "You're the first one who's noticed that one 'specially," he said. "She's the Jordan rose. 'Priscilla Jordan,' her name is, after the wife of the first master of Cliff House. Now ain't that funny, though? You're the very first one, Miss."

"And what does that signify, if anything?" Deborah asked and if she was embarrassed, she didn't show it. "Evidently the first mistress of Cliff House had the same exquisite taste in flowers that I have, Toby," she laughed merrily. "I'm afraid you're romantic," she chided, smiling at the old man. "But you have wonderful luck with your flowers."

"It ain't luck, Miss," he objected. "It's the care and love I give my flowers that make them what they are." He stooped and picked two buds from the Jordan rose and handed one to reach of his visitors. "Nary a thorn on them roses, Miss," he said meaningly. "Its scent is subtle and its heart is pure gold, you'll find." His very blue eyes twinkled as he went back to his digging.

Peter laughed and pulled Deb's hand through his arm as they wandered on through the maze of shrubbery to the summerhouse on the edge of the cliff.

"Toby's a bachelor, Deb," he told her. "For some reason he seems to have taken a fancy to you. I never knew him to cut one of his roses without being asked to. You should feel honored, my dear. I assure you Toby's quite a judge of female pulchritude."

"To hear you talk one would suppose girls and women flocked to Cliff House," Deborah challenged. "Is it public property?"

"Indeed it is not. But Harmony folk like to come up here once in a while, especially when they have guests from some big city. They seem to think Cliff House sort of justifies their living in the sticks."

"But Harmony needs no apology," Deborah protested. "I love it here. I think I am going to stay just as long as Mrs. Holcomb will let me have the place, and Polly will put up with me."

"Put up with you!" Peter objected. "Polly's your slave and you know it. And Polly's discerning, let me tell you. She doesn't give her friendship and loyalty easily or indiscriminately. My mother was happy here," he went on. "She was a Boston girl, but was perfectly contented at Cliff House until Dad's health failed. Now she seems devoted to California."

"I can understand that," Deborah agreed. "My mother was always stanchly American until she married my stepfather and now she's really terribly British. Talks about ancestry and heritage as if they were the two most important things in the world."

"And they're not?" Peter asked, not that he cared particularly about her answer but he liked to watch her vivid face below his cloud of wavy hair.

"Of course they're not. I've seen some anomalies since I became a nurse."

"I bet you have," Peter said. "And I bet you were a swell nurse, too. But come, I want to show you our own private beach and what do you say to a swim—right now?"

Deborah glanced at her watch. "I'm afraid not this afternoon, Peter. I promised Polly I'd drive her over to Buford at four o'clock. She wants to see a friend who is in the hospital. I won't go in with her, although she wanted me to. I can't." She shuddered and closed her eyes. "I just can't bring myself to visit a hospital or a sick person either. I'm ashamed of myself but—oh, I'll snap out of it after a while—I hope."

It wasn't until she was dropping off to sleep that night that Deborah remembered Peter hadn't told her about his ghost. But there was tomorrow. She smiled as drowsiness overcame her.

CHAPTER EIGHT

DEBBY!" CALLED POLLY QUICK from the foot of the stairs. "A caller to see you. Come right in, Peter. Seems like old times your droppin' in so often this way. But ain't you sort of rushin' things a mite, Peter? Seems to me Debby ain't had much time for anyone else since you came home three weeks ago. When's Nancy comin'?"

"Next week, I think, Polly," he answered, dropping into a cretonne-covered chair.

"I'm glad Debby's havin' a good time, Peter. She told me when she first came that she wasn't a man's girl, whatever that is: but they's a young doctor—Doctor Brown—comin' to dinner Sunday, and I'll guarantee he ain't comin' to see me." Polly laughed, then sobered. "I suppose that mother-in-law of yours'll be landin' down on you for a spell when Nancy comes, won't she? Land sakes, boy! Ain't you got no backbone? Why don't you put your foot down and send her a-kitin'? I thought the last time I see Nancy her disposition couldn't be worse but likely by this time 'tis: what with her and Eve, who's bad enough, land knows."

"I know, Polly: but what can I do? After all she's Eve's mother and Nancy's fond of her—and—of Eve."

"Fond of her! Fiddle-daddle! Why wouldn't she be fond of folks who allow her to do just as she pleases with nary a question or a nay? Peter Jordan, you're neglectin' your duty as a father and some day you'll rue it. Mark my words."

"But Polly——" he began, his voice suddenly harassed.

"Don't you 'but Polly' me, Peter Jordan. Those don't watch out. Spite of what you say, Peter Jordan, Eve's a—a vampire—one of these here life-suckin' vampires the movies tell about. You'll see. That specialist who told you to give your child to Eve was either a villain or a fool. I don't know which is worse."

"Oh, Polly!" the young man cried. "Be fair! Eve may be a little ineffectual and partial but she really loves Nancy——"

" 'Tain't only Nancy she loves, Peter, if you can call that jealous possessiveness love," Polly said surprisingly.

"It's Nancy's pa Eve Fowler's after. That's her game and don't you make no mistake about it. If you wasn't so dumb you'd have seen it long ago." Polly Quick shook a long finger at the grinning young man. "She never give you up to my way o' thinkin'."

"Now *you're* being partial," Peter said. "I'm no Clark Gable, Polly, and don't make me laugh. Eve and I fight like cat and dog: but darling, you must acknowledge that she's beautiful. As for her ever desiring me—why she simply treats me—well—like a sister would."

"Umph! That don't prove nothin'. When it comes to women, Peter Jordan, you're innocenter than a babe unborn," Polly told him.

"I guess maybe you're right at that, Polly," Peter agreed thoughtfully. "You're a mysterious sex and very, very artful: but," he flashed her a winning smile, "terribly attractive for all that. Tell me, my good woman, when will your charming mistress be able to see me? What the heck's she doing anyway?"

"Don't you 'good woman' me, neither, Peter Jordan," Polly cried, her pride offended. "And I'll have you to know that Debby ain't my mistress. She's my cousin's guest in case you ain't heard. Mistress indeed!"

"Oh, Polly, my darling! I was only spoofing," Peter told her, reaching a long arm and drawing her close. "You know I love you, so you should know I would never intentionally offend you." His voice was caressing while his eyes twinkled roguishly.

Polly slapped him sharply on one cheek. "Go 'long with you, Mister Jordan," she cried as she tore herself from his grasp. "You ought to take shame to yourself and don't let me catch you tryin' any of your blarneyin' on Debby. She's a sweet, innocent young girl and she's in my care and you see you behave yourself when you're with her or you'll answer to me."

Peter Jordan stood tall and straight and dignified. "Mistress Polly Quick," he said sternly, "you insult my manhood by your cruel doubts and insinuations." He dropped quickly to his knees before her. "Is this the way you reward my years of devotion to you? Is this my recompense for remaining true to you lo, these many years? Heartless, cruel wench! My soul writhes in sorrow at such wanton treatment. I——"

"What is this? A rehearsal?" Deborah asked as she paused in the doorway to contemplate the tableau before her. Polly's face was crimson and Peter Jordan scrambled hastily to his feet, stooping to brush imaginary dust from his white trousers.

"You needn't to do that, Peter Jordan," Polly said sharply. "I warrant my rug's cleaner than what your britches are."

"Yes," Deborah gurgled, enjoying Peter's confusion, "that was the unkindest cut of all. Don't mind him, darling," she told Polly. "He's just a mere man. We'll be back in time to eat some of that grand baked ham I saw cooling on the cabinet," she said as they reached the front door. "I have an idea Peter has already accepted, hasn't he?"

"Accepted!" snorted Polly, though Deborah saw that her eyes were twinkling. "He ain't even been invited."

"Oh, yes I have, Polly," Peter insisted. "Don't you remember years ago you told me to consider this my home and assured me the latchstring was always out for me? That constitutes a standing invitation, dear lady, and I hereby accept for the duration of my stay in this vale of tears."

"Ain't he the beatin'est, Debby?" Polly asked affectionately as the two went laughing down the steps. "All right, children. I'll be lookin' for you 'round six o'clock."

They waved as Peter's car took the curving drive amid a shower of loose gravel.

"Polly's a grand old girl!" Peter said as they swept into the afternoon traffic. "She's been wonderful to me all my life. Those she loves she adores and those she hates might just as well crawl off some place and die for she has absolutely no use for them."

"I didn't suppose Polly ever hated anyone," Deborah protested doubtfully. "Oh, I know she isn't fond of Mrs. Thompson and one or two others but I wouldn't say she hated them."

"Well, I know one person she hates all right with what she calls a righteous hatred whatever that is," Peter insisted.

"Surely no one in Harmony," Deborah said in astonishment.

"Oh, she doesn't live here but she comes quite often."

"Then it's a woman?"

"A girl, rather. At least I always think of her as a girl —a young and lovely girl."

"But why should Polly hate her? I can't quite believe it."

"Oh, well, let's forget it. I sort of wanted to go over to the island this afternoon and take our lunch but as long as Polly will expect us back for dinner I suppose that's out. Have you been up to Buford Glen? No?" as Deborah shook her head. "It's a lovely drive and a wonderful view from the top of the spire. And how's for coming swimming over to my place tomorrow morning right after breakfast?"

"Lovely!" Deborah agreed. "Jason says you have the best beach this side of the lake."

"I have. You like Jason Miller, don't you?" Peter stated rather than asked.

"Jason's a darling. He's been mighty sweet to me," Deborah told him.

"That's not strange," Peter smiled. "I can't imagine a man being anything else."

"Don't be silly. I'm not in the least a man's girl, Peter. In fact, I never had much time for men. Nurses live fairly busy lives."

"So Polly reported, yet she tells me you're having a young doctor to dinner on Sunday—from Medford. She told me his name—Brown, isn't it? A most uncommon name," he mocked.

"Well, Alec's a most uncommon man," Deborah said loyally and experienced a little thrill—new to her—at the other's tone.

"Is he a very special friend, Deborah?" Peter asked seriously.

"Special? If you mean more than a friend—no, Peter. Alec is a good friend and a splendid companion in trouble. We worked together a lot. All that seems very far away now," she murmured dreamily, leaning back against the leather upholstery of the powerful car. "I seem to be an entirely different person. I hope Alec isn't coming with the idea of inveigling me into going back. I—I can't—just yet—if at all. That—that terrible experience did something to me. I hate the idea of returning—of nursing. Maybe I shall never go back, And yet I'm ashamed of myself. It's as if I were lying down on my job. I feel like a slacker."

"Forget it." Peter spoke crisply. "What does it matter if you don't go back? Surely there are hundreds of girls ready to take your place."

"You sound like my mother," Deborah accused. "She never wanted me to be a nurse in the first place and Public Health Nursing was something quite beyond the pale in her opinion. She thought I had the worst district in Medford and I guess she was right as far as housing went. But Alice wrote me the city fathers have had a change of heart regarding the North Side housing. That's one good result from that fire."

"Your mother? You say she lives in England?" Peter asked curiously.

"Yes, in England. You see, she married an Englishman just last winter and they live abroad. But I told you that before."

"I know you did. So you're all alone over here?"

"All alone. But I don't mind," Deborah said. "I'm afraid I'm not an especially sociable person. I have never seemed to mind being alone. Perhaps it's because I've always found so much to do and think about that I haven't felt the need of other people."

"Well, I hope this Doctor Brown of yours won't succeed in upsetting you, Deborah," Peter said seriously. "I don't think you're in any condition to go back to that health work yet. The spirit may be willing but I'm sure the flesh is still weak and I have a notion the job you had called for strength of body as well as of spirit."

"Brave living. Sometimes those words haunt me, Peter," Deborah said softly after a moment. "That's what Doctor Hamilton, our chief, used to tell us. We Public Health Nurses have to live bravely—don't look for easy or especially lucrative jobs, but are content to take hold anywhere and lift."

"One doesn't necessarily have to live dangerously to live bravely, Deborah," Peter told her seriously. "Wasn't it Milton who said; 'They also serve who only stand and wait'? And I think it's a grand rule—brave living! I think your chief has something there—something applicable to us all. Only it takes greater courage sometimes to stand and wait—to be patient with trying conditions —to endure quietly without fireworks or an audience, than some of us possess, or wonder if we possess."

He turned to smile down at her and Deborah felt her heart contract. His eyes were brown with little gold flecks and just now there was a tender light in them. Peter was a dear! She wondered anew if the girl whose picture hung in the nursery at Cliff House had made him happy —if she had really loved him—just what sort of a girl she had been. She had avoided bringing Peter's name into any conversation with Polly for, once started, Polly kept nothing back. The whole history of the Jordans from the days of the first settler down to the youngest descendant would be spread out for inspection. Who married this one and who her people were. It reminded Deborah of Chronicles. "And Ner begat Kish: and Kish begat Saul; and Saul begat Jonathan," and so on. But she knew she was going to ask about Peter's wife when she got back to Harmony.

They reached Buford Glen to find the place full of picnickers and fled to the spire, a lofty peak approached by steps chiseled out of solid rock. There was a railing all round the base of the tall monolith and seats where one could sit and view the panorama that stretched for miles on all sides.

"You can look into four counties from here, Deborah," Peter told her, "and see five lakes. Look, off there to the south. There's Harmony and Polly Quick shaking her dust mop."

"Oh, Peter!" Deborah scoffed. "You can't see that far and, anyway, Polly wouldn't be shaking a mop in the afternoon. Where?"

Peter's arm drew her close as he pointed south toward the spot where Harmony should be.

"See her?" he asked, looking down at the lovely intent face so near his own. "She has on a pink dress. You're sweet, Deborah," he whispered and Deborah felt the pounding of his heart against her arm.

74

"I see something pink," she said a little breathlessly, "but I don't think it's Polly—in fact, I doubt if it's a woman at all."

"Have you no imagination, girl?" he asked after a moment in which Deborah quietly drew back from his encircling arm. "That could have been Polly."

"Mm-mm," Deborah shook her head. "Not at this hour of the day. I know Polly and her little ways altogether too well."

"I want you to have lunch with me tomorrow, Deb—at my house," Peter said irrelevantly. "There are a lot of things I want to show you," and as an added inducement he went on; "Toby's got a new rose he wants you to see. Tomorrow?"

"Oh, I'm afraid not tomorrow, Peter," Deborah said regretfully. "I promised Jason I would go over to his sister's for the day, and I can't go swimming at your place tomorrow either. I forgot I promised Jason more than a week ago. Make it next week, will you? I do want to—to see Toby's rose, Peter."

"Next week Eve and her mother will be there," he said.

"Your sister-in-law?"

"Yes. She's bringing Nancy home for the rest of the summer. She wrote that she'll stay a couple of weeks—she and her mother. Scott, Nancy's tutor, will leave in a day or two."

He spoke grimly as if he quite suddenly disliked the idea of their coming.

"It will be fine for you having your little girl with you, Peter," Deborah said and was annoyed that she hated the idea of this sister-in-law. "Is your—this Eve—young? But of course she must be."

"I thought I told you about her. Yes, she's young—well—comparatively—two or three years older than I am: but she doesn't look it. Yes, I'd say she's young all right and beautiful and very demanding, Deborah," Peter told her. "I had hoped we were to have a whole day to ourselves before she arrived. Sunday your doctor will be here." He spoke crossly.

Deborah laughed at him. "I'm afraid it isn't only Nancy who has been spoiled, Peter," she chided, "and don't call Alec 'my doctor.' He isn't, you know. This lovely sister-in-law doesn't keep you in chains, does she? Or does she? Don't tell me that you, a big strong man, are afraid of a mere woman no matter how beautiful she may be!"

"Of course not, Deb," he said a trifle sharply. "When Eve's at Cliff House things hum. She's always finding things that should be changed—improvements, she calls them: but her mother weeps—weeps for her lost daughter —my wife. Not an altogether cheerful atmosphere to say the least." He shrugged as if the subject were distasteful to him. "Let's drop it, Deb, and enjoy the rest of today. After all, one never knows what tomorrow holds in store." He took her hand and they went down the uneven stone steps to the glen below, and along the narrow trail to the entrance near which he had left his car.

"Five o'clock," Deborah remarked as they left the glen behind. "Polly will be expecting us any time now."

"How about tonight? Are you free and may I have it?" Peter asked as they sped along toward Harmony.

Deborah laughed. "Believe it or not, Peter Jordan," she said, "Polly and I are going to an ice-cream social at the Methodist church. Why not come with us?"

"All right. I will," he agreed. "I haven't been to a church social in years. Who all are going to be in your party?" he asked after a minute in which he eyed her suspiciously.

"Oh, Polly invited several of her friends," she answered noncommittally.

"Jason Miller, I suppose, and Philip Northrup and Robert Peck and all the rest of that half-baked crowd. What do you see in those youngsters, Deb?" he asked crossly.

"I like them," she told him sincerely. "They have been wonderful to me and—well, they make me feel young and attractive and desirable. Believe me, Peter, it has been a long time since I have felt that way."

Peter brought the car to a smooth halt and turned in his seat. "Do you actually need adoring adolescence to sasure you of that, Deborah?" he asked, his voice rough as he slipped his arm about her shoulders. Deborah drew back but she felt suddenly weak and helpless. She knew he was going to kiss her and turned her face into his shoulder for protection. He laughed raggedly and held her crushed against him. "You darling!" he whispered. "Don't you know I'm mad about you—you lovely girl!"

Deborah burrowed deeper and he took her chin in his hand and turned her face to his. She would not look at him. Her breath came in little gasps. His head bent closer and his lips met hers, met and clung for a long ecstatic, tremulous moment before, with a little sob of dismay, she struggled free.

"Oh, why did you do that?" she whispered. "You've spoiled things."

"I've wanted to do it ever since the night we met," he told her. "I think you're the sweetest girl in the world. You'll marry me? Say you'll marry me, Deborah."

"No, Peter, no. I don't think I shall ever marry any-one," Deborah protested, her lips trembling. "At least not for a long, long time, and we—we don't really know each other at all. A month ago you weren't aware of my existence."

"Oh, yes I was," he insisted. "Remember that day at the airport? You've been in the back of my mind ever since. That's why I gave the driver twenty dollars instead of one—I was gaga even then. It's fate. There are in-stances where time doesn't mean a thing, you know, Deb-orah." He gave her a little shake. "Don't you like me, Deb?"

"Of course I like you, Peter—I like you a lot," Deb-orah told him frankly, "but I've got to get used to the idea—I've got to know you better—— This is what is called 'so sudden.' "

Peter laughed joyously. "Suits me, Deb," he assured her. "I'd like nothing better than to move right in at Polly's so that I could devote all my time to you." He bent his head to kiss her again, but the girl protested and drew away.

A green roadster honked derisively as it sped past and Peter muttered an imprecation as he straightened and turned the ignition key. His car came alive and Deborah felt relieved. She was bewildered by his sudden proposal. She knew he liked her but then he liked other girls too and the people of Harmony had the idea he belonged to his sister-in-law. Anyway, in spite of his assertion to the contrary, time was important. What did she actually know about him?

They had gone scarcely a dozen car lengths when they noticed the roadster that had passed had stopped. A girl was getting out. She stood beside the car—tall, slender, arresting.

"Eve Fowler!" exclaimed Peter. Deborah sensed a sudden change in him. "She isn't due until Monday." He stopped beside her.

"Hello, Peter darling!" the young woman in the road cried and Deborah thought she had never in her life seen anyone lovelier. She reminded her a little of Cynthia Marvin. She felt Eve's inquisitive stare and managed a little smile although she shivered and said to herself, "Someone walked over my grave." That Eve was annoyed to find her with Peter was perfectly apparent to her.

"Hello, Eve!" Deborah thought he sounded embarrassed. "You're ahead of time. I doubt if things are ready for you at Cliff House. Deborah," he turned to the girl beside him. "this is Miss Evelyn Fowler, my daughter's aunt. How is Nancy?"

"About as usual," Eve told him, her blue eyes examining Deborah with obvious amusement. "She and Scott and Mother will be out tonight. I thought it better to come on ahead. I'm glad that I did—now." To Deborah's sensitive ears her tone implied possessiveness: that she had caught Peter in some mischief and that he needed looking after. "Peter didn't mention your last name, Miss——"

"Bradley, Miss Fowler," Deborah said coolly.

"Miss Bradley is living with Polly Quick for a few months, Eve," Peter explained. "We're due there for dinner right now. I'll see you again," he said and shifted gears preparatory to moving on. "Be a good girl. I won't be too long."

Eve Fowler stepped back but not before Deborah caught the look of jealous rage on her lovely face. "Poor Peter is going to catch it!" she said to herself and experienced a let-down feeling. What right had Eve Fowler to dominate Peter's life—if she did? How silly! Eve

Fowler was nothing to her nor to Peter Jordan either, if Peter had really meant the things he had been telling her. And yet how could any man remain unmoved by such beauty? Anyway, she had given him no definite answer to his proposal so he was perfectly free. Eve Fowler could have a clear field with no interference from her. Very likely they would not come in contact with each other, at least not often, for it was quite evident to her that the lovely Eve didn't approve of her friendship with Peter.

She was relieved when they entered Harmony. There was no more love-making—no more kisses. Eve's car kept just behind them. Deb could actually feel her inquisitive eyes boring into the back of her head.

Suddenly Peter smiled down at her. "What's the matter, Deb? Afraid of Eve? I bet you are, at that. Eve has a way of giving members of her own sex an inferiority complex, especially the beautiful ones, but don't let her get you down, darling."

"Why should I?" Deborah asked coolly.

"We-ll," Peter ruminated, "Eve's inclined to be arbitrary. You see, I married her younger sister and she's jealous if I so much as look at another girl."

"Jealous," asked Deborah, "for her sister or——?"

"Of course. Who else? I suppose she thinks when I marry again she will lose Nancy entirely. It's really sad——"

Deborah longed to use Polly's favorite expression of "Fiddle-daddle!" but merely murmured; "Isn't it?"

Peter went on earnestly. "And if you want time in which to get used to the idea of annexing a husband and to make plans for the future, it's perfectly all right with me. But Deborah, I'd feel better if you didn't have dates with other men—with Jason. I am sure he's in love with you. Can you manage that?"

"Of course not," she said crisply. "We're not engaged and you'll have to beau Eve Fowler about, won't you? Well, I don't relish the idea of being completely out of circulation for the duration of her visit. Let's not be silly, Peter, and anyway—anything might happen—— No, no. Not here, Peter," as he reached for her hand. "And when will you bring Nancy to see me?"

"Bring Nancy? But—surely you know—didn't you know?" Peter asked in surprise. "Nancy doesn't go visiting."

"Wh——— She doesn't? Why not?" Deborah asked in astonishment.

"Do you mean to say that Polly hasn't told you?"

"Why, no, Peter. Polly has never discussed you or any of your family with me. Why?"

"My daughter can't walk, Deborah," Peter said sadly. "Her spine was injured in the accident that killed her mother."

"Oh, no!" cried Deborah recoiling in sudden horror.

"Yes." Peter's voice became harsh. "I was driving the car that killed my wife and crippled my daughter. I think I won't stay to dinner tonight, Deborah," he went on grimly. "I had forgotten for a while that some people may consider me a murderer. You see, I escaped with just a few minor injuries—an arm and a couple of ribs. I ought to have been killed, too. Sometimes——"

"Nonsense!" Deborah interrupted, but her voice shook. "No one in his right mind could blame you. You wouldn't do such a thing—intentionally."

"Men have, you know." He opened the door and stood for a moment looking down at her. The afternoon sun brought out the ruddy lights in his wavy hair. Debs' heart went out to him. She put out her hand but brought it back as she thought of Eve. But Eve had disappeared. Peter's mouth twisted in a wry smile. "I'm sorry to miss that ham, Deb," he murmured, "but tell Polly that Eve's arrived and the ghost returns to Cliff House tomorrow. She'll understand."

Without another word he got back into the car and slammed the door. As he drove furiously down the quiet street a feeling of sick dismay mixed with hurt pride possessed Deborah. It might be that he was sorry to miss Polly's baked ham but he was certainly eager to get back to Cliff House—and Eve Fowler.

CHAPTER NINE

"BUT POLLY," DEBORAH exclaimed when Mrs. Quick had finished her recital of the accident that had taken the life of Mrs. Jordan. "You don't mean to say that anyone blames Peter. How could they?"

"Well, Debby, Peter and Marcy Fowler ought never to have got married in the first place. Peter's easy-goin' as an old gray mare and unsuspicious and don't think evil of nobody, and Marcy was ambitious and excitable and nervous as a witch—always a-grabbin' hold of a body's arm at the least little thing that startled her. Just sort of jittery-like. I always had an idee that that's what she done when Peter was driving her and Nancy on the day of the accident. Peter never said so, mind you, and when I asked him point-blank, he just shut his mouth and never made a peep. But I always had it in my mind that's just what she done. 'Twould have been just like her. Marcy's disposition would set a body's teeth on edge. I guess Peter didn't have the easiest time of it. But she did adore Nancy and the child worshiped her.

"You see, Marcy had money. That is, she had the life use of considerable. But it died with her. I've always wondered how Eve and her ma can keep on livin' in such grand style. I know that when Peter married Marcy, he saw to it that every cent of her money went to her ma and Eve: but I know for a fact that when Marcy died the fortune all went to her uncle's people who wouldn't give a cracker to a starvin' child.

"Marcy's ma kept Peter pretty much upset there for quite a spell what with mournin' over her daughter bein' killed and 'poor darlin'in' ' Nancy. They's ways of keepin' a wound open besides stickin' a crowbar into it. That child's like a cactus—full of sharp pricks. Would you believe it, the last time I see the little tyke, she told me she couldn't walk because her pa hurt her back. Believe me, I said a few things to her and the little brat sulked for days and wouldn't answer when I spoke to her. I was spellin' Anna, her nurse, then. Eve's the clever one, Debby. She's so everlastin' han'some the men fall like ninepins when she comes into a room and they flock after her wherever she goes. She winds Peter round her

81

finger. She can be so sweet and allurin' that Peter, like all men and some women, too, is her slave. And to keep him tighter in her toils she claims to be completely wrapped up in Nancy. He makes me so mad!"

"Tragic!" Deborah murmured—"for them all!"

"Ain't it, though? I've wished a hundred times if I have once that Peter Jordan would up and marry some good strong-minded girl who would take Nancy in hand. Get her right away from them Fowlers. But Peter just don't seem to cotton to girls, some way. Leastways they ain't been no evidence of it till now."

She peered innocently across the table at Deborah and smiled a little as she saw the color flood the girl's face.

"Peter's a fine boy, Debby," Polly went on, apparently noticing nothing amiss, "and the girl that lands him will be mighty lucky. He's well off and clean as a hound's tooth and that's sayin' a whole lot these days of crazy goin's on. Eve Fowler's always been crazy over him— even before Marcy married him. You see, Peter was Eve's beau before Marcy took him away from her. Leastways he brought Eve to Cliff House to visit his ma and pa before he married Marcy. We all thought 'twas Eve he was goin' to marry."

"Can't anything be done for the girl, Polly?" Deborah asked, ignoring Polly's other disclosures.

"Eve says not—insists not. Peter's had specialists up— some thought one way and some another—you know what them doctors are, Debby. Well, seems like everything that money can do's been done. Eve insists she'll not let the child be tormented no more. That woman makes me so mad!"

"But what is it?" Deborah asked. "What do the doctors say the trouble is? Paralysis, such as I have an idea hers is, has been cured, you know, by an operation on the spine. I've seen it done a number of times. There is probably pressure there that can be removed."

"I know," Polly wagged her white head. "Them specialists declare the spine's all right—that it's somethin' to do with nerves. Peter wanted to take her to England to that bloodless surgeon, you know. What's his name? Luther somethin' or other, wasn't it? He's died since. Well, no matter. They all made such a fuss that Peter had to give it up. Surgeons have come and doctors have gone and Nancy still lies on her back and keeps 'em all a-steppin', I can tell you."

"I feel sure from what you tell me that something can be done," Deborah declared. "Why do they give up? Why let that child be doomed to the life of a helpless cripple? My grandfather was a surgeon—I've seen him perform miracles and I've heard him say time after time that it wasn't for any of us to say a case was hopeless. That poor child!

I don't know as I'm wastin' very much sympathy on Nancy, Debby." Polly's lips were a straight line. "I don't think I ever seen a more disagreeable child. She's uncanny—she gives me the creeps. Yet she looks so much like her pa. The same brown eyes, only Nancy's are sly and calculatin': the same broad, high forehead and square jaw: but, in Nancy's case, the mouth instead of bein' sweet like Peter's is mean and peevish. Her hair's like Peter's used to be—red. I lay the whole blame for Nancy's condition on them Fowlers: anyway, her disposition's their fault. She used to be such a sweet baby."

"I don't," Deborah said sharply. "What ails Peter Jordan that he lets his sister-in-law rule him? I thought Peter was a man, but it seems I was mistaken. To let his little daughter be ruined just because he—he's probably in love with this Eve. No doubt he enjoys being dominated by her. If he does, why let him. I don't care. It's simply disgusting! Why doesn't he marry her?"

"Now don't you go off half-cocked, Debby," soothed Polly. "You don't know what you're talkin' about. They's always two sides to every question and remember that crazy specialist warned him that Nancy needed Eve and Eve needed Nancy—why, only he seemed to know. Eve don't forget it—not for a minute she don't, and she won't let Peter forget it either. What's more, you'd best remember it, too, for I've got a notion you'll have it called to your attention more times than once durin' the next few weeks."

"I?" Deborah asked in surprise. "Why should I be reminded of it? It isn't any of my business."

"No? Well, I reckon Eve's goin' to make sure it never will be any of your business either or I miss my guess, my girl," the old lady told her, "and if I was you I'd be hanged if I'd give in to her. I'd fight her every inch of the way. That's what I'd do."

"I fight her? But why, Polly? What have I done to Eve Fowler? Why should she interfere with me?" Deborah tried to appear surprised at Polly's advice but couldn't quite make it convincing.

"I guess you know all right. Anyone with an eye in her head can see that Peter admires you a lot. And bein' right in a front pew so to speak, I'd say he's been a-courtin' pretty steady," Polly said quietly. "An' it's no s'prise to you, either, Debby Bradley, or you ain't as bright as I take you to be."

"No. No, Polly," Deborah cried. "How could I—any girl care for a man so infatuated with another woman, however beautiful and inaccessible? I take it she's keeping him dangling or they would have been married long ago. Oh, Polly, I'm terribly disappointed in Peter!" It was a wail of despair and Polly shook her white head.

"You needn't to be, Debby. I guess you don't get the setup. You don't get the picture as it reely is. Remember outsides can always see more than them that are closest in. Peter's sort of bewitched by that girl because he thinks she's takin' his dead wife's place a-motherin' Nancy. If Peter happened to fall in love with a girl who could go in there and clean house, so to speak, and show Eve she ain't got a Chinaman's chance as far as hookin' Peter Jordan for a husband is concerned—'cause he's already hooked for keeps—'twould make a sight of difference—every way, you'd see. You don't know Eve's allurin' ways——"

"And I don't want to. I'll never fight for Peter or any other man. I came here to rest and get well and strong, not to go to war with a jellyfish's female relatives. I feel terribly sorry for the child. To think she had such a spineless parent as Peter Jordan! Don't let's talk about it any more, Polly. If we are going to that social or festival at the church, we'd better think about getting ready." Deborah was suddenly very tired.

"All right," Polly agreed, and set her lips in a manner betokening displeasure. Deborah went hastily to her room.

She didn't want to go to the social. She wanted nothing so much as complete rest—to be alone so she could think. Mrs. Holcomb had been wrong about Harmony being free from sickness and yet perhaps Nancy wasn't exactly sick, in anything but nerves and mind, which Deborah knew was one of the worst kinds of sickness and one of the hardest to heal. She felt a great sympathy for the child but shrank from seeing her. She had had so much of that sort of thing in her life that she was determined to avoid it as long as she could. She had no desire to come in contact with Eve Fowler again either and she felt different toward Peter Jordan, too. Her face flamed at the memory of his kiss. Why had she allowed it? And she had to acknowledge that his kiss had thrilled her as she had never been thrilled before. No. No. Peter Jordan wasn't the man she had thought he was. She would try not to see him soon again. She would manage to be busy or out with someone else when he called—if he called. He had seemed very queer when he left her this afternoon, almost as if they were strangers and as if what had happened a little while before had never taken place. She felt sure she couldn't possibly love a man on such short acquaintance any more than he could love her, and now that she knew about Eve Fowler, she was sure she never could—given all the time in the world.

"Debby!" Polly called. "You 'most ready? We best be startin' before all the strawberry shortcake's gone."

"I'll be right down, Polly," Deborah promised and hurried her dressing. She hoped and prayed that Peter wouldn't be there. She doubted if he would on Eve's first night at Cliff House. She thought of them together up there amid all that beauty—of Eve wooing him with her charm and allure. Her hands clenched as she recalled that Polly had said Peter had brought Eve to Cliff House while his parents still lived there. Polly had thought it was Eve he was marrying instead of her sister Marcia. No doubt Peter took lots of girls up there and—and——

"I must cut this out," she told herself grimly. "If he prefers to dangle after Eve Fowler why, it's none of my business and I shall absolutely refuse to play second fiddle to any girl—woman," she amended resentfully.

She picked up her purse and hurried from the room,

mentally dismissing all thoughts of Peter Jordan and the glamorous Eve Fowler, but she couldn't shake off a feeling of depression —disappointment.

"Brave living!" The phrase flashed before her mind's eye and she recalled what Peter had said. "One doesn't necessarily have to live dangerously to live bravely— 'they also serve who only stand and wait' " Her lip curled. Stand and wait—for what? Did he think for one minute he was living bravely? "Jellyfish!" she scoffed and went downstairs to join Polly in the front hall.

It had been years since Deborah had gone to a church social and it all came back to her as she parked her car in the space reserved for that purpose in the rear of the building. Tables and booths were set around a centre arena reserved for games. Polly and she were immediately surrounded by a bevy of young people and Deborah was borne off by Jason Miller, Mary and Philip Northrup, and the four found a place in semi-seclusion near one end of the lawn beneath a wide-spreading maple. Polly went off to help serve—that was her way. Deborah was sure she had never tasted anything quite so delicious as the huge wedges of shortcake filled with luscious berries and piled high with whipped cream. In the laughing, shouting throng, she forgot for a moment her disappointment and anger against Peter Jordan. Jason Miller brought it to her memory.

"I saw Eve Fowler today, Phil," Jason said between mouthfuls of shortcake. "Jeepers, but she's beautiful!"

"You've said it," Phil agreed. "I bet the original Eve was a lot like her. You know, a siren, though I must say I never had much use for Adam's rib. And I, for one, hate to think all her descendants have her seductive ways. 'It was the serpent,' sez she, the sly wench. Chances are the old serpent wouldn't have given her an eye at all if she hadn't tried to flirt with him. Two-timing her old man and so early in the game, too."

"She probably was bored to death," Deborah contributed. "After all, you know, Adam doesn't stack up very well himself in the final analysis. Didn't he hide behind Eve's skirt, or fig leaf if you prefer? I'm inclined to hold with that particular school of thought that insists it was a part of Adam's spine that was used to create a

86

mate for him instead of a rib. Certainly all that followed the incident of the apple seems to prove it."

"Hurrah for our side!" applauded Mary.

"Oh, I'm not particularly proud of old Adam's attitude regarding the apple incident, Deb," Phil said judicially. "But Eve probably did munch that crunchy, juicy apple tantalizingly close—right under her spouse's nose. And was he hungry for apples just then! No doubt he knew she had committed a grave social error and in order to place himself alongside her and so take part of the punishment, he made a grand gesture—he took a bite, too."

"I bet it was a good big bite," Mary opined. "I remember the ones you used to take. If I got the core I was lucky."

Deborah laughed. "But he spoiled the grand gesture by laying the entire blame on Eve." Her tone was unaccountably bitter—she was astonished to discover that she hated the name Eve. "He didn't have to submit to her blandishments, did he? He could have slapped her down for disobedience in the first place, couldn't he? But no, he ate and probably enjoyed his big bite and when his Nemesis appeared what did he do? He claimed complete exemption. 'The woman tempted me,' sez he—*cherchez la femme*, and all the Adams since have used the same alibi."

Mary Northrup clapped her hands. Phil and Jason refused to accept Deborah's explanation. "But Deb," Jason expostulated, "Eve did tempt him, you know. He acknowledged that he ate, didn't he? What he said was quite true."

"Oh, true—true!" Deborah cried and was immediately ashamed that she should be annoyed. "One can tell the truth without being so terribly explicit about it. Who cares about the contributory factors? The fact remains the man was a jellyfish or he never would have allowed himself to become so enthralled he had no will of his own—no backbone. I have no patience with weak-kneed people whether male or female."

"Miss Bradley believes in dangerous living, boys and girls," a new voice said. "She likes her men to be fighters —'he men,' I believe is the term. One must remember,

87

however, that bravery doesn't necessarily mean a display of brute force or great physical strength or even the use of high-handed measures. Bravery can be applied to the spirit and it often requires greater courage to submit to conditions than to fight them. Now that the lesson of the evening has been given, I'll leave you to your orgy of eating."

The four young people looked slightly dashed.

"Don't go, Pete—at least just yet," Jason said, jumping up and going after the tall figure in white. "Join us —temporarily. Deb is my date, remember, but we need reinforcements. We men ought to stick together. We have been discussing the epoch-making incident of the first stolen apple. Deb's argument was good, but somewhat weakened by the usual female traits—failure to. follow facts—lack of logic and—er—jealousy."

"The apple?" Peter asked, puzzled. The three at the table were watching, Deborah with a feeling of dismay. Did Peter imagine she was discussing him and his sister-in-law? How horrible!

"You know—Eve—the garden of Eden. Deb contends that every Adam since that day has blamed the woman when he missed his step or fell short of the Tarzan ideal."

Peter turned his gaze toward the table and his eyes met those of Deborah fixed upon him. So that was it? Then Deb actually thought him a poor creature—so completely under Eve's thumb that he inertly allowed her to control his life. She hadn't taken his proposal of marriage seriously. She didn't care for him at all. Maybe she even thought him careless at the time of the accident that had taken the life of Marcia and made Nancy a cripple. If that was the case then everything was over— ended. No doubt it was this Doctor Brown who was coming on Sunday, or Jason Miller. He shrugged his shoulders and turned to Jason.

"Miss Bradley should know," he said levelly, his voice perfectly audible to the three at the table. "Probably she has been unfortunate in her experiences with the opposite sex. I'm sorry."

He drew back from Jason's detaining hand and strode away, leaving a puzzled young man staring after him.

"Peter's out of sorts," Jason murmured as he sat down.

"Who cares?" Deborah was angry. How dare he use that tone to her!

"Probably Eve's sore at him because he wanted to honor our festival. He sticks pretty close to home while she's in residence. I wonder why he doesn't marry the woman and be done with it. He'll do it eventually so why not now? Lucky stiff!" Phil sighed loudly.

"Don't be silly, Phil," his sister said. "He hasn't done it yet and no man has to marry if he doesn't want to. Evidently Peter doesn't want to. It looks that way to me." She had been watching Deborah's face and was doing some wondering.

"I don't know about that," murmured Jason, thoughtfully. "Eve's mad about him and you know 'the female of the species——' "

"Rot!" exclaimed Deborah sharply, then quickly patted Jason's hand so near her own. "Don't be like that, Jason," she said sweetly, "and don't tell me you know any deadly females."

Jason caught her hand and leaned closer. "Like heck I don't," he whispered. "You've got me tight, Deb—I don't want to get away. You're in my blood. What if I am a year younger——"

"Ahem!" Phil warned. "The time, the place, the girl. Are we *de trop*, old pal? Shall we scram?"

Deborah laughed and withdrew her hand from Jason's. "Don't be silly. Let's go and play games with the children."

Peter Jordan didn't appear again that evening and all Deborah's protestations to the contrary, her heart was heavy. Not that she was the least bit in love with Peter—of course not: but she hated to see a man—any man—fall from his high estate to become a lackey—a mere slave to beauty. Even Phil seemed a bit enamored of the glamorous Eve. What was it Jason had said to her; "You are in my blood—I'm mad about you, Deb. Won't you give me a chance?" He had kept close all evening.

Jason was sweet. She liked him more than any of the others. She liked his family, too, and they seemed to thoroughly approve of her. She had rather neglected

Jason lately but she intended making it up to him. If he was in love with her he certainly couldn't love Eve Fowler. He was one man, anyway, who had managed to resist the siren.

"Oh, well," Deborah shrugged as she prepared for bed that night, "Alec will be here on Sunday—good old Alec—who has discovered by bitter experience that a lovely face can hide a cruel heart and an empty soul. But of course Eve is no doubt different. She must have something more than glamor to hold Peter, or has she? Dear Alec! It will be good to see him again, if only to bring me to my senses."

She tossed about muttering in her sleep and at last Polly came upstairs.

"Debby," she called and shook the girl's shoulder, "you et too much shortcake and cream. Here, you drink this and if you don't feel better soon I'll fix you a real dose."

Deborah sat up obediently but merely tasted the bicarbonate Polly offered her. "I'm all right, Polly, really. I'm not a bit sick."

"Then it must be a guilty conscience," Polly retorted, "and I don't know of nothin' any worse." The old lady departed, her voluninous nightdress swirling about her thin body and her straight back showing keen disapproval.

CHAPTER TEN

ALEC BROWN arrived in Harmony in time for Sunday morning breakfast with Deborah and Polly. He had driven as far as Buford the afternoon before, spent the night there and felt an urge to attend church with Deborah. Polly had been prepared to dislike the doctor, fearing a possible rival of Peter, but no one could resist the wholesome charm of the young man.

Deborah was aware that her mood was anything but devout as, a little late, they approached Saint Matthew's-on-the-Lake. She sensed the inquisitive gaze of several pairs of eyes as she and Doctor Brown entered the beautiful old church and followed the usher down the aisle. She felt rather than saw that Peter was in the Jordan pew and that beside him sat Eve Fowler in gleaming white. She was annoyed that the usher had taken them well down in front. She knew she probably looked all right, but Alec was attractive and rather distinguished looking but she would have preferred a rear pew—behind the Jordans.

The sermon that morning fell on deaf ears as far as Deborah was concerned. Her thoughts were chaotic. Although outwardly she took an active part in the service, she received little comfort from it. She called herself a silly goose for resenting the presence of Eve Fowler in the Jordan pew, but she knew the day was completely spoiled because of the advent of this other woman.

Peter had told her that his sister-in-law was older than he but she didn't look it. Deborah acknowledged her superlative beauty even though she heartily disliked her particular type. She wondered rather guiltily if her antagonism had been as apparent to Eve Fowler as the older woman's had been to her. And she wondered if, had she met this woman under different circumstances, she would have experienced the same inward shrinking.

The service was over at last and she and Alec prepared to walk up the aisle to the door. When she could bring herself to look, she saw that the Jordan pew was empty. Thank heaven for that! At the door they were surrounded by a group of young people and Deborah introduced Alec to them. Out of the corner of her eye she saw

Peter and Eve Fowler enter a limousine with a New England license and without a backward glance from either, saw the big car drive away. Again she was annoyed. After Peter's extremely friendly attentions of the past weeks, after what had happened between them just a few hours before, she had expected Peter to wait and greet her guest. Probably Eve objected to waiting. She bit her lip. "Jellyfish!" she shouted mentally and felt tears of anger behind her eyelids. If that was all he cared —if her friendship meant so little to him—she would put him right out of her mind. She forced a smile of goodbye to the group on the church steps and suggested to Alec that they drive around the lake before going home.

"I never saw you looking better, Deb," Alec Brown declared and went on to tell her how glad her friends in Medford would be to hear it. When was she coming back? They missed her and every time he called on one of her North Side families they asked about her. She had left a huge void that no one else could fill. Surely she was completely recovered. And surely she realized that her work was waiting.

"I don't think I shall ever come back, Alec," Deborah told him. "I hate the idea of sickness and suffering. I doubt if I could stand it, much less help anyone. Mother wants me to come to her for the winter and perhaps I shall go. I have never been abroad and it might help."

"There's only one thing that can break this spell— this phobia that has taken possession of you, Deb," Alec told her.

"And what is that, my dear doctor?" Deborah asked. The lake twinkling in the sunlight quieted her anger and unrest.

"Forget your own feelings entirely and wade right in. You'll find that your hand hasn't lost its cunning nor your lips their sympathetic smile. You're far too brave, my dear, to be beaten by the first real handicap you have encountered: too courageous to remain in the Slough of Despond without making an effort to get out. You're a nurse, Deborah, remember that. A nurse doesn't look for a soft berth with long vacations any more than a doctor does. We enlist for the duration of a war—a war on disease."

"But a nurse isn't like a doctor, Alec," Deborah protested. "Her enlistment isn't always for life. Sometimes a nurse marries, you know."

"Then she's a better wife and mother because of her enlistment. Are you trying to tell me something, Deborah?" he asked, his hands tightening on the steering wheel.

"Tell you? I don't know what you mean. I have nothing to tell, Alec, and I wish you wouldn't make me feel like a traitor. Truly I can't help feeling as I do. The very thought of looking at a sick person makes me almost ill. I hope it will pass, but just now——"

"Of course it will pass," Alec said crisply, "if you don't coddle it and yield to it. You've got to help, though. Better change you mind and come back—with me—now."

Deborah shook her head. "Not yet."

"Don't let yourself get soft, Deb," he urged her. "I could almost wish your mother had kept that money. You have been trained for hard work and this lazy life is enervating——" He stopped and went on, his voice low and earnest;

"Some day you will long to get back in harness, for there's nothing like work to keep one sane and happy, Deborah, remember that. When the time comes and you find idleness and idle people pall, come back to Medford and the Center where the work is endless and often unappreciated: where there are sick bodies to be healed and sick souls to be heartened. Don your old badge of service again and wade into the fight with the rest of us. We'll be looking for you."

Deborah shuddered. "Not yet," she repeated. Alec said no more. He felt it was for the good of the work that he wanted Deborah to return to Medford. Although he knew that her absence left an emptiness in his life that was at times almost intolerable, he felt sure it was purely a professional interest he entertained for this fine nurse. Alec Brown was confident that his experience with Cynthia Marvin had completely immunized him from further attacks of sentimental frenzies. He admired Deborah and

93

valued her friendship—that was quite all, he assured himself.

The lake was in a playfull mood this July day. Little waves slapped lazily at the shore with teasing, white-tipped fingers and slipped back to make room for others. A fleet of sailboats lay anchored opposite the Yacht Club, rocking gently in the faint summer breeze. A red canoe shot out from a distant cove: laughter drifted from the children splashing in the water just below them: swallows wheeled and dipped and skimmed over the water. Behind them lay Harmony, lovely, peaceful, satisfying. Deborah sighed. "Not yet," she murmured in her heart. "I'm not ready to go back yet."

Alec stayed the afternoon and evening but, in spite of Polly's invitation to remain with them, returned to Buford for the night. He must be back on the job by noon of the next day, and so departed, leaving Deborah more depressed than ever.

Monday she received a letter from Alice telling her that Paul was having a week's vacation and that they could come to Harmony for a few days right then if Deborah wanted them to. It was short notice but Paul hadn't known until he left work on Saturday that he was to have this time off. She wanted Deb to be quite honest and if it wasn't convenient they could put the visit off until later.

Deborah immediately put through a telephone call to the old apartment, only to be told that service had been discontinued. Evidently Paul hadn't overstated the financial conditions his bride would have to face after the wedding. So Deborah sent a wire instead. She would look for them on Tuesday or Wednesday at latest and they were to plan on staying just as long as Paul's leave of absence lasted.

"It will help them," she thought, and wondered how Alice was making out with her housekeeping. But perhaps she was taking hold better. Alice had written that she had given up her job and was devoting all the time she could possibly spare from housekeeping to her writing. She had sold another short story but the pay had been small. Paul had been promised a rise in September and

94

then things would be easier. But Alice sounded very happy and Deborah was eager to see her.

An answering wire arrived late in the day. Alice and Paul would arrive the next afternoon. Deborah sang as she helped Polly prepare for their visit.

"Can you get someone in to help you, Polly?" Deborah asked as she made out a list of extras.

"Don't be foolish!" Polly said sharply. "I'm quite able to take care of two extra folks without breakin' down."

"That may be," Deborah protested, "but I'm not going to have it. We'll get in someone to clean and wash dishes and so on."

"We'll do nothing of the kind. I guess I'm runnin' this house and I know what I want. If I need extry help, Mis' Sims will come over but I don't need no help. Maybe she'll want extry, though, for doin' the washin' and ironin'."

"Oh, I intend taking care of that. Find out about it, will you, Polly? And I do wish you would have help in for a couple of hours a day while they're here. I'd feel lots better if you would."

"Well, I won't, so feel as bad as you like. Land sakes, I been alone so long it's a real treat to have a sizable fam'ly to do for. Don't you worry about me, Debby. Do a mite o' worryin' about your judgin' Peter wrong. Now that's somethin' to worry about if you ask me."

Polly had tried in vain to sound Deborah out on the question of Peter Jordan but the girl managed to veer away from the subject and Peter hadn't been near the place since Friday. Polly was frankly worried. She felt she must do something about it. Deborah left the room wthout answering or giving an inkling of her feelings.

i Early next morning Deborah drove Polly to the market and it was while they examined chops and poultry that Eve Fowler entered and stopped to speak to Polly. There was an amused smile on her face as she nodded to Deborah that infuriated the girl even while she strove to appear unaware of it. Deb bowed coolly and ignored her presence.

"Well, how's your mother, Eve?" Polly asked, her hand on the pair of broilers she had chosen. "Here for long?"

"Mother's quite well, thank you, and we shall probably stay all summer, Polly," Miss Fowler answered. "Peter insists upon our spending the entire season at Cliff House and you know what a lamb he is and how insistent he can be, my dear." She smiled charmingly but her eyes slid for a brief moment to the girl beside the white-haired old lady. Deborah turned away. She couldn't help it, and there welled up inside her a feeling of such antagonism that she was startled and a little frightened.

"Don't know as I do," Polly sniffed. "Seems to me Peter's kind of easy-goin'. Nancy well?"

"About as usual. The poor child tries so hard to be brave." She sighed. "I can't seem to overcome the feeling of horror that these dreadful things had to happen to that sweet, innocent little girl. Her mother taken, her while life ruined: for, of course, there is absolutely no chance of her ever walking. It is fortunate that she has dear Mother and me," she smiled half-sadly. "She is my one excuse for living, Polly."

Polly shrugged. "Don't put so much weight in your importance to the child, Eve," she said bluntly. "Nancy's got her pa, ain't she? I guess they's others besides you and your ma who'd see the child had proper care, and prob'ly not spoil her so much either. Why don't you forget your 'maginary duty to Nancy for a spell, Eve, and do a bit of gallivantin' on your own hook? And why don't you get married—all the lone men in the world, and you——"

Deborah caught her breath. How would Eve Fowler take Polly's bluntness? But evidently everyone in Harmony knew Polly and her ways and took no offense at her outspokenness, for now Eve's tinkling laughter rippled out to be almost instantly stilled. One wondered if they had heard aright for there was no real merriment in the beautiful face.

"The same old Polly!" Eve said, her voice rippling again: then with sudden seriousness; "My care of Nancy isn't a duty, Polly. She is my beloved sister's child and as such is dearer to me than life itself, especially so since her father can give her so little of his time. Poor lamb—he has never recovered from the shock of that day. Perhaps it is to be expected and one cannot but sympathize. After all, life goes on. I tell him repeatedly that no amount

96

of regrets will bring Marcia back to him nor restore Nancy's health. Poor old darling! I wish he loved Nancy as I do. Doctor Davis was so right in giving her to me."

"Fiddle-daddle!" Polly sputtered sharply. "Peter thinks his eyes of that child. And after all, Nancy's a lot more Peter than she is Marcy—except in disposition——" she ended softly.

"Just what do you mean by that, Polly Quick?" Eve demanded, her eyes for a moment taking on a greenish glint.

"Oh, nothin', except that Nancy's the spittin' image of what her pa was at her age—all but her disposition which ain't sweet to say the least," the old lady said firmly.

"No-o," Eve agreed, "but I wonder if your disposition or mine would be especially sweet if we were doomed to lie on our backs all our lives." Her tinkling laughter bubbled up once more. "Oh, dear, I suppose Peter, the poor heartbroken boy, has been spilling his sorrow on you again, Polly. You must not allow it, dear. Peter must learn to carry his own cross without——"

"Nonsense!" Mrs. Quick retorted. "Peter ain't no one to tell his troubles—never has been. Maybe he'd be lots happier if he did—sometimes. He's that close-mouthed and loyal to his family and relatives that sometimes he gets my goat. 'Tain't wise to be too tight-lipped and to lean over backwards being honorable, sez I. 'Tain't appreciated in this here vale of miserable sinners. Here, Mr. Robbins, I'll take these two broilers and if they ain't up to snuff you'll hear from me."

Mr. Robbins chuckled and picked up the two broilers. "Anything else, Mrs. Quick?" His glance kept darting toward Eve.

"Two pounds of lamb chops and see they're tender and ain't all bone. That'll be all for now, and we'll take 'em with us. How's Molly, Mr. Robbins?"

"Fine. She's expecting you for that committee meeting on Friday afternoon. The ladies are lunching at our house. You're surely coming, aren't you?" Deborah saw he was growing jittery.

All this time Eve Fowler was tapping her foot impatiently while her quick eye sorted out the meat she wanted. Mrs. MacDonald always threatened to leave Cliff House after a few days of the Fowlers' stay there and it took all Peter's power of persuasion to make her change her mind. The Fowlers found Mrs. MacDonald and her regime amusingly out-of-date and one or the other insisted on doing all the marketing during their visits, quite conceivably, the housekeeper felt, to further annoy her. For some reason, Polly continued to engage the butcher in conversation. She examined a ham and found it too fat. She looked at beef and decided against it. She talked about the weather and the church, and Deborah knew that Eve was getting more and more impatient even while she wore a long-suffering smile. The young man helper fiddled about the shop trying to serve the lovely customer, but Eve, managing quite charmingly, would have none of him. At last Polly turned away for a minute and Eve and Mr. Robbins seemed to pounce upon each other. It was really very funny, Deborah thought.

"I'll have two of those broilers—better make it four, Mr. Robbins. They look especially fine this morning," she said sweetly. "Are these all the lamb chops you have? Oh, but Mr. Robbins, you surely wouldn't expect Mr. Jordan to like them! Oh, I am glad you have others. You're always so kind. I'll take that ham—no, the one you've just taken down. Peter enjoys baked ham more than anything."

Mr. Robbins turned to unwrap the ham, his florid face even ruddier. Deborah, who was waiting while Polly wandered about, saw that the butcher was admiringly obsequious. Another of Eve's slaves. Polly joined her and they left the market, leaving Eve examining the ham under the butcher's approving eye.

"Ain't that girl the beatin'est, Debby?" Polly asked. " 'My darlin' sister' she called Marcy and they never was any too fond of each other to my way of thinkin'. 'Poor lamb!' she called Peter and 'poor heartbroken boy!' Peter's a good ways from bein' heartbroken, I'll have her to know and he ain't nobody's lamb, neither. It's just that she never misses a chance to tell the world that Peter belongs to her and for others to keep their hands off her property. 'Twas all for your benefit I sort of fancy,

Debby. I see her slide her eye to you once or twice while she was a-talkin'. She'd give her eyes to land him."

"It would simplify matters if she did," Deborah said perversely.

"You don't mean that, Debby Bradley, and don't let me hear no more of such nonsense, either. Eve Fowler ain't fit to wipe Peter's shoes and why the boy don't see it wonders me. She's sort of put a spell on him same as she does on everything that wears pants and some that wears skirts, too. Trouble is, Peter never suspects nobody. He's so decent he thinks everyone's aboveboard. I always say Peter's got a lot more of the grace of God in his make-up than what I have. He feels like I do about them keepin Nancy all the time, but Eve keeps remindin' him of what that fool doctor said, when he was under her spell, no doubt."

"You mean he probably has a wide yellow streak down his back, Polly," Deborah said hotly and was instantly ashamed.

Polly didn't answer. She sat beside her, face front, every muscle rigid. When they reached the grocery, she said quietly;

"I'll get out here and you needn't to come in. I'll have the things sent out so you can just go on back to the house. I'll walk home."

"I'm sorry, Polly," Deborah said contritely. "I should not have said that about Peter. After all, I scarcely know him and anyway it wasn't kind. Please forgive me. I know you are fond of him."

Polly's look was one of reproach as she opened the car door and stepped to the ground. "Fond ain't the half of it. But I can do my buyin' by myself and I can walk home." She turned a straight back to Deborah and marched into the store.

Deborah waited for a minute then turned her car and drove back to the house. She was sorry and she had apologized. If Polly was going to hold a grudge because she was fed up with Peter Jordan and all his in-laws, it was too bad but she didn't intend groveling. She was glad that Alice and Paul were coming, for now she need not fear having to manufacture excuses to avoid being alone with him if he should call or if she should encounter him

99

anywhere. She hadn't been bothered with his attentions so far, she told herself bitterly. Since Eve Fowler's advent he had not made any effort to see her. Well, let him have his beautiful sister-in-law if he wanted her: no one was going to stop him that she could see. She tried to busy herself about her room, but Eve's lovely face and tall, lithe body kept darkening the day. Was it possible for a man to resist anyone so utterly exquisite? Even character or brains didn't have a chance against a beautiful face—history proved that. And Eve Fowler didn't look like a woman who could be easily discouraged. What she wanted she took if she had to wait years to get it.

Deborah shuddered. She thought of the vampires of fiction from whom it was impossible to escape once they fastened themselves on their victims, and laughed shakily. What a fool she was! They were living in the twentieth century—in a materialistic age. What nonsense to think that Eve Fowler could marry Peter against his will! And yet she had heard of women gaining their ends through many devious ways. She was being quite unfair to Eve she knew. Polly disliked her and Peter had called Polly discerning. That's the thing that made her so angry. He knew Polly hated Eve with what she called a righteous hatred—that she didn't trust her—and yet he refused to believe that Polly could possibly be right in her opinion. He refused to believe Eve anything but a devoted sister or her attitude toward Nancy less than purely maternal. What fool some men were! Or was Polly wrong? She would try to give Eve the benefit of the doubt.

Deborah was still in her room when the sound of a car on the gravel of the driveway made her rush to the window. Peter had brought Polly home. What was more, he was coming in.

Her hands icy, Deborah went to her dressing table, ran a comb through her hair and dabbed a bit of powder on a nose that didn't need it. She stood irresolute for a moment should she go down or wait until Polly summoned her? But Polly was peeved and maybe would not call. In that case, she would just casually descend the stairs and greet him as if nothing had happened. Cool and composed but perfectly friendly—that would be her attitude from now on.

When she reached the lower hall, she heard voices coming from the kitchen. They were laughing voices. Peter was teasing Polly about something. They had forgotten all about her. They didn't need nor want her.

"That you, Debby?" Polly called and Deborah felt relieved. Then Polly wasn't really angry with her after all. She walked slowly down the hall and stood for a moment in the kitchen door. Peter was sitting at the table, a great wedge of cherry pie on a plate before him. With his fork poised above it, he rose to greet Deborah.

"Hello, Deb!" he said and the girl wondered if it was just her imagination that all the intimate warmth of the past weeks seemed to have left his voice.

"Hello, Peter!" she replied and dropped into the nearest chair. "Did Polly tell you of our impending company? You see, Cliff House isn't the only place that's entertaining visitors." Then, on the spur of the moment, "I hope you and your sister-in-law will have dinner with us one night while Alice and Paul are here."

"I don't know about Eve, but I shall be glad to come," Peter told her in the same dispassionate voice. "Friends of yours, Deb? Here, have some pie—it's the best Polly ever made."

"Go 'long with you," Polly denied.

"I'll have mine later. Yes, Alice and Paul are very dear friends. Alice and I have an apartment together. She and Paul were married last month and are living there until I go back. After that I suppose I shall have the place to myself, unless——"

"You get married," Polly offered.

"Or get another housemate," Deborah corrected evenly. "Somehow that isn't an easy matter. People have to be congenial to live happily together in such close quarters as a four-room apartment. Alice and I made a success of it."

"You're easy to get along with, Debby," Polly observed and Deborah felt suddenly relieved. She couldn't stand having Polly displeased with her.

"I'll write a note to Miss Fowler and will you give it to her, Peter? Will day after tomorrow be all right,

Polly?" she asked, eager to put her good resolution into practice. She intended being friendly and uncritical. "That will be Thursday."

"It's all right with me, Debby," Polly told her. "Eve may not come, though. I imagine she's a mite peeved with me."

"Oh, no one ever stays peeved with you for long, Polly." Peter spoke affectionately. "Does the invitation hold for me if Eve can't accept?" he asked, looking at Deborah.

"Of course," the girl answered. "You'll like Paul and Alice and I do want them to enjoy their brief vacation. You see, Alice writes a little and hopes some day to have a book published."

Peter grimaced. "Who doesn't?" he asked and Deborah immediately took offense.

"Oh, I'm sure Alice won't be a nuisance to you. I doubt if she will even think of it while she's here and she need not know that you have the least connection with a publishing house. I'm sure I shall not mention it to her."

"That's something to be thankful for," Peter said coolly. "I, too, am on vacation and don't care to talk shop just now."

Deborah left the room to write her note and there was silence in the kitchen for a moment while she mounted the stairs.

"It's all off, Polly," Peter said sadly. "Deb thinks I'm a mighty poor fish—she likes her men two-fisted, knock-'em-down-for-the-count-of-ten."

"Fiddle-daddle!" Polly snorted. She's just jealous. Mad because Eve's here. The two of 'em glared at each other like Kilkenny cats this morning in the meat-market. Leave her alone for a spell—but get rid of Eve Fowler and her ma as quick as you can for all our sakes. I declare, Peter, Eve gets more buttery every time I see her."

"Look, Polly. I don't want her to take Nancy back with her. It will be a fight but I've made up my mind I'm going to stick this time. The child's impossible. Eve declares it's Cliff House that's bad for her which is of course complete nonsense. I paid Scott off, too, and told him I was hiring a governess for Nancy in the fall. Eve doesn't know this yet, or she didn't when I left home. I can't see why Eve was so insistent upon a tutor for Nancy—a girl of that age."

Polly snorted again. "You can't? Peter Jordan, you're just about the dumbest thing I ever see. Eve's afraid of a female teacher for Nancy. Scared to have one in the house with you. She thinks maybe you'd fall in love with her and then where'd she be? Get Nancy a female teacher, Peter, and pick out a pretty one. Maybe she can teach her manners and make a grandchild out of her yer ma and pa can be proud of. You might better have let your ma have her in the first place."

"No, Polly. I couldn't dump my responsibility on Mother. If the child were well, it might have been different: but not in her condition: it would tie her down too much. Eve seems to crave the responsibility and sometimes I feel like a heel that I'm so ungrateful to her. But it looks to me as if Nancy's too much for Eve——"

"I shall be looking for you both, Peter, and anything you can do to make Paul's stay pleasant will be much appreciated, I assure you." Deborah had heard Peter's last statement; "It looks to me as if Nancy's too much for Eve." Eve, Eve, Eve—thinking of Eve—never of poor little Nancy, whom Eve was spoiling. He made her sick. She'd held out the note to him and went back upstairs, while Peter turned and without a word went out.

Polly heard the screen door slam and a moment later the sound of Peter's car on the gravel drive.

"Drat the girl!" she muttered and banged the kitchen door with quite unnecessary violence. There was a protesting grunt and an indignant scratching outside. "Oh come on in, you pest," she said crossly, "and stay out of my way! Can't you see I'm busy?"

Lord Kitchener padded over to his cushion with heavy dignity but he turned when he reached his corner and his look was one of sorrow rather than anger as he lowered his great ugly head to his heavy paws. But Polly, usually quick to notice his moods, continued to set pots and pans down on table and cabinet with a heavy hand.

CHAPTER ELEVEN

THE SMALL, RATHER battered car of the Paul Hendricks' swept into the drive of the hospitable little house Deborah Bradley was at present calling home, and the two in the car sat for a moment inspecting the place. Roses climbed the white trellis each side of the attractive entrance. The grass was smooth velvet and the flower-beds a riot of color and fragrance. Lord Kitchener left the porch and waddled to the car where he lifted a snooty nose for investigation. Alice drew back with a little cry of alarm but Paul laughed delightedly and dropped one hand over the side of the car. If possible, the crumpled muzzle of the bulldog became even more wrinkled and the tip of a red tongue appeared with impudent effect before he turned his broad rear and, with a grunt, plodded back to the steps which he laboriously mounted with an accompanying gusty sigh at every step accomplished.

Paul got out and Alice pressed the horn. Deborah burst from the doorway and ran down the steps to greet them.

"Oh, this is grand!" she cried hugging Alice while Paul stood aside grinning happily.

"A swell place you have here, Deb," he said, admiring the gleaming white of wide clapboard and contrasting green of shutter and trim. "I've always wanted to live in a white house with green blinds. I think if I could live here for six months I'd never leave. My word, Deb, but Harmony certainly agrees with you. You look like a million. It seems like a grand little town."

"It is. And I love this house. Wait until you see your room and the rest of the place. And wait until you meet your hostess—Mrs. Quick," Deborah enthused.

"Hostess? I thought you had leased the house, Deb," Alice said. "I thought you had a housekeeper."

"Mrs. Quick lives here, Alice, never forget that. I'm merely a guest. She's a darling but proud as Lucifer. Now come on in and get rid of your luggage and make yourselves at home."

They entered the cool, shining hall and Deborah called;

"Polly, they've arrived! Do come and meet them."

The tall, white-haired old lady in crisp pink gingham greeted them cordially if a little critically. "So this is the girl who writes, is it?" her look said, "and this is her husband who don't make much money?" She decided they looked all right and felt sure they were the kind who would enjoy plenty of wholesome, hearty food. The quickest way to Polly's heart was by consuming with pleasure and appetite the good things she prepared.

"Debby'll show you to your room, my dears," she said warmly. "They's lots of hot water for baths and plenty of clean towels in the bathroom. When supper—I mean dinner's ready I'll ring this here gong and you'd best do a bit of hustling after that for I don't like vittles to stand and lose their goodness while folks dawdle. Go right on up."

"You see what I mean?" Deborah asked as she and Alice mounted the stairs followed by Paul with the luggage. "Don't make the mistake that I'm anything but a guest the same as you are. I don't mind in the least. Polly's a dear even if she does like to boss me and pry into my affairs."

"Pry into your affairs, Deb?" Alice asked as they reached the guest room. "What is there to discover even if——"

"For one thing, no one here knows I'm a nurse—I don't want them to and oh—well——" She broke off and held out her hands to the room before them. "Isn't it lovely?" She swung the door wide and stepped back.

A trio of windows looked out over the drive, the rose garden and the well-kept lawn of a neighbor. From the wide front window, the lake lay softly blue in the sunlight. It was a companion room to Deborah's across the hall and, except for the fact that this room contained twin beds, both canopied, and lacked the chaise longue, was similarly furnished.

Alice stood in the doorway, her eyes round with delight and awe. Paul peered over her shoulder and dropped the bags he carried.

"Gosh, Deb!" he murmured softly. "It's out of a book! Are we supposed to sleep in those beds?"

Deborah laughed. "Don't be silly, Paul. I'll say you'll sleep—like your never have before. There's something about this place that just soothes and quiets you until you forget all about the other side of life. I love it here. Maybe I shall never go back at all."

"If I were in your shoes I wouldn't," declared Alice, wandering about, examining the narrow framed silhouettes on the wall, the flounced dressing table and deep easy chairs. "This is the life, Paul. Let's build a house just like this when my book is sold."

Paul stood at the front window watching a sailboat putting out from a little bay and his face was that of an entranced small boy.

"I wonder if we have time for a swim before dinner—wait, I'll ask Polly," Deborah said impulsively.

"Oh, could we?" Alice breathed ecstatically.

Deborah was back in a minute and called through the door.

"Polly says if we go right now and don't dawdle, she can hold dinner until twenty minutes past six. So come on. Get into your bathing suits and let's go. I'll have my car at the side door in five minutes."

It was less than ten minutes' drive to the most popular of the bathing beaches along this side of the lake and Deborah and her guests came upon several of Deb's friends. They swam about in the cool waters until Deborah insisted they must return home or they wouldn't have time to dress for dinner. Polly would be displeased and they must know that was one thing that always proved disastrous.

"I'm going to love this place, Deb," Alice cried as they sped along the quiet street. "Everyone is so friendly and it's all like scenes in the movies. I'm having a grand time, aren't you, darling?"

Paul looked at his bride of a few weeks. "I hope this sort of thing isn't going to become a habit with you, Alice," he said grinning somewhat ruefully. "It's all very well for a change—a vacation, but for the rest of the year your life is going to be very real and very, very earnest, remember."

"As if I could forget," Alice retorted and then before he could take offense, "but when my book is finished, we'll begin to really live," she continued and added quickly, "Your raise is going to help, darling."

"I saw old Doc Hamilton yesterday, Deb," Paul said irrelevantly. "He sent you a message; 'Tell Bradley she'd better come back to Medford,' he said. 'We have two elegant cases of typhoid in Mercy Hospital from over on the North Side that we're tracking to its lair.' Raw milk, he thinks. 'Tell her that Philip Polycletus is proving a child wonder over in Ithaca and that the new apartment house is going up fast. Tell her we miss her like the devil and her vacation's lasted long enough.' There, I've got that off my chest. But when do you intend coming back, Deb? Or have you chucked nursing for good?"

Deborah shook her head. "I don't know," she replied. "I just can't go back now, anyway. Maybe some day——"

"Believe me, if I had the money you've got, the old Center would whistle for a nurse. I'd enjoy life while I was young and attractive. Do you know, Deb, you're a huge success as a loafer. You look like a society debutante. Certainly doing nothing agrees with you all right." Alice looked at the other girl a little enviously.

"About the apartment," began Paul.

"You keep the apartment until I decide what I'm going to do, will you?" Deborah urged. "Anyway, I doubt if I should ever get another housemate I could like as well as I do Alice and I wouldn't want to live there alone."

"What about this Jason chap?" Alice asked. "He seems to have fallen pretty hard for you, Deb."

They were turning into her driveway and Deborah laughed as she swung the little car in closer to the side entrance. "Why, Alice, Jason's a mere boy."

"Boy? I bet he's voted. Anyway, he's head over heels in love with you. Who is he? He looks pretty smooth to me."

"Oh, Jason's a native of the place. He's still in college and he's been terribly good to me and I think a lot of him. He's twenty-two but he seems years younger than I am and anyway——"

"Doc Brown was up here Sunday, wasn't he? Seems to me I heard Doc Hamilton mention it. How about Doc, Deb? Paul asked teasingly. "Darn nice chap, Doc; smart, too."

"Alec is nice, Paul. I like Alec, but I don't love him if that's what you mean and he doesn't love me, either." Deborah spoke with conviction.

"I'm not so sure!" Paul muttered but Deborah was already out of the car and up the steps, her beach robe held tight about her slim hips.

"Then who is the man?" Alice asked quizzically.

"Man, Alice? What man?" Deborah wrinkled her forehead at her friend.

"The man who has made you different—improved you—given your eyes a starry look and your voice new vibrancy—timbre, I think it's called. Come on, darling, tell me all. You may as well, for I'll find out anyway."

Deborah turned and went into the house. "Love does strange things to people, Alice," she said over her shoulder. "Just now you see people through rose colored glasses as loving and beloved. Make no mistake, my dear: no man is responsible for my improvement in health. It's Polly's cooking and the Harmony air. You'll see."

"Sez you!" jeered her friend. "I'll find out, Miss Bradley, and when I do I'll give you the old razzberry. You can't fool me, you know. I'm gifted with second sight, hence my success as a novelist—I hope."

Polly met them when they reached the hall and handed a note to Deborah.

"Peter just left it," she said. "I hope and pray Eve's decided she can't come to your party, Debby. Read it, do, and put me out of my misery. If I wasn't an honorable woman, I'd have up and read it as soon as it come."

Deborah scanned the brief epistle then lifted her eyes to Polly's. "You win, Polly. Miss Fowler sends regrets She feels that Nancy needs her. She explains that no doubt Peter will come and if he does it will do him worlds of good as he has been staying quite close to Cliff House since their arrival." Deborah tried desperately to keep the anger from her voice.

"Grand!" Polly cried, clapping her hands. "I foresee the success of your party, Debby. 'Twouldn't have been a safe bet if she had accepted."

"Did Peter say he was coming, Polly?" Deborah asked. She felt the hot blood rush to her cheeks at Alice's interested gaze.

"Oh, sure!" Polly told her. "Peter accepted yest'd'y mornin' when you first spoke of it, didn't he? He'll come all right, don't you worry."

"I wasn't worrying, Polly," Deborah retorted stiffly, "but it is better to know definitely, isn't it?" She started up the stairs, Alice close behind. "Worrying, indeed!" she scoffed.

"Oo, la-la-la," Alice crooned, "like heck you weren't! So its name is Peter——

> "Peter, Peter, pun'kin eater,
> Had a wife and couldn't keep her:
> Put her in a pun'kin shell,
> And there he kept her very well,"

she teased. "What's his last name? Does he live here? Deb, old girl, I'm crazy to see him."

"Don't be silly, Alice," Deborah scolded. "Peter Jordan lives up on the cliff in a place they call Cliff House." Then, as if to put the stamp of ineligibility on him, she went on; "Why, he's a widower, Alice, with a crippled daughter and a sister-in-law, beautiful as a poet's dream. I wanted you to meet her. Polly says she's out to become Mrs. Peter Jordan number two and I wouldn't wonder but what she's right." She slipped into her own room and closed the door.

"Ah-ha!" Alice murmured as she draped her robe over a chair. "And you don't intend letting her have a clear field. Is that it? Well, darling, more power to you, if, as I suspect, the man's worth while." She intended keeping her eyes wide open when Mr. Peter Jordan appeared and adding her own weight to that of her friend if this man passed the test. Deborah was such a baby where affairs of the heart were concerned. She hadn't the faintest idea on how to attract a lover, much less hold him or win a husband. Alice, married a month, felt there was much she could teach her friend.

The telephone rang while they were at dinner and Deborah rose to answer it.

"Would your guests like to take a ride in 'Firefly,' Deb? It's going to be a swell night and we could go over to Pirate's Run and dance. Some of the crowd are going in Pete Jordan's launch—he floated it this morning. Sure hope it's okay. It certainly was a mess last fall. Well, how about it?"

"Wait a minute, Jason, I'll ask them," Deborah said, all the time wondering why Peter hadn't invited them to join this party. She asked Alice and Paul and they accepted with enthusiasm. It would be fun. No, Polly preferred the dry land. She didn't hold with all this gadding about on the lake at night, and she hoped they wouldn't be late coming home, either, for one never knew when squalls might come up on Penguin Lake—which was noted for its peculiarities.

"But Polly," Deborah said when she had given her acceptance to Jason, "this isn't what you would call squally weather. It's clear as a bell and it hasn't rained in a week."

"Go 'long with you, Polly said. "I was only makin' excuses as to why I don't hold with gaddin' about on the water. It's likely all right for them that likes it, and if they don't jiggle about none."

"We won't jiggle," Deborah promised and they went upstairs to dress.

Paul changed quickly and the two girls could hear him in the kitchen talking with Polly. Deborah and Alice visited across the hall as they dressed.

"This seems like old times, Deb," Alice laughed. "It's grand and I love it here. What sort of a place is this Pirate's Run? Sounds sort of spooky."

"It's very swank, Alice. High class orchestra and grand food. It's one of the most popular resorts in this section although the cover charge is outrageous. But don't worry about that. Jason will take care of everything—it's his party."

Alice lowered her powder puff and stared unseeing at her reflection in the mirror.

"Oh, Deb, you wouldn't embarrass Paul, would you? You know we haven't much money——"

"Shut up, Alice. Who's embarrassing Paul? We are going as Jason Miller's guests and he'd be terribly insulted if any of us dared offer to pay for any part of the evening's entertainment. Tell Paul he mustn't attempt it. I can return the compliment while you are here. That's the worst of getting used to Dutch treat or paying one's own way all one's life—you feel like a chiseler when anyone else pays. But I'm getting used to it now, Alice, and it doesn't faze me a bit any more."

Alice picked up her powder puff once more and began on her neck. "I guess maybe it's being so absolutely destitute, Deb, that makes me that way," she explained apologetically. "I get so nervous when we go places for fear we'll have to stay and wash dishes to pay for our meal that I don't half enjoy it. That's why I won't let Paul take me to very ritzy places. If I could only have kept my job——"

"Why didn't you, then?" Deborah asked, shaking out the thin muslin frock she took from the closet. It was yellow and had tiny sprigs of maidenhair fern sprinkled over it

"Oh, Paul didn't want me to keep on working. He had some obsolete idea that he wanted a wife who would meet him at the door with a kiss and a hot dinner when he came home. He gets the kiss but not always the hot dinner—especially this kind of weather. But we do have fun, Deb, even though it's hell being so darned poor that I have to count the grains of salt I use in the potatoes."

"How's the book coming?"

"Slow. Somehow it's harder to feel inspired when you know the alarm clock is due to bust out yelling; "It's time to put the meat in the oven!' Some day I'm going to take that blasted clock and throw it right through old Bedlow's near-plate glass window into his prize hot-bed. I hope it smashes every pane of glass in the darned thing, too."

"Bad as that, Alice?" Deborah asked, worriedly, coming to stand in her guests' doorway.

Alice made a grimace at her reflection in the glass, then swung around on the bench. "Don't mind me, Deb. It's only when Paul's out of hearing that I dare blow off steam. He's swell, Deb, and we're happy as dimwits, only there are times when being poor gets me down. I made a vow to myself when we came up here this morning that when we got back to Medford I was going to finish my book if I had to stay up all night every night to do it. It's going to be a swell book and when it's done I'm going to send it to Oliver Cromwell Turner's publishers. I felt his visit was a gilt-edged tip and I'm going to make the most of it."

Deborah opened her mouth to protest such presumption, then closed it quickly. Why shouldn't Alice send it to Crane, Fish and Company? They could but turn it down. After all, Alice was clever and her conversation was bright and witty. Maybe Crane, Fish and Company would snap it up and Alice's book go over big. Some of the most inane books were best sellers. She hoped with all her heart that Alice would make good.

"After all, Alice," she said sententiously, "happiness isn't dependent on money——"

"No?" her friend interrupted ironically. "Sez you! I hope you never have to put it to the test, darling." She jumped up and ran to Deborah. "Don't mind me, angel," she whispered. "It's just that I'm jealous—envious of anyone but me having this darling house. I love it!"

"So do I," Deborah said, "and I dread the thought of leaving it. I intend staying just as long as I can, but of course it belongs to Mrs. Holcomb who probably wouldn't think of selling it."

"She might," Alice murmured, smoothing down the bed cover with a gentle, admiring hand. "I think I'll set my heart on it and every morning I'll will her to part with it and will Paul and me the wherewithal to buy it. I understand there is something in this mind-over-matter business. If there is I'm going to have this house and before I'm as old as Methuselah, too."

"Yoo-oo!" sounded outside and Deborah ran to the window overlooking the drive.

"It's Jason," she reported, "and he's got his father's big car. Come on."

The two girls ran down the stairs and joined Paul who was already seated beside Jason.

"You be careful!" warned Polly as she waved from the porch and Jason called back;

"You bet, Mrs. Quick. Careful's my middle name."

Pirate's Run was thronged with the summer crowd from all sides of the lake. A famous orchestra held forth each season and the place was becoming increasingly popular. On the wide brilliantly lighted veranda the newcomers were welcomed boisterously. Deborah was now one of them and, as Deb's friends, her house guests were accepted with keen delight. Alice was lovely with her beautiful hair and almost childlike eagerness to make everyone happy. Paul, tall and good-looking, smiled often these days. Deb felt they were a huge success.

"Where's Pete Jordan?" someone asked, his eye scanning the newcomers.

"Eve Fowler's at Cliff House." The explanation appeared adequate. Several of the men complained of Pete's dog-in-the-manger attitude but Deborah caught Jason's hand.

"Let's dance, Jason. Oh, I love this." She sang softly with the orchestra as, followed by the others, they entered the pavilion.

"I'm having a grand time, darling," Alice whispered some hours later as she and Deborah met for a brief moment near one of the long windows. "Where are you bound for?"

"The beach, for a breath of fresh air," Deborah replied. "It seems a shame to spend all the evening indoors, even if you're dancing."

"And solitude," Jason added meaningly.

Alice laughed and made a little grimace. Which was it, she wondered, Peter Jordan or Jason Miller? And why, if it was Jason, wasn't he invited to Deb's dinner?

"You look eighteen tonight, Deb." Jason's voice was low and he drew her closer as they strolled along the moonlit beach.

"Looks are deceiving, my dear," Deb told him. "I'm twenty-three—almost twenty four."

"What of it? Love recognizes no age. I've read that somewhere and it's true. What does a year or two or ten matter?"

"But Jason, there's your law course to consider. You ought not to think of marrying yet. And you'll probably fall in love a dozen times before you meet the right girl."

"You don't mean that, Deb," Jason said indignantly, "and what if I am in law school? I can take care of you." His voice roughened as he went on earnestly; "Darling, we can be so happy—just to have you near me always

113

is all I want of life. My people love you—they approve of you, sweetheart. Won't you give me a chance?"

"Oh, Jason, you're sweet!" Deborah whispered. "I —I—but I don't think I love you—like that. You seem so young——"

They had reached a secluded nook some distance from the pavilion.

"Stop treating me like a boy—as if I were adolescent and you a grandmother or something." He gave her a little shake, his hands firm on her slim shoulders. "Is there someone else, Deb?" he asked. "That doctor who was here Sunday or—or—it can't be—no——"

"No, Jason—at least——"

Suddenly she was in his arms, his eager young mouth hard against her own. Deborah didn't struggle. This boy's ardent wooing soothed and healed, in a measure, the hurt bewilderment of the past few days. Her lips were soft beneath his and they stood for a long moment completely oblivious of their surroundings.

It was a shrill laugh a few yards away that caused them to move swiftly apart.

"You do love me, Deb!" Jason was triumphant.

"Oh, I don't know. I—I—oh, Jason, please don't let us make any mistake. Let's just be friends for a while— until——"

"Not too long, darling," he laughed softly: "but I'll let you sort of get used to the idea of becoming Mrs. Jason Miller, wife of the sometime eminent jurist."

"But—but—I haven't promised——" Deb stammered.

"Oh, here you are. We've been thinking of dragging the lake." The owner of the shrill laugh and her escort joined them.

"Paul and his bride are becoming jittery," the escort added a bit tipsily. "I knew about this 'Lovers' Retreat' and offered to bring you back alive and still in your right minds. Have I succeeded or is everything signed, sealed and delivered, Jason, old top? If not, you're no longer the smart lad we've been led to believe you are."

"Maybe you know what you're talking about, Slacks," Jason said shortly, "but I think you're tight."

"There's a pal for you!" the other muttered inanely, "an' I wouldn't blame Deb if she gave you the air. Come

114

on, Toots. I guess I know when I'm s'perfl—not wanted. Right, eh——or——"

"Blast him!" Jason muttered as Deb hurried him back to the pavilion. "Forget him, darling. I'll be along tomorrow and——"

"Not tomorrow, Jason. You see——"

"Well, we thought you had gone back without us." Alice ran to meet them.

"Silly!" Deborah put her arm through that of her friend and Paul fell behind with Jason. "But it is getting late and we must go home. You and Paul had that long drive up without a bit of rest. Polly will scold me."

There was a light in the hall when Jason stopped his father's car beside the front porch, and Polly came out to greet them.

"We didn't jiggle the boat, Aunt Polly," Alice told her, "and we had a grand time. You should have come. I was scared once, though," she went on impishly. "You see, Deb and Jason got themselves lost but fortunately they were together and——"

"Nonsense, Alice!" Deborah's laugh showed embarrassment. "We knew where we were all the time—at least, Jason did."

"I'll warrant," Polly muttered as Paul and Alice joined her. "I'd ask you in for a snack, Jason," she called, "but I know you've got a long drive ahead of you and—well, it might rain." She peered up at the starry summer sky and added hospitably; "Come again, my boy. They'll be a new batch of fruit cookies the last of the week. Be careful goin' home or your ma'll skin me alive for lettin' you stay so late. Good night!"

It is doubtful if Jason heard one word of what she said. Deborah had lingered. "Good night, Jason," she whispered. "Thank you for a lovely evening."

"I don't suppose I dare kiss you right here, with that bunch staring at us. Why don't they go in and mind their own business?"

Deborah drew back. "Heavens, no! Good night, and thank you again," and as she turned to join the others, he called softly after her;

"Goodnight, dar-ling," and quickly shifted gears.

CHAPTER TWELVE

PAUL WAS THE first one downstairs next morning and he and Polly had their breakfast together. The girls were to sleep later. But Paul had scarcely left the guest room when Alice padded across the hall and crept in beside Deborah who sleepily protested she wasn't going to get up for hours and that Alice could just go to sleep as she had no intention of talking at this hour.

"This hour!" jeered Alice, who wanted to talk about the ride, Pirate's Run, Jason and oh, heaps of things. "It's half-past seven, my pampered darling, and I remember the time when you used to yank me out of bed long before this and with no gentle hand either. Oh, Deb, wake up! You can't possibly need all this sleep. You're getting lazy."

Deborah rubbed her eyes, stretched and yawned widely. "I guess that's just it, Alice, I'm lazy. Sleep? I sleep like a baby—just simply wallow in it. Maybe I was more tired than I knew."

"Your man, Peter Jordan, wasn't at the party, was he? I wonder why," Alice asked.

"I wouldn't know," Deborah replied. "And don't call him 'my man.' Probably Eve needed him for something or it might be he was out of town. He is connected with some business in New York and flies down there quite often."

"But he was here this afternoon, Deb. Don't you remember, he brought you a note from this Eve?"

"Oh, well, what does it matter? He missed a grand party and I doubt if anyone missed him. At least, his name wasn't mentioned that I know of."

"I missed him," Alice said. "What sort of looking chap he is?" She wriggled to a more comfortable position and went on; "Let's talk about our beaus, Deb, like girls always do when they're bedfellows."

Deborah laughed. "You're the limit, Alice. Here you've been married a whole month and you act like a schoolgirl. Anyway I haven't any beau."

"I bet you have only you won't tell."

Deborah yawned and frowned crossly. "Oh, go on back to your own bed!"

  " 'Debby's mad and I'm glad
  And I know what will please her.
  Give her a treat to make her sweet
  And Peter J. to squeeze her!' "

Alice chanted wickedly in a singsong voice. "Or should it be Jason M.?"

"Say, what goes on up there?" Paul called from the lower hall. "If you two are awake you'd better get up pronto. Aunt Polly's made muffins and I never tasted anything like them. I smelled 'em in my sleep and they drew me as nothing else ever has—not even you, my darling wife."

Feet padded back across the hall and although Deborah turned over and tried to recapture slumber, she found it quite impossible, for Alice was singing at the top of her lungs.

Paul lounged on the little porch outside the small breakfast nook while the girls ate Polly's hot muffins. The morning was glorious as so many of the mornings had been this summer, Deborah noticed. The lake was a dazzling mirror in the brilliant sunlight and through the open windows came all the delightful sounds and smells of summer. Her face ecstatic, Alice sat with half-closed eyes making soft murmurs of exaggerated content as she ate muffin after muffin. Deborah watched her in delight. She hadn't realized how very much she had missed her housemate. Polly was enjoying these two guests. Paul seemed to have crept into her heart and it was "Paul" and "Aunt Polly" almost at once. But Paul was like that. Deborah had always felt a sisterly affection for him and was happy to be the means of giving him and Alice this holiday, brief though it must be.

The girls were still at breakfast when Eve Fowler cantered up to the little porch on a spirited black mare and introduced herself to Paul who, with Lord Kitchener between his knees, was ragging the girls. The bulldog rumbled low in his throat and the mare sidled off, dancing on her hind legs. Paul held Kitchener firmly with both hands and called to Polly who left the kitchen to find out what the early morning visitor wanted.

"Oh, Polly, I dropped in to see if Miss Bradley and her guests would come out to Cliff House for luncheon this afternoon. This is one of Nancy's good days and she does so enjoy meeting new people."

Polly eyed the girl on the horse for a moment and then called to Deborah who had been keeping perfectly quiet. She had no desire to talk with Eve Fowler. But Alice was excited.

"Tell her we'll come, Deb. I'm crazy to see her at close range. They tell me she is absolutely criminally beautiful."

Deborah left her chair and pulled Alice to her feet. "If that's what you want, come on and meet her. Anyway, perhaps you'd better protect Paul from her fatal charm." The two girls went to the little side porch and Deborah felt the caller's eyes appraise them, that same irritating amusement in their blue depths. They lingered longest on her and Deborah's head lifted, unconsciously.

"I'm sure we shall be very glad to come for luncheon this afternoon, Miss Fowler," she said with cool formality. "It was kind of you to invite us. This is Alice Hendricks, Miss Fowler, and Paul Hendricks, her husband."

The lady on the fidgeting mare scrutinized the bride and groom almost rudely, Deborah thought. "I suppose she thinks that her beauty and wealth give her the right to stare," she said resentfully as the visitor disappeared down the drive. "In anyone else that would be considered ill-bred and I'm not sure but it is in her case, too."

"Oh, I don't mind," Alice declared. "I guess maybe I've been guilty of considerable staring, too, since I've been here. Haven't you, Paul?"

"Gosh, Deb, the dame's gorgeous! But just what have you done to her that she should treat you with such amazing, almost triumphant condescension?" Paul looked puzzled.

"Then you saw it, Paul?" Deborah exclaimed.

"Saw it!" sniffed Polly. "I felt it. Drat the blasted woman!"

"Where is this Cliff House?" Alice asked interestedly. "It sounds like a place of mystery where deep, dark deeds are perpetrated. The lady won't poison us at this luncheon, will she? We're so young to die," she whimpered, "and have been married such a short time!"

"Don't be a nut!" Paul grinned.

"Not with food, my dear," Polly said. She thought Alice a "clip"—a word dating from her long ago childhood. "Not with food, she won't poison you—she uses words—sugar-coated poison words and they're far more deadly to my way of thinkin'."

"Pooh!" scoffed Alice.

> "Sticks and stones may break my bones:
> But words can never hurt me,"

she chanted.

"I don't know about that, Alice," the old lady demurred. "I know lots of cases where poison words have well-nigh wrecked people's lives. Best be on your guard, children, when you're in Eve Fowler's vicinity. She'd find the agony of a pin-stuck fly amusin'."

"Flies don't have feelings, Aunt Polly," Alice informed her. "If we thought they had we wouldn't be so keen to swat them."

"But we swat 'em dead," the old lady insisted.

"I'll say we do," Paul agreed. "After that they can't feel."

"Well, all I can say is you better be on the watch for nasty scratches and such."

"We will," Paul assured her, "and we'll form a hollow square of protection about Deb, too, so that no little barbed words will sneak through and strike her. Just who is this dame, anyway? Nature certainly pulled a boner when she created that exquisite creature if she left out the soul."

"I know who she is, Paul," Alice chirped. "She's the other woman."

"What other woman? I didn't know there was one," her husband said.

"You'll see, sightless one. And may virtue triumph over mere fleshly beauty once again, my frans," she said oratorically.

"Don't be silly!" Deborah snapped and left them.

Alice made a wry grimace and prepared to follow then thought better of it. She tucked her arm into Polly's and led her back to the kitchen.

"Give me the low-down, Aunt Polly," she whispered. "Spill all the dirt. What's going on here, anyway? Tell me so that I can put my oar in and maybe help bring the frail bark of true love into port."

"They ain't nothin' to tell that I know of," Polly said, eyeing the pretty girl beside her.

"All right for you, Polly Quick!" Alice warned. Then she tried a new tack. "Is the great Peter Jordan really fond of our Debby, or has this Eve person put her brand on him for keeps?"

"She'd like to all right," Polly muttered vindictively.

Paul had followed them and now spoke. "Don't tell me that the fair equestrienne has matrimonial designs, Aunt Polly! I had the distinct feeling she had fallen heavily for me, and I was about to break it gently to my clinging bride that our marriage was a sad mistake, that at last I had found my perfect woman. Oh, but I'd adore painting her—if I had some paints—and was a painter. Such coloring, such eyes, such hair and such a figger! Alice, my love, give me back the heart you stole from me, lo, these many years agone! She can't be very old, Aunt Polly. Twenty-five or six, maybe?"

"Eve Fowler's thirty-four," Polly pronounced firmly. "I ought to know for Marcy was six years younger than she is and Marcy would be twenty-eight if she'd lived. She's four years older than Peter——"

"Tut tut, Aunt Polly, and fie fie! That's no crime," Paul said smiling at her vehemence.

"Let's see," murmured Alice meditatively, "Marcia was Peter's wife and Eve's younger sister. Right? Well, according to certain authorities she is due to become the future Mrs. Peter, but somehow the affair hasn't jelled yet, so to speak. I get the set-up now. This very desirable young man has shown a marked interest in our Debby, eh, Aunt Polly? But where does Jason come in?"

"Come in? Where?" Polly wanted to know.

"That's what I'm asking. He's head-over-heels in love with Deb, you know."

"Puppy love!" sniffed Polly.

"Oh, but Aunt Polly," Alice insisted. "Jason's a perfect peach! Is this Peter nicer even than Jason?"

"Nicer? Umph!" was the extent of Polly's comment.

"Umph me no umphs, darling," persisted Alice. "What I want to know—has this Peter man been making passes at our Debby?"

"I ain't talkin'," Polly said firmly.

"You don't have to, old dear," Alice chortled. "He has and hence the sweetly sticky glances from the glamorous Eve." With her fists raised in belligerent warning after the manner of one Ajax defying the lightning, she intoned;

> " 'Shoot if you must this poor red head
> But spare my lovely friend!' she said."

Polly stood transfixed, her eyes round and her mouth open. Paul gave his wife a little shove. "Shut up, you nut!" he rebuked, grinning fondly at her nonsense. "Don't mind her, Aunt Polly. She's only half-baked."

"Ain't she the beatin'est!" Polly murmured, her eyes affectionate.

Deborah dressed very carefully for the luncheon at Cliff House and Alice inspected her critically before they went downstairs.

"If my opinion were to be asked, I'd say offhand that Eve hadn't the ghost of a show, my girl," she said as she watched Deborah adjust a wide, flower-trimmed straw hat on her shining brown head. "Tip it just a wee bit, darling. It gives you a sort of rakish air, a to-hell-with-the-lot-of-you effect so earnestly striven for by all us females—if we tell the truth. Now let me give you just one little bit of advice, Deborah. Leave the chip at home. You're positively irresistible when you're your own natural self, but I never knew anyone so utterly capable of becoming a human ice machine on the least provocation. Honestly, Deb, you freeze up for the simplest things! Just be the sweet young girl you are and forget you have a mad on this Peter person because he's temporarily bewitched by Eve the glamorous."

Deborah had been angry with Alice for her persistence

regarding Peter Jordan but discovered again, as she had long ago, that it was quite useless to try to change her friend's nature. Now she laughed, if somewhat dubiously, tipped the hat at the desired angle and turned a lovely, amazingly youthful face to her guest.

"Think I'll do all right? I confess I'm more scared of meeting the child, Nancy, than I am of any of the others. After all, they're not going to eat us.'

"You look sweet enough to eat at .that, Deb," Alice told her. "I love that frock."

"You look pretty delectable yourself, Mrs. Hendricks," Deborah returned the compliment. "That part of your trousseau?"

"Uh-uh. Like it? Nineteen-ninety-five at Marshall's. But I did have some pretty things—I've always loved clothes, Deb, and believe me I stocked up before I got married knowing it would be quite a while before I bought any more. It's lucky I brought my prettiest things with me—going out in such swanky society and all."

"Isn't it, queer, Alice," Deborah mused, "but I never thought of the people here as particularly rich until Eve Fowler came. They appeared just a nice, friendly crowd who were quite prepared to like me and help me enjoy my summer. Now, they all seem different, somehow. But I don't intend letting my imagination spoil my vacation and I defy her or anyone to intimidate or patronize me."

"Atta girl! That's the spirit!" applauded Alice. She struck an attitude and cried in ringing, martial tones;

> "Beauty to right of her,
> Envy to left of her,
> Jealousy fronting her
>   Warned of a rival.
> Decried by older belle
> Proudly she strode and well
> Into the mansion 'Cliff'
> Into the arms of—well?
>   Strode our sweet Debby.

Hurrah for our side, darling! More power to you and we're right behind you to give you a poke should the old courage fail."

"It won't," Deborah promised and led the way downstairs.

Peter was not in evidence when the three arrived at the lovely estate known as Cliff House. The maid who answered their ring remembered Deborah and smiled as she ushered them into the long cool drawing room. Alice gazed about in exaggerated awe while Paul grinned and shook his head at her. Deborah refused to acknowledge that her knees felt weak and that she was glad to sit down in the nearest chair. What an idiot she was! She bit her lip and thought of Alice's cure for self-consciousness; "To hell with the lot of you!" and she was smiling when Eve Fowler entered from the end of the room to greet her guests.

"So happy you could come," she smiled sweetly and Alice's expression said plainly; "Liar!" while her lips smiled mechanically. Alice was intensely loyal to Deborah and felt that in some way this lovely woman was hurting her. "Mother is in Buford attending a Colonial Dame luncheon," the charming voice went on.

Alice, two-thirds gamin at heart, murmured in her turn; "Oh, is your mother a Dame, too? How interesting!" Deborah restrained a giggle with difficulty.

Miss Fowler looked sharply at the pretty red-headed girl but Alice's face was guileless as that of a child.

"We are having luncheon on Nancy's veranda," she explained, suddenly losing a bit of her air of lady of the manor. "She is eager to know you all. Won't you remove your hats—no?" as Alice shook her head. Her hat was new and vastly becoming and Eve Fowler nor anyone else should take it from her. "Come this way, please. Nancy's suite is one flight up. We think the air is better for the poor darling and there is less noise and confusion."

They mounted the broad, shallow stairs and Deborah discounted the reason given for Nancy's room being on the second floor. The place was quiet as the grave. In such a huge place, so massively built, all sounds were minimized. Even their footfalls made not a whisper on the thick carpet. Deborah was forcing herself to go on. Every nerve in her body protested against this visit—this looking upon suffering and perhaps disfigurement.

They passed through Nancy's sitting room to the wide veranda overlooking Penguin Lake. Against her will, Deborah's shrinking glance flew to the reclining chair and the girl who lay in it and she gasped. How very like Peter she was! And yet how very different—almost as if some vandal had deliberately altered certain features of the face.

Miss Fowler went directly to her and took a small hand in hers. A large, raw-boned, elderly woman in white, sitting near, rose. Her cold unfriendly eyes appraised each visitor in turn before she turned abruptly and left them.

"I've brought a bride and groom to have lunch with you, darling, Eve said and drew Alice nearer the invalid. "Mrs. Hendricks, Nancy, and this is her new husband, Mr. Hendricks. Sit down, do," she went on and after a moment swept a hand toward where Deborah stood and murmured; "And this is a friend of your father's, sweetheart, Miss Bradley—it is Bradley, isn't it?

The little girl, who had shaken hands quite amiably with the others, stared coldly at Deborah who held out her hand and smiled down at the child. Her throat felt thick with tears. Nancy made no effort to put her hand in Deborah's, however, and when the caller took it in her own, she found it cold and unresponsive. The child's bright brown eyes had something repellent in them. She looked up at Deborah sullenly, and withdrew her hand at once.

Miss Fowler was immediately apologetic. "Please don't pay any attention to her, Miss Bradley. You know one never knows about children. They take the strangest fancies—likes and dislikes, you know, and very often they change so quickly it is hard to follow them.

"Do you find it so?" Deborah asked coolly.

"Oh, children always adore Deb," Alice said quickly, longing to wipe that sullen look from Nancy's face.

Paul was uneasy and watched his hostess curiously. She interested him. He had never met a woman like her, so lovely—so flawless in every detail—so poised and assured. What was there about her that drew and yet repulsed him? And just what was the reason for Aunt Polly's intense dislike of her?

A car entered the drive below and a man's voice floated up to them. Paul saw Eve's slender body stiffen and her bright blue gaze dart to Deb's face. He hoped she hadn t noticed the girl's added color and the sudden light in her gray eyes. Maybe he was imagining things for Deb's greeting of Peter Jordan was quite impersonal, while the man's manner was merely cordial. His sister-in-law, however, laid a slender white hand on his arm and laughed gaily.

"Naughty boy, to have vanished at the first sign of visitors! What am I going to do with you?

His daughter continued to sulk and appeared quite unaware of his presence in the room. Peter colored and looked unhappy. He found a seat beside Paul, and both being ardent fishermen, they fell to discussing the virtues and effectiveness of various flies. Alice set about dispensing a bit of cheer in what was proving a very dull visit. Her amusing chatter brought an occasional grin to Nancy's sullen mouth and even a thin tinkle of laughter that surprised her guests and caused her aunt to shake her head warningly. Deborah thought, however, that Peter looked relieved and even a bit grateful. Eve Fowler had little to say. Her looks told plainly she was tolerating them for Nancy's sake, finding the situation oddly amusing if somewhat trying. For the most part, Peter's conversation was of generalities. The food, however, was delicious and daintily served. Nevertheless, Deborah was relieved when the time came for them to depart. As they said goodbye to their small hostess, she surprised everyone by saying in her thin childish voice;

"I'll shake hands with you now, Miss Bradley."

Deborah pressed the tiny hand in her own and murmured; "It was a nice party, Nancy. I hope you will come to one of mine some day."

Eve shook her head. "I'm afraid not, Miss Bradley, she said with sad finality.

"Afraid?" Deborah asked. "Afraid of what? Surely she has ridden in cars." She turned to Peter. "Why can't you bring Nancy over to spend the day with me?"

Eve spoke quickly. "We think it unwise, Miss Bradley. And I doubt if Peter would care to take the responsibility

—against Doctor Davis's advice. But we are grateful for the invitation, aren't we, darling?"

But Nancy had withdrawn into her shell of sulky silence.

"I'm sorry," was all Deborah could manage to say.

Alice called a gay goodbye to Nancy and with her arm through Deb's left the veranda. Before they reached the stairs, however, they knew Nancy was having a tantrum. They could hear Eve trying to soothe her and then cajoling, harsher tones, probably the nurse, Anna.

Eve joined them at the foot of the stairs, her descent a symphony of grace and beauty. Peter wore an air of listening, almost of anxiety, as he and Paul talked with the two girls at the foot of the long stairway. He answered Alice's eager inquiries as to the identity of the portraits in the hall rather absently, Peter who was so proud of his forebears!

"Waiting for Eve," Deborah told herself bitterly.

Now Eve stood beside him, her arm through his, a possessive smile on her perfect lips. She gave him a little shake.

"Darling," she cried, affectionately, "don't be such a bear! You really should learn to control your feelings. People might not always understand."

Peter who had scarcely looked at Deborah during their stay now turned to her, his gaze begging her to understand.

"I'm sorry Nancy was cross, Deb," he said as he held her hand closely. "Next time I hope she will be on her good behavior."

Eve chuckled: the sound was like that a tiny spring makes as it ripples over pebbles in an ecstasy of freedom.

Paul marveled anew.

"Poor lamb!" Eve murmured. "Nancy's moods are such a trial to him. But we don't bother him long as a general thing, do we, darling?"

Peter didn't answer, and, Deborah thought, very gently withdrew his arm from her clinging hands and stepped to the porch beside Paul.

"See you tomorrow, Jordan," Paul ventured. "You've got a grand place here."

126

"Oh, I love it, Peter," Alice cried. "I hope you'll invite us again."

"The latchstring is always out for all of you," Peter answered but he said it soberly, with none of his gay comradery that was such a part of him. Peter was obviously worried about something.

As Paul shifted gears, he muttered; "There, my dear, is a plot for a story. But could any woman faithfully and artistically put on paper Eve Fowler as she actually is? I doubt it. It would take a Rider Haggard or an Edgar Allan Poe to do that. What a woman?"

"Piffle!" scoffed Alice. "It would take a woman to understand her and only a woman, my darling husband. The world's full of her kind. Jealousy! The base of every triangle. And plots like that can be bought for a dime a dozen."

Paul shook his head. "You've missed the point of the whole setup," he said. "And you think you're a novelist!"

Deborah said nothing. She was thinking that it was perfectly fiendish to doom that child to the life of a helpless cripple on the advice of one man. Criminal, until every resource known to science had been exhausted. Suddenly she felt a wild surge to be back in the midst of the fight. She felt strong once more. Why was she loafing here in luxury while there was work to be done?

Of course she could do nothing regarding Nancy Jordan. That was entirely up to her natural guardians. But there were dozens of youngsters without a single chance for life, liberty and the pursuit of happiness unless she and her associates kept on the job—fought tooth and nail for them. Then and there she decided to go back to Medford and to her work on the North Side.

CHAPTER THIRTEEN

DEBORAH DIDN'T MENTION her decision to go back to her job in Medford. She would forget it—forget everything sad or serious for a little while longer. She wanted Alice and Paul to have a carefree, restful vacation and, anyway, she had leased the house until October 1st. However, she made up her mind to go back before her lease expired.

"You fix the table, Debby," Polly advised next day as they sat at luncheon. "They's plenty of flowers you can choose from and you set the table for four. I ain't a'goin' to set down with you. Now you listen to me," as Deborah protested that Polly sit at the head of the table as usual. "I aim to tend to the vittles and wait on table." She set her mouth stubbornly, and Paul defended her stand in the matter.

"I think you've got something there, Aunt Polly," he told her. "After all, you're mistress here and you've got a perfect right to do as you like. Personally, I shall feel lots more like enjoying my dinner if I know you're at the controls. And," he lowered his voice and spoke directly to her, "I'll be out to eat a snack with you later. Never could do complete justice to a meal when company's present."

Deborah said no more. After all, Polly was enjoying the guests and was probably pretending they were all her children. She acted like it. Bless her!

Peter drove into the yard soon after six o'clock that afternoon. The spotless white of his informal dinner clothes added inches to his slim height and made the deep, healthy tan of his skin even more pronounced. But Deborah thought as they shook hands:

"He's unhappy and worried. Why does he put up with it? Surely he doesn't have to. If he wants her why doesn't he marry her—or else?"

Polly called to him from the kitchen where she was beating something in a glass bowl. "Pe-ter! Did you tell her yet?"

Peter went down the hall to answer. Deborah could hear the sharp staccato of Polly's questions and Peter's deeper voice replying though she did not understand what they said, but when Peter returned to the living room, his face had lost some of its dark, tragic look. She was glad. It somehow hurt her to have him unhappy, even though he exasperated her for allowing Eve to make a fool of him.

Alice and Paul came downstairs and greeted the guest with enthusiasm.

"I love Cliff House, Peter," Alice chirped youthfully as she shook hands with him. "It's like a movie set— any minute I expected someone would shout; 'Lights, camera, mu-sic!' How can you take it so casually—such beauty and grandeur?"

"I'm glad you like it, Mrs. Hendricks—well, Alice, then," as Alice looked offended at his formality. "You see," he smiled, and Deborah thought; "How it alters his appearance—that smile of his! "It's just home to me. No doubt when Great-grandfather built it, materials and land were cheap and the old boy was something of a David Harum in his day and made some pretty close bargains. Grandfather added to it and my father, too. It's been in the family four generations with but little change. Nancy makes the fifth generation—poor youngster!" His face darkened for a moment and he shrugged as if to shift the load and turned to Deborah.

"The child seems quite unwell today. Eve blames the excitement of her party. But as it was her own idea, she must hold herself wholly responsible. Anna was opposed to it and in consequence we're all in the doghouse. Mrs. MacDonald, however, thinks there's nothing to worry about. Nancy has these upsets occasionally.

"Is there absolutely no hope of her ever walking, Peter?" Alice asked, pity in her eyes and voice. Before he could answer, Deborah said positively;

"Nothing is absolutely hopeless, Alice. Miracles are happening every day and very likely something will be discovered to help Nancy. I have watched too many apparently hopeless cripples given back the use of their legs to ever make the statement that any case is absolutely incurable. If there is no pressure there, then there are means, aside from an operation, of effecting a cure. It is wicked to give up hope—it's the defeatist attitude. Ours is a profession of hope——" She paused and flushed in embarrassment. "Forgive me, I forgot——'

"Forgive you? For what?" asked Paul who had been watching Peter's face. "For jacking up the faint hearts of doubting Thomases? Don't be foolish, darling. We should know that if ever man that is born of woman had cause for hope it's in this twentieth century. Of course, I'm discounting dictators and wars and such and speaking from the standpoint of science and art—the science of healing and the art of helpfulness, and now it's my turn to apologize for preaching." He laughed and turned to Nancy's father.

"I suppose you're both right," Peter said somewhat morosely.

"Of course they're right," Alice interrupted quickly, "and that being the case, let's dance a little before dinner. Will you play, Deb, or no, let's use the radio so you can dance, too." She ran to the hall and called; "Aunt Polly! I'm rolling back the living room rug and we're going to dance a little. Do you mind? You know I'm a Methodist, too—at heart."

"You're nothin' of the sort," Polly said, her head appearing through the kitchen doorway. "But go as far as you like. If 'twasn't that I'm too busy I'd come in there and do a cakewalk like we used to do it over in Deacon Walker's barn—after prayer meetin'. Ain't nothin sinful in dancin'—it s what's in people's minds, sez I." The head was withdrawn and there came the sound of brisk beating of spoon against bowl.

"Ain't it the truth?" Alice muttered as she pulled chairs and tables close to the wall while the two men rolled back the rug. Deborah was at the radio trying to get her favorite orchestra. Here it came flooding the room with rich, warm melody.

"I missed the party night before last, Deb." Peter murmured as he and Deb floated down the long room in the wake of the other two.

"It was a grand party," Deborah replied. "The lake was smooth as silk and Alice and Paul enjoyed it all immensely. I was so glad that Jason thought of it. He's sweet."

130

Peter said nothing and Alice began to sing in her high sweet soprano. Soon Peter and Deborah joined her and Paul suddenly stopped. "Sa-ay," he demanded, "let's either sing or dance—I can't do both—not proficient enough in either. Now, my friends, which shall it be, sing or dance?"

"Dance," Peter said. Alice pouted as she agreed with him. Alice felt like singing. She was ecstatically happy and had to express it in every way she could. She gave her young husband a shove.

"All right, sourpuss, go dance with Deb. Peter and I will dance and sing if we like. I want to improve my acquaintance with the master of Cliff House. Now tell me all about your lovely sister-in-law," she said surprisingly. "She intrigues me."

Deborah caught her breath. How dare she? Really Alice was being a little too naive and it was queer, too, for she wasn't naturally so. Pert and modern, rather.

The living room was large and Deborah could hear nothing of the conversation that went on between her two guests. She stole a glance at Peter to find him smiling down at Alice as the girl gazed up at him with eager, wide blue eyes. Paul chuckled.

"Picture of a novelist in search of material," he grinned. "She's barking up the wrong tree as I told her before. Jordan's the last person in the world to give her a lucid and critical analysis of Eve Fowler, her life and character. He's too close to her and anyway she has him completely blinded—buffaloed. But Alice won't believe me. Refuses to take any stock in me as a student of human nature. I'm merely her husband. Oh, well, let her go her own gait—maybe she'll learn after a bit but more than likely she never will."

Deborah experienced a feeling of panic. Then Paul, too, thought Peter was infatuated with Eve Fowler. She stiffened and Paul looked down at her. "What is it?" he asked.

Deborah laughed. "I just thought of something, Paul," she explained. "I should have written, Mother today." It was the first thing that came to mind.

"How is your mother, Deb?" he asked. "Still want you over there?"

"Yes, but it isn't likely I shall go. I'm going back to Medford and to the North Side. I didn't mean to tell——"

"Good for you!" Paul applauded and met Peter's questioning glance above his wife's bright head. "When did you decide that?"

"Yesterday. Do you know that Nancy Jordan is the first sick person I could bring myself to come in contact with since I left Medford more than three months ago? I expect to go back around the first of September— perhaps a little before. But don't mention it to Alec or any of the Medford crowd. I want to thrash this out myself and I won't be hurried."

"Okay, sister. I won't even tell the wife. But don't you think you could prevail upon Jordan to have Gilbert give Nancy the once over? He's a whiz, you know, even if he isn't big time—yet. Brown is no slouch either— your Alec, I mean."

Deborah shook her head. "What good would it do to convince Peter? You yourself said it's his sister-in-law who's boss. And just try to convince her of anything she doesn't want to believe! No, Paul, it's none of my business and while I think it's positively criminal, I can't do anything about it."

"You might stage another fire, Deb, and save the chee-ild," he said whimsically, and went on: "Philip Polycletus got his chance, remember."

"But the Polycletus family are paupers. Nancy's people are wealthy. I doubt if even a fire would budge that woman." Deborah's voice was bitter and Paul laughed at her.

"Don't let her get you down, darling," he told her giving her a little shake. "That's her aim. Can't you see that?"

Polly came to stand in the door. Peter deposited Alice in a nearby chair and caught the old lady in his arms. She was light as a feather and the two made the circle of the room before Paul cut in. Peter joined the girls on the long divan.

"In her youth Polly was the best dancer, besides the best all-round nurse, in these parts," he told them, "and she hasn't lost the knack even in her sixties. She's a grand old girl!"

The dancers reached the door and Polly slipped into the hall. "Dinner'll be ready in two shakes," she announced, "if it ain't spoiled by my makin' a fool of myself. I'll ring the gong and mind you come in proper."

Deborah smiled. It was just as she had thought. Polly was pretending they were all her children or perhaps her girls and their beaus or her sons and their sweethearts. It was really Polly's party. The gong sounded and the four stood up, the young men bent slightly from the hips in grave formality, crooked their arms and the girls slipped their hands through them and they started slowly with measured tread toward the dining room across the hall. Alice began to hum the wedding march and the others joined in. Tum-tum-ta-ta. The old lady stood just inside the room near the kitchen beaming happily upon them.

Deborah put aside her disappointment and Peter his strange aloofness. Alice and Paul kept up a continuous merry chatter and soon the others were entering into the conversation as happily as they. Polly changed plates and served silently and efficiently. She refused to linger or have anything to say during the entire meal. It was a very successful dinner and, when the last mouthful of dessert had been eaten, the four left the table and invaded the kitchen where Polly was giving Kitchener his evening meal.

"Aprons—aprons!" they shouted in unison. "We demand aprons!"

"What is this?" Polly asked in bewilderment.

Peter caught her in his arms and carried her, scolding and struggling, to the living room where he deposited her on the divan. The others followed.

"You sit there, Polly Quick," he ordered, holding her down, "until we call you. You provided us with but one waitress. You're going to have four—and handsome ones at that. Now, my darling, where are your aprons?"

"Don't be foolish, children," Polly chided, but her eyes were bright and her face flushed with happiness.

"I'll find them!" Deborah promised and fled to the kitchen from where in a minute she called; "Eureka! Come and get them!"

Polly sat quietly on the divan in the disordered room and smiled mistily. What dear children they were! If her two had lived they would be coming home to her like this and probably bringing her grandchildren. From the kitchen and dining room came sounds of laughter, hurrying feet and the clink of china and glasses, the ring of silver and once in a while a mild expletive, no doubt when someone spilled something or perhaps scorched a finger. At last the gong sounded and the slow measured tread of marching feet. Paul and Peter entered and each offered an arm and between them the old lady walked to the dining room across the hall. The two girls, wearing white aprons and paper napkins in lieu of caps, stood ready to serve her. It was all beautiful and there were tears in the old lady's eyes. Paul, however, saved the day by sitting down across from her and saying in a loud, solemn voice;

"Service! I like your samples and you may now bring me large portions of everything you have. Service, I say!" He hissed the last and the girls fled. Peter seated himself nearby and thought he, too, could eat something more, perhaps a bit of chicken or just a sliver of that delectable ham. Surely it was the best meal he had ever eaten.

The girls brought in fresh platters of food and gasped in astonishment when the young men helped themselves and, throughout the entire meal, kept pace with Polly.

"Well," Alice said in disgust when she brought in the coffee, "I have heard that a man's appetite knows no appeasement and that his stomach is absolutely bottomless, but I never quite believed it. I do now—and how!"

"We'll do the dishes, Polly," Deborah said as Polly laid her napkin beside her plate. "You've done altogether too much as it is. You look tired."

"Fiddle-daddle, Debby! I ain't had so much fun in a coon's age. Don't you go makin' an invalid out of me yet. This old mare's just as good as she ever was and don't you make no mistake about it."

"Just the same——"

"Anyway, Mis' Sims is comin' over to clean up by and by. I told her about eight or somewhere there. Don't you worry about me, child. You go on and enjoy yourselves. They's a bridge table in the hall closet and cards in the cabinet."

"How's for staying quiet—out on the side porch, say?" Paul suggested softly, patting his belt buckle, as the old lady left them.

"If you will make a pig of yourself, Paul Hendricks," exclaimed Alice, "you'll just have to suffer. Where do you put it, and you, too, Peter? All right, let's go outside and sit then, but I warn you if two attractive young men come along looking for partners for the evening, Deb and I are stepping out."

"Over my dead body," Peter declared. He hadn't had such a good time since he was a youngster. How natural and homey it all was! This was the way to live— the way he would have life if he had boys and girls home on vacation.

"Let 'em go, Peter," Paul yawned and muttered uncomfortably, "then we'll have some peace. In action is what I crave just now. The bigger the inaction the better."

And when, a few minutes later, Jason Miller and Phil Northrup came over with invitations to an impromptu dance at the Country Club, the girls accepted joyously and refused to allow the two overfed young men to leave their comfortable chairs. As they drove off in the elder Miller's big car, their merry laughter floated back to the men they had left behind.

"We'll drift over there in a couple of three hours and see what's going on," Paul said as he groaned in discomfort. "Why in heck did I have to eat that last piece of cake? I tell you, Pete, I'm altogether too sentimental and now I feel terrible!"

Peter laughed ruefully. "I don't feel so hot myself, old chap. Perhaps if we walked about a bit we'd feel better. Like me to get you some bi-carb?"

"And let Aunt Polly know I can't take it? Not on your life! I'd die first and I guess maybe that's what I'm going to do. Oo-ow!"

"Let's go down to the drugstore and get something,"

Peter suggested. He hadn't eaten such quantities as Paul had although he had tried to hold up his end. "The walk will help, anyway, and then we can come back——"

"And eat some more, I suppose. But all right, let's go."

Walking helped materially. The sparkling glass of soda water that was served them at the fountain helped still more. When they returned to Polly's for Peter's car they felt able to face anything—except food.

At the Club the girls were having a gay time. Alice was like a child and Deborah, who had been feeling guilty for running away from her guests, relaxed and entered into the spirit of the impromptu party. That was one thing about Harmony she had liked from the first. One never knew when someone would telephone or run in with an invitation to some get-together at Club or home. It was all so informal and delightful that any strangeness one may have felt disappeared immediately. She would miss all this friendliness and gaiety when she went back to Medford, but as Alec had reminded her, idle people and idleness were sure to pall after a time. When one was trained for active duty there was no permanent happiness in idleness.

Deborah was dancing with Gordon Meade, guest of Phil Northrup and possible suitor of his sister, Mary. He was one of those men who talk little while dancing and Deborah's thoughts wandered. Suddenly she heard him give a startled exclamation and looked up to see him staring at the door. Following his glance, she was surprised to see Eve Fowler entering with a tall, rather distinguished stranger.

"Do you know who that girl is?" he asked.

"Yes. Miss Fowler," Deborah told him. So this was the reason why Eve turned down her invitation to dinner. Nancy indeed! And Peter had known it, probably. Was that the reason for the tragic look on his face when he arrived this afternoon? "Beautiful, isn't she?" she went on.

"You've said it, sister," the young man muttered. "Just who is she?"

"Wait," Deborah said, having no desire to listen to his ravings over Eve Fowler. "Mary knows her better than I do and will no doubt be glad to make the necessary introductions."

"Not Mary," the youth protested, somewhat shamefaced. "There's Phil—let him do it."

They swung over to one side where Phil stood watching the dancers. Deborah told him of Gordon's request. Phil grinned and slapped his friend on the back.

"Moth and flame, Gordy old son. Take my advice and give that dame a wide berth. If ever a female mowed down everything in pants, that gal does. Scarlett O'Hara had nothing on her nor Cleopatra either. Beware!"

Gordon Meade glared at Phil and muttered; "So she turned you down, did she? I don't wonder, you old busybody! Come on, pal, do the decent thing. Maybe she hasn't met a *man* lately."

"Your blood be on your own head and don't say I didn't warn you," Phil declared and piloted him to where Eve Fowler stood surrounded by a group of admiring males. "Remember, old top," he hissed as he left him, "all sirens don't have red hair."

Deborah felt Eve's eyes on her once or twice but refused to acknowledge her presence. Alice, on the other hand, waved her hand as she passed and called a gay "Hello!" Suddenly there was a little stir near the door and Deborah saw Paul and Peter Jordan enter. Peter frowned when he saw his sister-in-law but Deborah's heartbeats quickened as she watched his glance slide from Eve to wander about the room and come to rest on her. She smiled and waved to Paul who immediately cut in. She was annoyed when Peter didn't follow suit but turned and left the room. "Afraid of offending Eve," Deborah told herself bitterly.

Eve and Gordon Meade passed close to them and Deborah felt nauseated at the dying-calf look of adoration on the young man's face. Poor Mary! Evidently she had seen it, too, for she had disappeared. Deborah wondered if she really cared for Gordon. If she did it was tragic. Love could be terribly cruel!

But Eve soon wearied of Gordon's admiration, for Deb saw her surreptitiously summon her escort who came obediently and the two left, moving in the general direction of the Club bar.

It wasn't until after Eve's departure from the room that Peter returned and cut in on the dance Deborah was having with Jason Miller who protested vigorously. He made no explanation of Eve's presence here and Deborah asked none. It wasn't worth it, she felt.

"Let's get out of here," Peter whispered as the music stopped, and drew her through the nearest exit.

"No, you don't, Peter old boy," Jason muttered, catching Deb's hand. "This next is mine. Get yourself another girl, my fran. Deb's my date—see?"

Peter said nothing and Deborah was annoyed at herself for being annoyed at Jason. Did he think he owned her?

It wasn't a very late party and Jason took the girls and Paul home soon after midnight. Peter left at the same time but went back to Cliff House. Deborah didn't see Eve again during the evening and was amused and a bit cynical as she saw Gordon Meade's frantic efforts to make his peace with a cool and very aloof Mary.

"Darling," Jason whispered as they neared home, "have you been thinking of me—us?"

"I'm afraid you'll have to forgive me, Jason, but I've been so busy I haven't thought of anything. Let's forget it. I—I——"

"Never!" Jason said emphatically. "I almost told Mother yesterday——"

"Jason—you didn't!" For a moment she was angry. "There's nothing to tell," she said more evenly. "I told you I felt sure I didn't love you the way you ought to be loved and——"

"I said I'd take a chance on making you. I mean it, darling."

Deborah shook her head and drew away from the shoulder pressing her own.

"All right, all right, darling," he whispered, sensing her withdrawal. "I'll be good, but you will think about it, won't you? Promise?"

"No. I won't promise, Jason," Deborah said firmly. "Love isn't something one can manufacture. It has to be spontaneous. Let's be friends. I'm—I'm really very fond of you but——"

"A girl couldn't possibly fall for a man who has been completely infatuated with another woman for ages, could she?" he asked sulkily.

"I'm not—of course she couldn't." Deborah found she was trembling. How dare he! "I've got to have time—I won't be hurried—I want to be by myself—to go away somewhere and think," she stammered.

"You'll have time," the young man muttered. "I'm going to New York with Mother tomorrow. I told her I wouldn't go, but I've changed my mind. When I get back maybe you'll give me an answer. Oh, Deb darling, I'm sorry I said that—that I even hinted——"

"Oo-oo! Aunt Polly!" called Alice as they entered the drive. "Got a snack for us?"

"Oh lord!" groaned Paul.

Jason refused the invitation; turned and drove swiftly away.

"What were you and Jason scrapping over?" Alice the inquisitive wanted to know as she and Deborah stood in the upper hall later.

"Scrapping? Jason and I? Why, we never quarrel, Alice. He's a dear, but almost too adolescent at times."

"You probably mean, my dear Deborah, he's just finding out that he's a man and in love. What are you going to do about him, Deb? It wouldn't be a bad match at that although my money's on Peter."

"Don't be crazy, Alice!" Deborah snapped and shut her bedroom door with a sharp click.

"Just the same"—muttered Alice as she prepared for bed—"something's very wrong or maybe it's just love running true to form. Oo-la-la! What a prickly creature Love has turned you into, my sweet Debby, Paul, who are you betting on—Peter or Jason?" She stared suspiciously at the occupant of the other bed. He couldn't possibly be asleep already. Paul's eyes were shut and a faint but slightly exaggerated snore answered her. "Oh, darn!" she exclaimed not too softly. She didn't give a hoot if she did wake him up. What business had he going to sleep so quickly anyway? Paul never moved. She gave her pillow a vicious punch and sighed lustily, Men were so exasperating at times—especially husbands. She felt in the mood for a long confidential chat. She lay down with her indignant back to the other bed. She didn't see one of Paul's eyes open experimentally and his mouth twist in a satisfied grin. Now he could really sleep.

CHAPTER FOURTEEN

THE DAYS OF Alice and Paul's vacation flew and Harmony did its best by them. And when on Sunday morning the two guests made ready to depart, there were many expressions of regret from the group that came to wish them goodbye.

The house seemed very quiet and a little dull after their departure. Deborah decided to hurry her plans for returning to work. She saw little of Peter during the last days Alice and Paul were with her, and never alone. Peter came to take Paul fishing twice and once they went on a big picnic to the Island but, on that occasion, Peter had to leave early because of a business engagement at Buford. Eve, she saw not at all and was thankful for it, although she wondered just why. Polly enlightened her. It was a day or two after Alice and Paul had returned home.

"Debby!" she called, coming in from market that morning. "Come on down. I got news for you."

"We-ll?" Deborah smiled at the excited old lady as she joined her in the kitchen where Polly stood transferring meat and vegetables from her big basket to the refrigerator and work-table. "You do look as if something important has happened."

"Somethin' has, Debby, and I'm no end pleased that the boy's at last got his dander up enough to insist on Nancy's remainin' with him. He's goin' to hire a nurse and a governess. Eve threw that old fake Davis in his face but the boy never budged a mite."

Deborah's heart missed a beat. She felt suddenly weak and dropped into the nearest chair. What a silly fool she was! It was nothing to her.

"She's gone, Debby, this mornin', she and her ma and that Anna with her. I ain't got the hull rights of it yet but Peter'll tell me. He's told me things since he was knee high to a grasshopper—things he wouldn't tell another soul."

"Who did tell you, Polly?" Deborah asked.

"Mis' MacDonald. I saw her over to the market. She said Peter looked like death and Eve took on somethin' turrible. The servants was all up in arms. They all admire her but I don't think any of 'em ever reely liked her—she's too demandin', and I guess they was plenty s'prised and shocked at her goin's on all right. She threatened to have the law on Peter—imagine!—on Nancy's own pa! Crazy! She called him a wanton murderer and crool monster. She said she'd make such a scandal he'd not dare show his face in Harmony again. Crazy—all of it. What could she do? Peter's a Jordan and Jordans have been the first fam'ly in Harmony for mor'n a hundred years. Then she tried coaxin' and soft-soapin' him—called him 'darlin' ' and 'poor lamb' and 'precious' till it was fair sick'nin', Mis' MacDonald said. But Peter kept gettin' whiter and whiter and stood there sayin' nothin'. I could have told her plenty if I'd been there, but Peter ain't quarrelsome and he was brought up to honor women and I guess 'twas pretty hard to stand up to her—to tell her he wasn't satisfied with that Davis's opinion, and was goin' to make some changes. Oh, Debby, I'm so glad he done it. Now p'raps Nancy's got a chance and her pa, too."

"None of this would have been necessary if Peter had acted like a man and a father in the first place, Polly. If he hadn't been so completely infatuated." For some reason, inexplicable even to herself, Deborah felt perverse. "There's something to be said for Miss Fowler. In a way, one can't blame her for wanting to keep Nancy. She has had her four years now, hasn't she? and probably grown so attached to her that it's going to be terribly hard to give her up. Why it's almost cruel and I suppose she can't understand Peter's sudden right-about-face. Until now, he has been perfectly willing she should have the responsibility of his daughter."

Polly stared at the girl opposite in open-mouthed amazement. Had Eve contrived to weave her fatal spell over Deborah, too?

"He was not willing—never has been willing," Polly declared emphatically. "He fought against it tooth and nail but this Davis and Eve between 'em made him believe 'twas Nancy's life. 'Twasn't till he see how Eve's ruinin' the child that he knew somethin' had to be done and done right quick, too. I hope to heaven Peter finds some good girl who ain't afraid to tackle the job of mother-in' the youngster. She'll have her hands full, I grant you, but some girls ain't afraid of the hard things in life. If I was younger he'd not have to look no farther, but I'm too old to tackle it, now."

"I take it, then, that Eve isn't marrying him at once?"

"Marry him? Marry Peter? She'd take him in a minute if she got the chance. Like everyone else, he admires Eve—lord knows she's beautiful enough!—but I'll eat my best hat if he ever wanted her. Oh, I know what folks say, but I know——"

"You're prejudiced, Polly. You see I do believe what the people here in Harmony say. I believe Peter is infatuated with her—everyone knows it."

"Fiddle-daddle!" Polly exclaimed crossly. "Then why ain't they been married all these years?"

"Oh," Deborah tried to speak airily, "probably the lady couldn't make up her mind."

"Debby Bradley, you make me so mad sometimes!" the old lady exclaimed. "Peter Jordan can marry anyone—anyone he wants to——"

"Then his troubles should soon be over. The sooner he gets himself a wife the better."

"Wife!" Polly exploded. "I wasn't talkin' about a wife. What Peter needs right now's a governess for Nancy. One who'll teach her self-control and manners and such. Know of anyone who might fill the bill, Debby?"

Deborah shook her head. "Now, if it were a trained nurse he wanted, I know of several who might do very well."

"He wants a nurse, too. I told you, but you was prob'ly wool-gath-rin'. Mis' MacDonald's sort of pinch-hittin' till he finds one. She's got to be young and pretty with good manners and a sweet disposition," Polly explained carefully.

"The woods are full of them," Deborah explained, "but I think the most essential thing would be that she be endowed with a tough hide. She'll need it in Cliff House I imagine."

Polly looked at Deborah with searching blue eyes. "Sort of soured on Peter lately, ain't you? Scared, are you, Debby? Scared to tackle the job of stepmother?

Fie, girl, don't be such a baby! Life ain't easy no matter what kind of a job you got and you nor nobody else ain't got any right to expect to always travel a road without bumps to jar you and sloughs to dampen your spirits. 'Tain't reasonable and 'tain't nat'ral."

Deborah laughed without much mirth. She had always enjoyed listening to Polly's philosophizing: but today she felt the old lady was going too far—taking too much for granted. In her eagerness to serve her adored Peter, she was willing to fight for him—take any and all chances to bring about his future comfort and happiness. Well, Deborah had no idea of being laid on the altar of Polly's devotion and the sooner the old lady knew it, the better.

"You're really very funny, Polly," she said. "I assure you I haven't the slightest intention of becoming a stepmother. As for Peter Jordan, I don't give him a thought. I am sorry that his little girl is crippled—of course I am -any normal woman would feel sorry. And I do feel that it is no time for him to give up the fight for her complete recovery. I told him that. But really, Polly, I can't see how any of this affects me one way or the other. Soon our lives will diverge and very probably we shall never meet again."

"Soon? What d'you mean, Debby? You're here till October, ain't you?"

Deborah shook her head. "No, Polly," she said slowly as if the words were being dragged from unwilling lips. "I'm going back to work in another week or two."

"Work? What did you work at, Debby Bradley?" Polly demanded skeptically.

"I'm a nurse, Polly. A Public Health Nurse on the North Side—the worst district in Medford," she said quickly.

"You a nurse!" Polly's face was an open book. Here was the solution of Peter's problem. "Then you can take the job, Debby. You're exactly the one to do it. Oh, my dear, Peter will be so happy to know that his worries are over."

"*His* worries!" scoffed Deborah. "I'm a Public Health Nurse, Polly. Don't you understand? The people I nurse and help are poor—dreadfully poor—destitute, many of them, and ignorant and superstitious. Most of them are

144

foreigners who can't even speak English. They understand us only because we use the language of love and helpfulness. The Jordans are rich. Nancy can have a dozen people to take care of her. No, Polly, I'm going back to Medford's North Side."

Polly's blue eyes snapped. "You're just as crazy as Peter is. He'd lean over backwards bein' courteous to women; always givin' 'em the benefit of the doubt. So honorable it hurt mor'n once, I can tell you. You lean over just as far backwards in doin' your whole dooty. You think all them poor folks you talk about are more important than what rich folks are. They both got souls, ain't they? They both got feelin's, ain't they? And if some folks are cleaner than what others are, is that a sin? Seems to me your dooty's been planked down right smack under your nose, Debby. You're just the girl to make somethin' of that poor child—the only one who could mend what Eve Fowler's broke, or at least, bent in the wrong way."

Deborah shook her head. "You don't understand, Polly. I can't, that's all. Peter will find someone to take charge of Nancy without any trouble. My duty lies in Medford and I'm going back. Don't look so disapproving, my dear. Eve Fowler expects that I will go to Cliff House. I think that may be her plan."

"Her plan?" puzzled Polly. "How—her plan?"

Deborah hesitated. It sounded like some old-fashioned novel in which the villain laid a well-baited trap to ensnare his victims. But the thought had occurred to her while Polly was talking that perhaps Eve had planned to create a scandal if she went to Cliff House as nurse to Nancy. But could she? Deborah was afraid Eve would stop at nothing to gain her ends. If only Eve hadn't seen Peter kissing her on the day she arrived in Harmony! Then, too, feeling as she did toward Peter and being thoroughly aware of his changed attitude toward her, she was sure flight was the better part of valor.

"You told me that Eve threatened Peter with a scandal, Polly. Perhaps she thought I might try to take her place as Nancy's governess or nurse or maybe just as a friend. You know, Polly, Eve imagines I am a rival for Peter's affections."

"But Eve don't know you're a nurse, does she, Debby? Why should she think you'd take a job as Nancy's nurse then?" as Deborah shook her head. "And if she thinks you're her rival—well, you are, ain't you?" she ended, bluntly.

"I am not!" Deborah was indignant. "I told you before that I'm not interested in men—Peter Jordan least of all. I did like him until—well—I was disappointed in him. I don't like men who will take anything from a woman just because she happens to be beautiful. He's weak, Polly. The men I know best are strong. They may not be as polite or as cultured as Mr. Jordan, but they are a heap more courageous."

"I see they's no use in arguin' with you, Debby," Polly said at last. "They's none so blind as them that won't see. I'm sorry for I want to see Peter happy. Poor lad, life's played him some pretty mean tricks but he ain't beat yet—he'll manage to grin and bear it, same's he's done before. I tell you this bein' a gentleman can be mighty wearin' on a man's soul. Some folks don't 'preciate that fact. When you aimin' to leave, Debby?" As far as Polly was concerned the incident was closed. Deborah saw that, and felt a little shiver of dismay.

"Perhaps by the end of the month—maybe sooner. Oh, Polly, I hate leaving! You have been so sweet to me and I do love this house and Harmony and—and—— But I'm well again and must get back to work—I've been a slacker long enough. For the next few days, though, let's forget it, shall we? I want to enjoy every minute of my stay, for it will be months before I get another vacation."

"But your lease runs till October," Polly pointed out.

"I know—but—suppose I send you a couple of girls who would enjoy your cooking and your lovely home? Could I do that, Polly?"

"Depends, Debby. Who are they?" the old lady demurred.

"I'll find out and let you know. Mrs. Holcomb probably will suggest someone. Do you know, I envy them, whoever they are. I've had such a grand time here that I'm getting selfish."

146

"I wish Alice and Paul could come up again. They're nice folks. I like 'em both."

Deborah laughed. "Did you know that Alice is willing Mrs. Holcomb to sell this place to her?"

"Sell? Oh, Abby wouldn't do that," Polly said, "and I thought Alice and Paul was poor."

"They are. But Alice is writing a book and expects to make barrels of money when she sells it," Deborah explained.

"I hope she does although if she's set her heart on this place she'll just have to un-set it again. Abby won't sell—I know that."

"Don't worry, Polly. Alice isn't going to make a fortune right away," Deborah told her. "Anyway, they couldn't live up here—miles away from Paul's business. It was just one of Alice's dreams. She has them quite often."

"She's a nice girl," Polly murmured.

CHAPTER FIFTEEN

THE INSISTENT ringing of the telephone roused Deborah from her first deep sleep. She sat up in bed and pulled on a light. Two o'clock. Startled, she slipped her feet into mules and drew on a robe as she ran down the hall to the stairs. The bell rang again—long, insistent; menacing, Deborah thought with a shudder. Why was it, she wondered, that night calls always seem so much worse than those during the day? In daylight we take them quite as a matter of course—the easy, delightful method of reaching friends or doing errands that would otherwise require much time and energy.

"What is it?" Polly poked her head into the hall from her bedroom as Deborah reached the stand on which the instrument stood.

"I don't know, but I'll find out," Deborah told her. "Hello?" She spoke into the mouthpiece, lowering her voice to a mere whisper as one does at night.

"That you, Deb?" It was Peter and he sounded frightened.

"Yes. What is it?" Deborah found her knees shaking and her heart beating suffocatingly. Really she seemed to have completely lost her grip. What on earth ailed her?

"It's Nancy. She's terribly ill, Deb. The doctor can't possibly get here for an hour at least. Will you and Polly come up now—at once? Mrs. MacDonald is worried. Please, Deb."

"Of course, Peter. We'll be there in just a few minutes. I'm sure it's nothing serious, Peter. Children often appear much worse than they are. Don't worry."

She replaced the instrument and turned to face a white and shaken Polly behind her.

"Get dressed, Polly. Nancy is very ill and Peter is scared to death. I told him we would be right out. I'll run up and dress and get the car out while you do what you have to."

Deborah was halfway up the stairs before she finished speaking. Polly nodded emphatically, and disappeared into her room. As Deborah dressed she was surprised to see how calm she felt—how competent and confident.

She was in her element now—a nurse, no longer playing at being a social butterfly.

The car sped through Harmony in the warm summer darkness with neither of its occupants saying a word. Thunder muttered in the distance and forked lightning zigzagged down the sky. They turned into the cliff road and began to climb. The headlights made a wide path through the dense undergrowth and huge, softly swaying trees. Once a rabbit paused hypnotized in the glare of light and Deb braked so quickly that Polly jerked forward in her seat, her glasses sliding suddenly down her nose.

"I'm sorry," Deborah murmured, "but that fool rabbit would stop right in front of us." She touched her horn and the little animal darted away. On they went and turned into the driveway of Cliff House to find the place ablaze from attic to cellar.

Peter met them as they stopped and a boy who evidently was Johnny, the man-of-all-work, drove Deborah's car to the garage. Peter looked worn and disheveled. Polly took his hand in hers, patting it maternally, as they mounted the steps to the porch and entered the brightly lighted hall. It was the first time Deborah had seen the place at night and she was impressed anew with its immensity.

"I haven't uniforms with me, Peter," Deborah told him, "but I can quite easily send for them if you like."

Peter's face relaxed and Polly smiled at her. Deborah bit her lip. Now why on earth had she said that? She had no intention of staying on here. Peter could easily get a trained nurse for Nancy, and she was going back to the Center, anyway. Oh, well, she could stay until the doctor arrived and no doubt he would suggest someone.

Deborah went directly upstairs to Nancy's room. Polly and Peter talked for a few minutes in the hall before Polly followed. Peter remained downstairs to await the coming of Doctor Barnes.

Mrs. MacDonald looked up when Deborah entered the room and breathed a sigh of relief.

"You're a trained nurse, Mr. Peter tells me. Good! How do you think she is! I have never seen her like this before."

Deborah saw that Nancy was very ill. Her temperature was high, her breathing rapid. Under her finger the pulse was quick and shallow.

"One hundred four and two-tenths. Of course that doesn't necessarily mean much in a child, Mrs. Mac-Donald," she said as she shook down the thermometer. "Who is this Doctor Barnes? Has he attended Nancy before? Does he know her?"

"Oh, yes. That's why Mr. Peter sent for him. He lives over on the Buford road about eight miles from here, but he's camping up on Silver Mountain. He said he'd be here in an hour. Do you think it's anything serious, Miss Bradley?"

"I don't know. I hope not. Some children run a temperature very easily. I imagine Nancy is one of them. We'll know when the doctor comes and in the meantime perhaps I can make her a bit more comfortable. Suppose you go lie down for a while. I'll stay with her now, Mrs. Quick came with me and we are all going to help."

Polly came into the room and she and Mrs. Mac-Donald held a whispered conversation before the housekeeper left. Polly came over to the bed.

"Poor little mite!" she murmured pityingly. Her gentle hand brushed the thick red curls back from the broad forehead. She was very like her father now. In repose her face lost its unpleasant qualities. A low moan came from the slightly parted lips and Polly drew back. "Don't let me bother you, Debby," she murmured. "You go right ahead with what you plan on doin'. If you want me for anythin' I'll be out here in the other room. If Eve Fowler wasn't miles away from here, I'd swear to goodness 'twas some of her deviltry. I ain't sure but what 'tis, even yet. I've heard tell of people puttin' an evil spell on folks before this."

"Nonsense, Polly!" Deborah said severely. "I'm ashamed of you—a good Methodist!"

Polly's face puckered for a moment and she turned and left the room. Deborah continued to moisten the parched lips and refill the ice pack on the burning forehead. From time to time the girl moaned as if in pain and Deborah searched closely for a possible cause but could find none. She would just have to wait the coming

150

of Doctor Barnes. He came within the hour and shook his head in a puzzled manner.

The two worked over her for what remained of the night. Morning found conditions much the same. Examination showed her heart good which was one thing in her favor. In mid-afternoon, however, her temperature dropped a degree and the doctor looked relieved, but toward morning it rose to its peak of one hundred four and two-tenths again. And that was the way it went for several days. On the fifth day the fever abated considerably and they were all encouraged, especially when it failed to rise after midnight as it had been doing. From then on, Nancy appeared to improve. She still grew delirious at times and muttered amazing things that shocked Deborah but made Polly nod her head understandingly. There seemed, however, every reason to believe she would recover.

Deborah saw little of Peter during these trying days. He would stop in every hour or so to gaze wistfully down at the thin face on the flat pillow, then leave without a word. Deborah took her exercise in the lovely gardens and Toby Wren often entertained her with stories of his flowers. But Peter never joined her. Deborah felt hurt and angry that he should treat her so summarily. Well, just as soon as Nancy was definitely on the road to recovery, she would leave Cliff House with its ghost of Eve Fowler lurking in every nook and cranny of the huge place. How had she ever admired this great, gloomy mansion? There was something almost sinister here.

Once down near the south entrance she came upon a strange man who looked at her intently. She thought he might be going to speak to her but evidently he thought better of it and turned away, sauntering on through the winding path to the summerhouse on the cliff.

Deborah made friends with Romulus and Remus, the two Irish setters, and often they accompanied her on her walks. She saw the stranger on another occasion when she was walking along the woods road outside the estate. She had wanted to slip over the stone wall and get a view of the lake from the edge of the cliff. She had heard there was a clear drop of six hundred feet to the beach below. The man touched his hat to her and asked after Nancy.

"Doing nicely, thank you," Deborah said and walked on. Who was he? She would ask Polly or Mrs. MacDonald when she went back to the house.

She decided against going through the woods this morning and turned back. The man had disappeared. Her nerves tingled warningly. Suppose this man had designs on Nancy. She hurried back to Cliff House and ran upstairs to Nancy's room. The child lay motionless in her bed, staring sullenly up at the picture of her mother. Polly sat knitting beside her, crooning softly as her shining needles slipped in and out of the bright colored wool. Better not disturb Polly, Deborah thought and went in search of the housekeeper. Mrs. MacDonald knew nothing. She became excited and Deborah wished she had not mentioned it. Out in the garden she saw Toby busy with his roses and stopped to ask him what he knew. Toby winked at her and whispered:

"He's a dick, Miss. Mr. Peter's taking no chances with kidnappers, he ain't. Better not mention it to the girls, though. They get excited over nothing."

"I'm glad you told me, Toby," Deborah said, breathing easier. "Did Mr. Peter tell you that he was a detective?"

"Sure. Suppose I'd take the dick's word for it? Not me. Mr. Peter's worried but I tell him no one could get in here and me not know it. But Joe's a fine detective— nothin' gets past him."

"I know you're very keen, Toby. But just the same I'm glad he's here. There he is now. I'll go speak to him. I rather snubbed him a little while ago."

But the man had vanished and Deborah went back to the house. She wondered just why Peter was afraid. Surely Eve wouldn't dare attempt kidnapping Nancy. She met Peter as she entered by a side door and saw that he looked positively haggard.

"You ought to get some rest, Peter," she said kindly. "First thing you know I'll have two patients on my hands."

"Don't worry about me, Deb," he smiled bleakly.

152

"I'm all right. By the way, have you seen any strangers lurking about the place lately?"

"Only your detective, Peter. He frightened me for I felt sure he had evil intentions, but Toby explained that you had hired him to watch the place. Can one man do that, Peter?" she asked worriedly.

"Oh, Toby and Johnny and I are on the job, too, Deb," he told her and swayed on his feet.

"Do go to bed," Deborah urged. "If you break down what good will you be as a protector?"

"I guess I'm not much good at anything," he said bitterly. "No good as a husband nor as a father and now you accuse me of failing as a protector."

"Don't be silly, Peter," she said irritably. Deborah was tired and felt impatient at the man who seemed to be demanding pity from her. Well, he wouldn't get it. "What's the use of bemoaning what's past?" she went on, crisply. "Rather look ahead. After all, each of us is master of his own fate and captain of his soul. Of course you feel low this morning. You're tired. Go to bed and sleep until dinnertime. I'll guarantee you'll feel a million times better and quite capable of 'licking your weight in wildcats' as once upon a time you boasted you were. Remember?"

Peter Jordan drew himself to his full height of six feet two and said coldly: "Thank you, Deborah. I forgot for a moment that you are here in the capacity of nurse. I certainly must be in a bad way if I thought anything else."

He left her abruptly and Deborah felt as if she had been soundly slapped. Perhaps she had been a bit unsympathetic, but he had it coming to him. He had brought all this extra worry on himself, hadn't he? Letting his infatuation have complete sway over his intelligence. What could he expect? Her breath caught and she bit her lip impatiently. Of course he looked terrible—who wouldn't after days and nights without sleep and under the constant strain of his child's sickness? Her head lifted and she went with determined briskness up the stairs to her room.

From that time on it seemed to Deborah as if Toby, was the only sane person in the place. The maids spoke in whispers, their eyes darting into shadows, scared of every sudden sound.

Mrs. MaDonald, placid and efficient under ordinary conditions, looked worried and answered both back and front doorbells personally, a thing she confessed she had never done before. Johnny kept pretty close to the house and always carried a gun loaded with birdshot. It all appeared melodramatic yet Deborah found herself acutely aware of untoward sounds and continually searched the shadows whenever she left Nancy's bedside during the night.

"Deborah Bradley, you're a nut!" she scolded herself. "You have always prided yourself on being free from silly nerves, and here you are jittery as an old woman! Snap out of it! Brave living!" She grinned wryly to herself. "Is there a possibility for such a thing in a world harboring so much evil? Of course it's utter nonsense that Eve Fowler will attempt to kidnap Nancy. How could she hope to accomplish such a feat in the first place? Certainly not with the aid of any of the help at Cliff House. They are all absolutely loyal to Peter and the family."

Deborah had come downstairs to breakfast determined to be sensible. In the light of day, her fears and worries appeared mere figments of an over-active imagination. Nothing ever happened in Harmony—why, the natives even boasted of its tranquillity and absence of anything that might lead to notoriety. Cliff House, high as it was and seeming to stand solidly for peace and freedom from all that might disturb, looked a veritable fortress—a haven of safety. The garden was particularly attractive and she left the house for a brief walk before going to bed. Oh, it was grand this morning. Why should there ever be illness, sorrow or troubles? No doubt most of them were imaginary.

She looked up to see a man talking to Toby who appeared to accord him but scant attention. The stranger was tall, gray-haired and distinguished. She stopped in the path wondering where she had seen him before. He turned, saw her and lifted his hat. Why, he was the man who had been with Eve Fowler at the Club dance the evening of her dinner. She hadn't seen him since. What was he doing here? Phil Northrup had told her he was an attorney and had wondered what mischief Eve was cooking up." Let's see, Phil said his name was Harding, and he came from Albany or was it New York? But his name meant mischief, according to Phil.

Now he came toward her, hat in hand, while Toby sat up on his heels and watched. Suddenly he began to whistle tunelessly and as the man turned his head, returned to digging industriously. It was like a play, Deborah thought. She saw Johnny hovering in the shrubbery and a minute later, the big, raw-boned figure of the detective loomed near the side entrance. He was hatless and had just dropped the handles of a wheelbarrow. Toby kept on whistling and Deborah's weariness left her. She felt stimulated and excited.

"Good morning, Miss—er—Bradley, isn't it?" the man smiled ingratiatingly. "Lovely morning, isn't it?"

"Beautiful," Deborah agreed coolly. "Did you want something?"

"Oh, no. I called to see Miss Fowler, but the gardener tells me she isn't here. Can you tell me if she has gone back to Boston or to some other place? She invited me to Cliff House to see the garden and to lunch—I had not heard she had changed her plans."

"I'm afraid I can give you no information, Mr. Harding," Deborah told him. "I barely know Miss Fowler and so, of course, she would scarcely tell me of her plans."

"Oh, I had an idea you were a friend of the family—an intimate friend. Is someone ill? I believe you are a trained nurse, are you not?" he said smoothly.

Deborah was surprised. No one in Harmony knew she was a nurse with the exception of Peter and Polly. She was not wearing a uniform. How did he know she was a nurse? "I am sure you can't possibly be interested in my business, Mr. Harding. I wish you good morning." She attempted to pass him but he caught her arm. Deborah stiffened and looked him coolly in the eyes. "I don't understand," she said, drawing back.

"I think you do understand, Miss Bradley," the man murmured meaningly. "Why did Miss Fowler leave Cliff House? What happened? You better tell me for——"

"What's going on here?" The detective had left his

barrow and stood just behind the tall stranger. How Joe arrived in just that position at that opportune moment, Deborah didn't know, but there he was looking solid and dependable. "Who are you and how did you get into these grounds? Don't you know you're trespassing?"

"Trespassing?" The man laughed amusedly. "My dear fellow, I am merely keeping an engagement."

Joe glanced questioningly at Deborah.

"Oh, Mr. Harding's no friend of mine," Deborah said quickly and felt an impish delight at the man's change of color. "I never saw him before—except once. Then he was with Miss Fowler."

Joe's eyes hardened, but he merely reiterated the fact that this was private property and the owners didn't relish trespassers.

Harding turned and started for the entrance. Johnny followed, keeping well behind the concealing shrubs. A car started. He was gone.

"I wonder what his game is?" the detective asked. "Just looking the ground over, likely. He wouldn't try any funny business in broad daylight. And I doubt if he would do anything anyway. He ain't the type, not for rough stuff. His kind go in more for slander, blackmail—white-collar jobs."

"Just what are we all afraid of?" Deborah inquired.

"Mr. Jordan's afraid his sister-in-law's planning to snatch his daughter. He says she threatened to and if she succeeds it will kill the child. Is that right? I mean is she that bad?"

"That's drawing conclusions, Mr. Detective," Deborah said noncommittally. "But it would be a risky thing to do under any conditions—risky for the child and for the culprits, too. But with you on the job I'm sure Mr. Jordan need not worry." She smiled into the broad, ugly face beside her and the man grinned sheepishly.

"Oh, he'll worry all right even if there's no need to—that's a way parents have. But I don't think this dame'll succeed in her plans, Miss, though from what I hear tell, she's wild to get the kid."

"Then you don't know her? No?" as the man shook his head. "Well, she's one of the most beautiful women I have ever seen."

"Hmm," muttered the officer. "Yeah, I know. They're the worst. Think they have a right to everything they want. Mr. Jordan's popular, ain't he? Good family."

Deborah felt queer discussing her host with this man but knew he was merely being friendly. Perhaps, though, he was cross-examining her to see which side she was on. Johnny returned, his boyish face eager and his hand tightly grasping the shotgun. Joe grinned at him.

"Be careful that don't go off accidentally, Johnny," he warned. "You might hit the wrong person."

"Oh, no, I won't," Johnny promised. "When I shoot, it'll be at the one I aim t' hit. If that guy'd done any detourin' I'd o' filled him s' full o' birdshot he'd have t' get a derrick t' raise him."

Deborah laughed. "I guess the rest of us don't have to worry with you three on the job. Toby, the siren to warn and you two husky men to guard the premises. I shall go in now and sleep like a top, knowing that the marines have landed and have everything well in hand."

"Right you are, Miss." Joe grinned and slapped Johnny on the back as he stared at her, his round eyes puzzled.

"He thinks I'm a nut," Deborah smiled as she went back to the house. "And maybe I am to get mixed up in a family scrap. Just what did that Harding mean by his insinuations? How on earth am I supposed to know why Eve Fowler left Cliff House and where she went? I suppose she has gone although there are times when I feel her lurking about. I suppose it's that picture of her sister. They are alike. I wish the thing was out of there. I have a feeling the woman doesn't approve of me for some reason—though knowing her sister as she did, she should realize that Eve was a bad influence over her daughter for years and that anything is better than the care, or lack of it, she was giving her. I wish I dare suggest moving it from Nancy's room or perhaps moving the child. She lies and stares at it constantly. Some bright landscape or even a Galahad such as hung in my bedroom at home or even the Dionne quins would be much better for her. Anything but what that portrait stands for. The youngster will never forget while she has that picture to keep reminding her."

157

She wondered if Peter was sleeping. She hoped so. Poor boy, he looked completely fagged. She stood for a moment at one of the windows in her room, looking down at the densely wooded hill and on beyond at the lake, blue as lapis lazuli, smooth as glass. Polly would say a storm was brewing when everything was so still. Well, it didn't look much like a storm but one never could tell about this part of the country.

She undressed quickly. She was more tired than she had realized. It was good to lie down even if she wasn't particularly drowsy. She yawned and stretched and pulled the cool sheet close under her chin. A thought jerked her into wakefulness as she prepared to slip into unconsciousness. How had Harding known she was a trained nurse? She toyed with the question for a few moments then sleep overcame her and she knew nothing more.

CHAPTER SIXTEEN

POLLY WOKE HER. "It's near six, Debby, an' dinner'll be ready in no time. Have a good sleep? You look rested. Peter's been to bed, too. He tells me you ordered it. I'm glad of it. Poor boy! Jason asked for you to call him sometime this evenin'. That boy seems turrible cut up on account of your bein' up here at Cliff House."

"Cut up, Polly? But why should he be?" Deborah asked eyeing the old lady seated on the foot of her bed.

"Well, you see, child, he ain't got no idee you're here in a business capacity. It seems the boy fancies he's in love with you."

"Don't be ridiculous, Polly!" Deborah said and yawned and stretched like an awakening kitten. She had completely forgotten Jason.

"That's just what I told him—that he was ridiculous when he sputtered about your bein' imprisoned up here. He said he was comin' to see you one day and Johnny told him he'd better not: that they didn't encourage strangers nowadays. I told him you'd talk to him when you got up and he shouted at me 'Got up!' like he thought I was crazy. I didn't dare say anythin' for I don't know that Peter wants anyone to know Nancy's sick."

"I'll talk to Jason, Polly," Deborah promised and disappeared into the bathroom for her shower.

Polly chattered while Deborah bathed and dressed. Said there was no change in Nancy's condition that she could see. She was perfectly conscious, Polly knew, for once or twice her eyes had flickered and her mouth had twitched when she had read something comical or sang to her.

"D'you know what I think, Debby?" Polly asked after a minute in which she admired, with a pang of regret for her own lost youth, Deborah's lithe young body as it slipped into the few tiny sheer garments girls nowadays affected. "I have half a mind to speak to Peter about that picture of Marcy that's a-hangin' at the foot of Nancy's bed. I've thought of it before but now I've just about made up my mind to do somethin'. The child jest lies there and stares continual, and it ain't healthy. It must bring up mem'ries—unhappy ones—and keep remindin' her of her aunt, too. Marcy and Eve was a lot alike 'though Eve was so much older."

"Do you think Nancy loves her aunt, Polly?" Deborah asked.

"No, I don't," the old lady said emphatically. "She might have got used to her like you get used to a pack on your back, but once it's gone and you're free—why, they's nothin' like it—it's heaven! She'll get over missin' her aunt Eve quicker, too, if that picture disappears. Any suggestions as to how to go about it, Debby?"

"No, I haven't. But I can see how a constant reminder might harm Nancy and retard her recovery," Deborah said slowly. "Whose idea was it, hanging it there in the first place? It's much too large for the room—it dominates it and—oh, Polly, I just don't like it. I don't know why—perhaps it's because Eve Fowler might have posed for it. I think the best way would be to suggest moving Nancy to another room—another part of the house. Do you suppose you could work it that way?"

"I won't do any suggestin', Debby," Polly said. "I'll simply tell Peter we think Nancy's needin' a change of scene. We'll move her over to the other side where there ain't no veranda but what they call a picture window. It looks out over the village. A right nice view, too. Ready? Come on then. Mis' MacDonald is settin' with Nancy while I eat."

Deborah wore a plain wash dress. She hadn't sent for her uniforms after all. Polly said it was foolish and that it would no doubt be better if Nancy didn't know she was sick enough for a trained nurse. Peter met them at the door of the dining room and seated Polly at the head of the table. He and Deborah sat opposite each other.

They were having coffee when Polly broached the subject of moving Nancy over to the other side of the house. Peter looked surprised at first but Deborah saw approval dawn in his dark eyes and he nodded his head.

"That's an idea, Polly," he said. "She may have grown tired of her own room and moving might interest her. Shall you move her bed too, or give her a complete change, bed and all?'

"Let's change everything," Deborah suggested. "I

wonder why she hasn't a regular hospital bed—one that can be adjusted to her comfort."

"You mean one that winds up?" Peter asked.

"Doctor Barnes suggested that but, you see, Nancy can't sit up. So Eve vetoed it. Do you think it could be used to her advantage here? She has never had one, I'm sure, but if you think it best I'll order one right now."

"You can borrow one from Buford Hospital, I imagine, until you are able to have one shipped here," Deborah told him. "Any hospital will rent you a bed. They always have a surplus, you know."

"I'll do that." Peter left the table and went into his study to telephone. He was gone but a minute and returned with the information that the bed would be out within an hour.

"How did you manage that, Peter?" Polly asked, her blue eyes twinkling. "Bribery, I suppose. Money can do about everythin', seems though, don't it?"

"Oh no, it can't, Polly," Peter objected, sadly.

"But it can go a long way toward it," Deborah said. "Lack of it creates tragedy and misery in countless cases."

"I'd give all that I possess if Nancy could be like other girls—if——" He shrugged and smiled apologetically. "What's the use?"

"Well, we'll try what a change of room'll do for the child," Polly said quickly. "I'll have the bed took down and moved out of that other room and then when the hospital bed comes they won't be nothin' to do but set it up and move her right in. It's a right pretty room I think, and'll be lots more interestin' for her, too. Didn't that used to be your sister Barbara's room, Peter? I thought so," as he nodded. "If it's like it used to be it's got some right cute pictures on the wall."

"Oh, Babs chose her own pictures: her favorite heroes and scenes. I'm glad you thought of it, Polly. Babs was happy there."

"It was Debby's idee, reely," the old lady said. "I only offered to ask you about it. You see, I know you some better than what Debby does and she being just the nurse and all——"

"I see," Peter said quietly. "Then I'm glad you thought of it, Deb," he amended.

"It's my place to consider my patient, Peter," Deborah reminded him and wondered why she should feel squelched.

Mrs. MacDonald and Polly superintended the removal of the bed in Barbara Jordan's room and made ready for the hospital bed. The room was aired and fresh linen brought in and, when the truck arrived with the new bed, it was immediately set up and Peter carried his daughter carefully through the long hall and laid her down in her fresh surroundings. The girl had said little from the time she had regained consciousness and now she sighed as if she were very tired. Peter and Deborah looked down at her, so frail and white, and smiled encouragement. For a moment they thought she was going to return their smile; but instead she scowled and turned her head from them. Peter left abruptly.

Deborah busied herself about the room then sat down at the small desk to write letters. There was not a sound from the bed and, after a little, Deborah stole a glance that way and saw the wide brown eyes moving from wall to wall to rest at last on the "picture window" which filled the greater part of the east wall. The afternoon sun was reflected on the windows of houses in the village below so that they shone like jewels. Deborah was reminded of the story of the house with the golden windows and wondered if Nancy knew it. She saw the heavy lids falter at last and droop sleepily and decided to let nature have her way. Soon the child slept. Deborah finished her letters and laid them in a little pile on top of the desk to await mailing. Peter stole silently into the room shortly after nine to stand for a moment beside his daughter's bed.

"I think this is going to help, Peter," Deborah murmured comfortingly and saw his face lighten a bit.

"I hope so," was all he said before he turned and as silently departed.

Deborah liked this room. Typically a girl's room, it seemed to breathe normality and sanity. There were several very good water colors—scenes along Penguin Lake, she imagined. The popular sepia of Galahad and a really charming print of the Child Jesus. There were several photographs of a lovely young girl in her early teens, Barbara, probably, one astride a shaggy pony, one in a bathing suit of a generation ago, one in a swing, hair flying and ruffles a-swirl. Not a gloomy note in the room. Even the Child Jesus wore a happy, friendly expression as if he had not yet come to feel the burden of the sins of the world he was born to carry. Yes, Deborah told herself, it was a good room. Bright chintzes covered chairs and a chaise longue and draped the wide windows. The rug was gay with roses and the wall was a neutral tint to harmonize with everything. She was glad she had suggested the change—but most of all she was relieved to get away from the huge portrait of Marcia Jordan.

She had experienced considerably difficulty with Jason Miller. He was hurt and angry that she had shut herself away from him and could not be made to understand that she had come because Polly was staying at Cliff House. Jason had assured her there were any number of homes in Harmony open to her. His, for instance. That she didn't have to go there just because Polly went. He didn't like it and what had she to say to him? Didn't she realize how he felt?

"Please don't be like that, Jason," Deborah pleaded.

"How do you expect me to be?" he demanded. "Up there with him after all you've said——"

"Listen, Jason." Deborah's voice suddenly became icy. "You've said quite enough. I don't think I care to talk any longer."

"All right," he shouted. "I'll go with Phil, then. He's driving to the San Francisco Fair. Goodbye!"

She heard the slam of the receiver as he ceased talking. Of course she was sorry to have it end this way but perhaps it was best. She hadn't told him she was leaving Harmony herself within a week or two. There was no use in stirring up any more trouble and anyway Jason ought to realize that she was much older than he was—probably not in actual years, but in experience and in feeling. And while she liked him she positively did not love him and never could. She dismissed Jason from her mind.

With the coming of darkness the wind rose and Deborah closed one of the windows. Outside the great trees writhed and twisted. A fork of lightning threw the whole cliff into view. In that instant Deborah saw a car without lights coming up the cliff road and wondered about it. Probably campers caught in the valley and hurrying to beat the storm. She knew there was a camp settlement about a mile from Cliff House. The storm must still be a considerable distance away for it was some time before lightning showed again and then Deborah noticed the car had disappeared, probably hidden by trees which were thick all along the cliff road. She pulled the cord, closing the slats of the Venetian blind against the recurring glare of lightning.

Cliff House was too solidly built to be affected by the storm. Doors didn't bang nor rafters creak and the shutters stayed firmly put. Only the sighing of the trees and the moaning of the wind could be heard and Deborah, who loved Nature in all her moods, listened and felt her nerves tingle and her spirits soar. How she would have loved being out in this storm! She let her thoughts wander. Before she left Cliff House for Medford, she intended trying to prevail upon Peter to let Doctor Gilbert examine Nancy. If the trouble was mainly neurotic as she thought, then special baths, massage and exercise together with certain occupational therapy tending to rouse and interest her, might work wonders in her condition. She wondered just why Eve had objected to further scientific experimenting in Nancy's case. Then she swerved back to the old riddle of why Peter had submitted to Eve's arbitrary sway. Even though Eve was amazingly beautiful and possessed all a siren's wiles, after living with one siren for half a dozen unhappy years, according to Polly, how could he remain enamored of her double? Perhaps Eve had some hold on her brother-in-law. But Peter didn't seem like a man who was easily frightened, nor one whose past held a sinister secret.

Deborah brushed her hand across her forehead which was creased in a frown. No, it was just that Peter, like so many others, was completely infatuated—Eve's slave —always eager to do her bidding. What had broken the chains that bound him to her? Probably Polly. Her lip curled in disdain and she determinedly switched her thoughts to Alec Brown. Dear Alec, with his fearlessness, his spiritual integrity and his complete forgetfulness of self! She wondered if he would be glad to have her back on the North Side. She hadn't answered his last letter. She wasn't sure just when she could leave here. She wanted to be certain she had done all she could for Nancy. Polly had been so wonderful to her that she felt she owed this much to her friends.

Twelve musical notes came faintly to her from the grandfather clock in the hall below. Midnight. Deborah left her chair and drew aside the curtains of the great picture window. The storm was nearer now. Lightning flashed almost continuously; thunder muttered and crashed; the trees twisted and writhed as if trying to tear themselves from the earth that bound them. She could hear the surf pounding against the cliff and imagined the grandeur of the lake in its orgy of rage, or was it merely exuberance? With a terrific crash thunder cannonaded along the sky. The wind died to a soughing of tired exhaustion. The rain fell in torrents. Through it all Nancy slept quietly and Deborah looked at her wonderingly. Just what sort of a child was this daughter of two such unlike people? Just now she was a small replica of her father. Deborah's eyes filled and she longed to take her into her arms—to hold and comfort and will her back to health. There was a sound near the door and she turned quickly. Polly crept in.

"How're things goin', Debby?" she whispered. "Bad storm, wasn't it? Most over though."

"I loved it, Polly," Deborah said. "Nancy slept right through it all. Run back to bed, my dear. You ought to be able to sleep now."

"I ain't sleepy, Debby," the old lady said. "Somehow I feel excited—as if somethin' was happenin' or goin' to happen."

"It's the storm," Deborah told her. "It always affects me that way, too. But you'll calm down now it's over."

One of the dogs barked suddenly—a snarling, ugly bark and there was a wild yelp of pain.

"What was that?" Polly whispered. They were on the wrong side of the house and could see nothing. "That was either Remie or Rommie, I'm certain. I'm goin' to find out."

Before she reached the door, there were sounds of several shots in quick succession, or was it a car backfiring on the steep cliff road? Deborah couldn't be sure. She went to the window and stared into the night. There was pale moonlight now and lights flickered along the shrubbery. Dark shadows darted in and out among the trees. Out on the road a car raced down the hill and disappeared from view.

Polly opened the door and ran down the hall to Nancy's old rooms. One French window opening onto the veranda was wide open and she recalled getting up to close them all before the storm broke. Not much damage had been done except for huge muddy footmarks and an overturned chair. The bedroom door was ajar and she went in. The bed covers had been thrown back and the imprint of the same huge muddy feet marred the beauty of the soft gray rug. So that was it. Polly closed and locked the window again. She saw that one of the panes of glass had been neatly removed. She put out the light and returned to Deborah. Peter met her in the hall outside Nancy's door. His face was livid with rage and he was soaking wet.

"I know, Peter," Polly told him. "But it didn't work, did it? Lucky thing Debby thought of changin' Nancy's room, wasn't it? The child slept right through the whole commotion. Did you get 'em?"

"No, damn them!" Peter's voice trembled with suppressed passion.

"They left plenty of tracks in Nancy's rooms and on the porch. Can't they be traced by footprints as well as fingerprints? Mebbe they's fingerprints there, too."

"They didn't get into the house, Polly?" Peter whispered, his face fearful to look at.

"Either them or someone with an awful nerve, for they left enough mud to sink a scow," Polly told him. "Come on and see."

"Just a minute. I want to look at her," Peter muttered and Polly drew back while he softly opened the door to Nancy's room.

Deborah looked up as he peered in and shook her head

understandingly. After a moment he closed the door and followed Polly down the hall to the child's old rooms.

"Now, now!" Polly soothed as Peter stood with clenched fists and flaming eyes in the centre of Nancy's sitting room. " 'Tain't no use. It didn't happen and I don't think they's much chance of them tryin' again right soon. I'm a-wonderin' what happened to Rommie and Remie. I heard a lot of barkin' and snarlin'. Are they all right?"

"I don't know, Polly. I ran to the house at the first alarm. I was down near the road. I thought I heard a car and went down to investigate. They must have come in through the upper entrance—you know, the old road that hasn't been used in years. Anyway, that's the way they went. The car that left the front entrance had only one man in it and he didn't come into the grounds. He disappeared while Johnny and Joe were chasing the others through the garden. I saw him distinctly as he raced away. I tried to telephone, but the wires have been cut. It s Eve's work, Polly. She said she'd get Nancy. What an idiot I've been—what a blind fool! What does she expect to gain by all this? The woman's a devil, I tell you, and my child has been under her influence all these years! God forgive me—I shall never forgive myself. Yet God knows I've been decent to her. Sometimes I have thought she resented the income I have provided her and her mother since Marcia died. When Davis insisted she keep Nancy for both their sakes, one of her arguments was that it would make her feel less dependent. How could I have been so blind! Why did she do it?" he groaned again.

Polly said nothing. She knew he didn't know what he was revealing. She had had her suspicions of course but now she knew he had generously taken upon himself the added burden of supporting his mother-in-law and her remaining daughter. That explained a lot of things that had often puzzled her. She understood Eve's method of handling Peter. Her argument, backed by Davis, that by keeping her with her she was providing the mother-care Nancy so sorely needed at that time and which she had been deprived of by that unfortunate accident. And, Polly went further, supplying an added reason for Eve's wanting her niece—the possibility that it might be the means of regaining Peter's love for herself. "Mother love" was a grand combination of words and had been known to trap more than one wary male.

"Mother love!" sniffed Polly and wasn't aware she spoke aloud. But Peter hadn't heard or at least he made no comment.

CHAPTER SEVENTEEN

DEBORAH WATCHED the first rays of light touch the tip of Saint Matthew's spire. Everything looked clean and fresh and a faint breeze moved the gauzy curtains and fluttered the pages of the book in Deborah's quiet hands. The picture window looked out upon Harmony in the little valley—upon the toy houses and tiny plots of garden fresh and green in the first golden rays of the morning sun. Nancy slept on and Deborah's heart warmed to her. Flat on her back, with a small, half-open palm each side of the thin waxen face, she looked like a doll. The long dark lashes curled up at the tips and Deborah thought what havoc to masculine hearts those lashes would wreak if their hopes for the child were realized. She must strive to find the little girl hidden in that hard, unchildlike shell of misery and suspicion. She would do what she could before she went back to Medford. She somehow found it necessary to keep reminding herself that she was going back to the North Side in Medford. There were times when she knew she didn't want to go, when she wanted to live all the rest of her life right here in Harmony among these people whom she had grown to love. But she knew she must go. Peter had changed. Sometimes she felt that her brief romance with him was just a figment of her imagination. It had never really happened. Well, it was a good thing she hadn't accepted him—hadn't become engaged to him. Then it would have been something to weep and gnash her teeth over. As it was, nothing had happened and everything was just as it was when she first came to Harmony, except—— She didn't finish the sentence but left her chair to watch more closely the awakening of the village to life.

Cars darted along the streets, no doubt filled with boys and girls on their way to an early morning swim. She would like one herself—right this minute. Toby passed beneath the window and she leaned out and whistled softly to him. He waved a hand in greeting, his very blue eyes looking as clean and rain-washed as the rest of the world. One of the dogs raced to meet him and he stopped to pat his head. Which was it? Rommie or Remie? And where was his twin?

"I'm hungry," came from the bed and Deborah turned with a start.

"So am I," she smiled. "I wonder if anyone else in the whole house is awake yet. Do you suppose they are?"

"Make them get up, then. I'm hungry and thirsty, too," the querulous voice insisted.

"Well, I'll see what I can do about it," Deborah said. She rang not too optimistically for it was scarcely six o'clock. But after listening to Polly's graphic account of what had happened during the storm last night, she would not leave Nancy alone for one minute. Mrs. MacDonald answered the ring and Deborah was sorry she had brought her all the way from her room downstairs.

"Cook's getting breakfast," the housekeeper said, "and Rose didn't get much sleep last night what with the storm—and everything," she went on, looking meaningly at Deborah whose face remained blank. "Did the storm disturb you, Miss Bradley?"

"Oh no, I was awake anyway, you see, and I love a good sharp storm. There's something exciting about hearing the wind roaring with laughter at the great blustering giant, Thunder god, who really wouldn't hurt a flea. I love watching the trees waving and dancing their branches back and forth while the lightning chases the thunder just to hear him roar. It's all great fun and old Mother Nature always feels better after she has had a fine romp and scrubbed all her children clean with a good drenching downpour. Just look out this window, Mrs. MacDonald. Isn't it a morning to make you thankful you're alive?"

"I'm not thankful I'm alive," Nancy said peevishly. "I'm too hungry. Why don't you stop talking and do something?"

The housekeeper turned immediately and started for the door.

"Nancy doesn't mean to be rude, Mrs. MacDonald," Deborah apologized. "If you will stay here I'll go down and prepare her tray."

"I do too," the child insisted. "I shall be just as rude as I like and I want Mac to make breakfast for me."

"Oh, do you like being rude, Nancy? Most girls don't," Deborah said matter-of-factly.

"Most girls aren't cripples," the child snapped.

"But you're not always going to be a cripple. That is, of course, unless you like being a cripple."

Mrs. MacDonald turned startled eyes on the nurse. Deborah never turned a hair. Nancy stared at the lovely face smiling at her.

"Well, do you?" Deborah asked.

"What do you think?" The voice was a snarl and the brown eyes glowed with passion.

"I'm sure I should not like being crippled—especially in my disposition," Deborah told her, "and what's more, I should try to do something about it. I don't think I should ever give up. I'd make myself be pleasant at least five times every day and I'd smile at least seven times. I should want to ride like the lovely strong Aunt Barbara in that picture there and swim and play tennis and skate on the ice in winter, and I believe I would, too, if I made up my mind to do it; but if I couldn't, I'd make believe I could and pretend I was a seal, maybe, or a mermaid or maybe a circus rider."

"Oh, ye-ah!" sneered the girl in the bed, glaring at Deborah malevolently. "It's easy for you to talk; you're not a cripple. Get going, Mrs. Mac—I'm hungry, I tell you."

The housekeeper ducked out as if she were dodging some deadly missile. Deborah pretended not to have noticed. She went to the tiny jewel of a private bathroom and brought in a basin of water, soap and towels and proceeded to give Nancy her morning bath. The child made it as hard for her as she could by pushing her hands away and complaining bitterly that she was hungry and thirsty; that she hated everyone and that everyone hated her, especially her father. Deborah felt sure she said that last expecting a reprimand and decided to ignore it entirely.

Mrs. MacDonald knew the prescribed breakfast. She had watched Deborah fix Nancy's tray every morning since the child had been able to eat again, and Deborah felt sure everything would be satisfactory. She was tying a yellow satin bow on Nancy's shining curls when the housekeeper entered with the breakfast tray which Deborah arranged attractively on the table within reach of small hands. Then she proceeded to wind up the bed slowly and gently so that Nancy, her eyes on the tray, was entirely unaware of a change being made. Just a few inches the first day. The child took her orange juice through the usual tube and reached for her cereal which Deborah noticed she ate much more easily this morning even with the slight change in her position, than she had been doing.

"Just why," Deborah asked herself, "did Eve Fowler insist that Nancy should not have an adjustable bed?"

Nancy ate a normal breakfast and decided she wanted a book to look at. Deborah adjusted the rack for reading and found the book Nancy wanted. Mrs. MacDonald picked up the tray and prepared to leave with it, saying she would return to relieve Deborah at once.

"I can fix that bed so it will be more comfortable for you, Nancy," Deborah offered tentatively, smiling at the child.

"Oh no, you can't," the child told her. "It isn't good for me to have my head too high."

"Why not? What's the matter with your head? Most little girls of your age have their heads in the clouds half the time," Deborah smiled. "This is a magic bed. You'll see. There?" she said when she had given the crank a few more twists. "See?"

"I shall be sick now," Nancy cried. "You want to get rid of me, I know you do, so Daddy won't be bothered with me." She was working herself into hysteria and Deborah promptly lowered the bed to its original position wishing devoutly she had let well enough alone for the first day in the new room. "Darn you, Eve Fowler!" she muttered to herself as she smoothed the spotless pillow and again adjusted the book rack. "I hope you pay for this!" Aloud she said quietly;

"There's no need to get excited, Nancy. The bed is flat again and if you like it better that way all right. Only I thought you had more grit. I hoped you were like your father, strong and brave and kind." Her voice was

172

calm and even. If she longed to speak sharply, she didn't show it. "There!" she said to herself as she prepared to go downstairs to her own breakfast, "I've done my good deed for today and I hope it's given you food for thought, you poor little spoiled brat!"

Polly joined her in the bright little breakfast room directly off the kitchen and the two ate the morning meal together. Peter had gone to the village directly after Joe had driven to the nearest telephone to report the affair to the Buford police. Already strange men were examining footprints in the garden and in Nancy's suite and the pane of glass from the French window was carefully wrapped and deposited in their car. Polly had related what she knew of the affair to Deborah who shuddered anew at the thought of what might have happened if Nancy hadn't been shifted to another room.

"God watches over children and fools, Debby," the old lady said positively when she had finished her recital. "I hope none of this lurid tale'll leak out to Nancy. It ain't healthy for young'uns to know so much about evil doin's, sez I. It's bad enough for us oldsters to have to come in contact with it without passin' it on to children."

"I doubt if she will hear anything about it, Polly. But did it ever strike you that Nancy is terribly—tragically old for her years? It's pitiful."

"It's wicked, that's what 'tis. And I think they's a special hell for women like Eve Fowler." Polly's usually kind voice crackled with indignation. "Seems to me she could have spent a little time lovin' the poor young'un instead of wastin' it all on a man who don't care two buttons for her."

Peter came into the kitchen in search of Polly. He held a telegram in his hand and his eyes looked sunken in his haggard face. He held the wire out to Polly and dropped into the nearest chair with a groan, his head in his hands.

"Here, you read it, Debby, my other specs are upstairs," the old lady said, handing the paper to Deborah with a shaking hand. "Oh Lord, what now?" she moaned.

"EVELYN FOWLER INSTANTLY KILLED THIS MORN-

173

(Signed) ANNA BURTLESS."

Deborah's voice was perfectly expressionless as she read the brief message. It just couldn't be true. Someone was playing a ghastly trick on Peter—maybe Eve herself, to bring him to her.

Polly sat motionless, her face a gray mask. "Peter," she said at last, "you sure? This ain't another trick, is it?"

"No. It's true all right. Bob Nellis at the Post Office said Wilton had been trying to reach me by telephone but that something was wrong—Central couldn't make connections. I had an idea Eve and her mother hadn't gone back to Boston. They must have taken rooms in a summer hotel in Wilton which is only about forty miles away. The wire came after Wilton failed to get through by telephone. I guess that's the way it was. I don't know. It is all so horrible—so useless—so unnecessary! I'll have to go at once. Joe is having an extra guard around the house tonight so you need have no fear. They will be up to fix the telephone right away." He rose and started to leave the room.

Deborah wanted to ask how it happened but couldn't bring herself to speak. She was unutterably shocked. Polly asked shakily if there were any particulars and Peter told her he knew only what the telegram said. He was driving to Wilton at once.

After he had left the room, the two at the table stared at each other unable to speak for a long moment. Deborah's face was white, her eyes enormous. Polly looked old and strangely shrunken.

"I wasn't goin' to say I was sorry, Debby," she said, her voice quavering, "for 'twould have been a lie. I ain't sorry—not reely. It just had to be that way. Eve Fowler didn't care how much sorrow and mis'ry she handed out to Peter, nor how she ruined that poor helpless young'un upstairs there. He called her a devil last night and that's just what she was."

Deborah was too stunned to take in Polly's disclosures.

Polly went on: "I ain't hated her all these years without a mighty good reason, Debby. You can bank on that. I always felt that because she hated Marcy for marryin' Peter, she took revenge on Marcy's child."

"Oh, no, Sally. No sane woman could be as fiendish as that."

"Sane? I don't think she was sane, Debby, and that's the most charitable thing I can say about her."

Deborah went to bed and tried to sleep but found it quite impossible. She dressed and went down to the garden to talk to Toby. Romulus was quite badly hurt but the veterinary was confident he would recover although he would always be a little lame. But he had put up a game fight. If only Johnny could have reached him in time the rascals wouldn't have escaped. But Johnny was watching the front of the house and Joe hadn't been quick enough for them. However, they hadn't accomplished their fiendish purpose. Toby was surprised to hear they had climbed to the upper veranda and entered the child's bedroom.

"How did you know that, Toby?" Deborah asked in surprise.

"Mr. Peter told me about it. He said you had just moved the child to another room. That was God's mercy, Miss. Why did you happen to think of it?"

"I don't know," Deborah murmured although she knew the reason. But now she felt grateful to Marcia. She felt sure she would never again dislike her portrait. If she hadn't resented the pictured face of Nancy's mother staring with what she felt was supercilious disapproval down at her from the wall of the nursery, Nancy might have been killed—mentally injured at least. She determined to visit the room and pay silent tribute to Nancy's mother.

"It was strange, Toby," she said after a moment in which conflicting thoughts raced through her head, "but I had a feeling that a change might do Nancy good. At least it has done her no harm and it did probably save her a nasty shock."

"I'm glad you're here, Miss Bradley." Toby's blue eyes looked searchingly into her gray ones. "Cliff House ain't been a 'specially happy place lately. I mind when Cliff House was the merriest place in these parts. Boys and girls flocking in here—dances and parties and dinners. That's when the old folks was here and Mr. Peter was in school—before he got married. Mr. Peter's changed a lot, Miss. He ain't the happy-go-lucky boy he once was."

"Life has a way of sobering us, Toby," Deborah said seriously.

"Don't it though, Miss?" Toby agreed.

Deborah walked on. She ought to have put on rubbers for the grass was very wet: but no matter, she would slip into bed as soon as she walked herself tired. Toby called to her as she turned back.

"Mr. Peter told me about the accident, Miss. It was a terrible thing, of course; but I can't help feeling that the world is a wee bit better with one hate less. Hate poisons everything it touches. I shan't profess to mourn her, Miss, for I believe 'twas the Lord's will."

"I know," Deborah murmured, "and life is far too short to spend one tiny part of it in hating, which after all is a boomerang with the hater suffering most."

"Ain't it so, Miss?" Toby muttered, squatting down beside one of his roses. "Curses like chickens come home to roost. Cliff House will be happier after this—you'll see."

Deborah went back to the house and up to her room. She undressed quickly and got into bed. Toby, too, thought of Eve as the embodiment of evil just as Polly did. She had always heard that the dividing wall between the two great passions, love and hate, was so thin that often the one was mistaken for the other and that love could change to hate in the twinkling of an eye. If that were true, then perhaps it was hate that dominated Eve Fowler and not love as so many of them thought. Paul had spoken of it on that day they had lunched with Nancy——"Hell hath no fury like a woman scorned." She hadn't understood why he should say that. She shivered as if a sudden chill had crept into the sunny day. Poor Eve! Beautiful, wealthy, young—what a waste of splendid womanhood, sacrificed on the altar of hate! Poor Eve, to have missed so much!

On the edge of slumber, Deborah suddenly remembered something she must do. She slipped into a robe and mules and went quickly through the hall to Nancy's old suite. The rooms had just been cleaned for there was now no evidence of the intruders of last night. She went into the nursery and directly to the portrait of Nancy's mother. Was it her imagination or did those painted lips seem to smile? Deborah gazed intently and wondered just why she had thought the face anything but lovely. The blue eyes held the faintest trace of amusement as if the girl pictured there was wondering why all the fuss and bother when it was all so quickly over.

"I don't dislike you, Marcia Jordan," Deborah whispered whimsically; "it was just that you didn't seem to understand, but you do now. I see that you do."

What it was the girl smiling down from the wall didn't understand Deborah didn't say, for she turned and hurried back to her room and fell asleep at once.

CHAPTER EIGHTEEN

TOBY WREN'S predictions proved true for Cliff House seemed to brighten. Something sinister that had lurked about the place, dampening and subduing every happy thought, every spontaneous delight, vanished and Cliff House and its occupants breathed easier. An alert guard was still kept about the place, however, in spite of Toby's assertion there was no longer any need.

To the general public, Peter gave an expurgated account of the accident that had taken Eve Fowler's life and that of Lansing Scott, Nancy's tutor. Perhaps Polly was the only one to whom he talked freely. Anna Burtless, maid and close confidante of both Eve and her mother, told of Eve's rage at the failure of her plans to have Nancy brought to her by Scott and his henchmen. In a mad frenzy, she had vowed to accomplish that which her hirelings had bungled. All Scott's entreaties, her mother's pleadings and Anna's warnings failed to swerve her from her purpose. She and Scott started. Eve appeared insane. No doubt she was insane. Half an hour later, word reached them that one of the front tires of her powerful car had blown out, sending the machine down a steep embankment where it was completely demolished and both its occupants instantly killed.

Polly shook her white head. "Young Scott seemed such a nice boy, too," she murmured.

"He was. But he was Eve's slave. Anna said that when Eve refused to give up her scheme, Scotty insisted that he be the one to carry Nancy. She knew him and wouldn't be frightened and he would be gentle with her. Do you know, Polly, I'm glad Scotty's dead? It would have gone hard with him otherwise."

"How about the others?" Polly asked. "They must have been four or five at least."

"Three, we think. Anna didn't know anything about them. Scotty's the only one we positively know anything about and he's gone. You know, Polly, I thought of Scott when we found Nancy's rooms had been entered. I felt sure that someone familiar with the place must have been involved."

"How's Mis' Fowler?" Polly inquired.

"Bad. She's had quite a severe paralytic shock and has two nurses besides Anna. She was still unconscious when I came away. She may recover—partially—but the doctors hold out little hope. Polly," Peter went on after a pause in which he stared bleakly into space, "the misery and tragedy that girl has caused! I've suspected for more than a month that her influence over Nancy was bad. Oh, I know you told me it was, all along, but you never liked her. However, on the day she left Cliff House, she called me a poor blind fool. She said she had always hated me—hated her sister for marrying me—hated our nasty little brat. She swore to get her back if it was the last thing she ever did and she'd ruin me into the bargain. I knew she was angry; that she probably didn't mean nor even know what she was saying; but I still refused to let Nancy go with her. She was like a mad woman— like a devil! And yet as she lay asleep, surrounded by veritable mountains of flowers, she looked like an angel of light. How could I know this would happen?"

"You couldn't, Peter," Polly assured him. "The girl was crazy—no doubt born with a screw loose some'ers. No sane person would have done the things she persisted in doin', and Peter, it's God's mercy she went like she did or lord knows what mischief she'd have brought about before she fin'ly died. Don't you worry, Peter; you done your best—a thousand times more'n what any other man in your shoes would have done. Forget it and her. You can be happy now. It's like losin' a heavy burden or like sunshine after a long, rainy spell. Life'll be sweeter from now on, you'll see."

Harmony had been terribly upset when word of the attempted snatch leaked out. The older folk shook their heads and wondered who would have dared attempt such a dastardly crime. They murmured sententiously that "trouble never comes singly" when news reached them, at almost the same instant, of Eve Fowler's tragic passing. They seemed more shocked at the untimely taking off of young Lansing Scott who had seemed such a likable chap and played a smashing game of tennis. They were philosophical about it, however, for they had never considered Peter Jordan's handsome sister-in-law as one of them and, of course, young Scott was just a summer

179

visitor. Only the youthful element regretted the untimely death of a woman physically so beautiful, and thought it quite romantic that Lansing Scott had died with her.

Deborah received a long letter from Alice full of affection and crammed with news. She passed lightly over Eve's death. Scott she didn't know even by reputation and thought if he had been enamored of Eve, he was merely running true to form. All men fell for a pretty face. Neither Deborah nor Polly had mentioned young Scott's connection with the attempted kidnapping, so he was just a name to Alice. There were much more interesting and important things to write about to Alice's way of thinking. The first was a profound secret and Deb must promise not to mention it to a soul. Alice had received a letter from Oliver Cromwell Turner apologizing for his haste in leaving her at that last meeting and offering to help her with her novel. Not collaborate, Deb must understand, but give her the benefit of his wider experience. She had sent him the first draft of her novel and was anxiously awaiting his reactions. She had slaved night and day on it and felt sure it wasn't hopeless and with the services of such a well-known, brilliant novelist as O.C.T., why, she was practically made. Now, at last, Paul began to take her seriously Oo-la-la-la! What a time she had had with him!

"I know whom I have to thank for this wonderful break, darling," she wrote. "Having met the famous Oliver, I am confident pressure was brought to bear in order to make him unbend. But he, too, swore me to secrecy, so mum's the word, old dear.

"Paul and I went out to celebrate our second anniversary (months, you know) last Wednesday night and whom do you suppose we ran smack into at the Cosmopolitan? He sat at the very next table to ours and we visited back and forth. Alec Brown, no less, and with him was a girl named Phyllis Carter. Do you know her? She's a P.H. Nurse. She's pretty—a little like you. And isn't it a strange coincidence that she should have your old job on the North Side? But she told me on the q.t. that she's not very keen about it. I have a hunch it's Alec who's the attraction and not the dirty dozen or two or three who dwell over there. The great unwashed make no appeal to her maternal instinct as they did to yours, my dear.

"Alec seemed quite impressed, however, and she is attractive, I'll grant that. He asked what we had heard from you and I told him you were having a grand time and that if you ever came back to Medford it would be over the dead bodies of some forty admirers not to mention Aunt Polly. I've heard since that he's really keen about this Phyllis girl. When I heard it I was darned glad your heart interest was elsewhere.

"Aunt Polly's letter was full of your exciting time at Cliff House. You always were the luckiest thing in the world, Deb. Why couldn't I have been on the spot? I, with my nose for news and my itching fingers to put that news on paper. Paul's still crowing over me that he saw through the glamorous Eve and insists she's back of the kidnapping attempt. Don't tell Peter this, though, and why not wake up, darling, and make hay while the old sun shines?"

There were pages of like nonsense and Deborah tossed the letter aside and wondered bitterly if she wasn't needed in Medford any longer. So her place had been filled, had it? Not only on the North Side but in Alec Brown's friendship as well. The world was a fickle place. But perhaps Doctor Hamilton could use her still. He had called her his greatest success. But did he mean it? Anyway, she had said she would go back and now she must. There was no help for it.

Polly was still spending most of her time at Cliff House although Deborah suggested getting in two trained nurses to fill the places she and Polly would leave vacant when they returned to take up their own lives. Peter told her that new nurses would be forthcoming in due time. Nancy was getting used to Deborah although Deborah now doubted if she would ever trust and love her. If she did it would take time and that was one thing Deborah lacked—time for Cliff House.

Before she should leave, however, Deborah succeeded in inducing Nancy to let Doctor Gilbert come up to Cliff House and prove her right in her contentions that Nancy could learn to walk, run and even dance and be like other girls. It was a struggle and required every bit of tact, strength, grace and courage that Deborah possessed to bring it about. And when Deborah told Peter that Nancy had consented to let Doctor Gilbert look her over, the man gasped in surprise.

"Don't you see, Deb?" he cried. "Don't you understand that you are what Nancy needs? You have done more for her in the few weeks you have been here than all the others put together in four years. Can't you see that this is your job?"

But Deborah shook her head. "No, Peter," she replied, her gray eyes serious. "Nancy has everything that money, a loving father and devoted servants can provide—every advantage known to science. My North Side people have nothing except what we at the Centre can give them. Don't you see, Peter, that I have to go back? I've got to take the hard road. It is what I trained to do and what I must do, I'm a Public Health Nurse." Her head had lifted and her gray eyes seemed to the man before her to glow as no doubt the eyes of the crusaders glowed centuries ago. "Our slogan is 'brave living,' Peter. I feel sure Nancy will improve under different treatment—treatment that Doctor Gilbert will indicate and that any trained nurse he will recommend can give."

"I see," Peter's face clouded. "Of course it is for you to decide. I am sure I have no wish to influence you— to impose further on your kindness."

Deborah watched his tall, white clad figure until a closed door hid it from view. She turned blindly into a shady path, her heart beating hard. She suddenly hated the idea of any other nurse taking charge of Nancy, quieting her terrors, soothing her sudden fits of passion, laughing with her on those rare occasions when the child's latent sense of humor crept to the surface, and trying, oh, so slowly, to change her deep-seated fear and hatred of her father. She shrugged her shoulders and frowned.

"Don't be a complete idiot, Deborah Bradley!" she mentally scourged herself. "Peter Jordan cares nothing for you—any more, if he ever really did care. He has shown it in countless ways. Have you no pride, girl? Better get away while you can or Peter will want you to marry him so that Nancy can have a mother to help her. I could quite easily learn to love the child—maybe I do even now—a little, but I refuse to be married for the sole purpose of mothering another woman's daughter."

She tried to recall if Peter had ever told her that he loved her. He had kissed her. Even yet Deborah could feel the pressure of his lips. But even when he had asked her to be his wife—away back there before Eve appeared —love was not mentioned. Perhaps he had taken it for granted, but what girl is satisfied with that sort of proposal? No, she doubted if Peter had ever loved her and was certain that he did not now. Maybe if the truth were told, he even disliked her a little for ever considering him weak and vacillating.

"I shall leave directly Doctor Gilbert has given his opinion and recommended a trained nurse to take my place," she told herself. "I'm definitely retiring from the picture."

Doctor Gilbert, a big, raw-boned, rather ugly man, arrived two days later. Deborah had known him but slightly and if he remembered her at all, he gave no sign that he did. Nancy made the examination as difficult as possible. Polly urged Peter to keep out of the way but he insisted on staying close at hand. Perhaps he might be needed. But he wasn't. The doctor knew all about cases such as Nancy's and he confirmed Deborah's suspicions that Nancy's trouble was wholly neurotic—a neurosis brought on by shock but fostered, encouraged and pampered until it had become a fixation.

"This is a case where patience, courage and faith are needed, Nurse," Doctor Gilbert told Deborah. "Yes, and a sense of humor. I understand the child is motherless. Well, it will be your privilege to know pain and travail that this child may experience a rebirth. You must literally will her to use her legs; to sit up alone: to walk step by step, to swim, to dance and run. Mr. Jordan tells me you have done wonders already. I am glad to know that, for you are undoubtedly the proper one for the job. Let me congratulate you, Miss—er—thank you—Bradley, you will find yourself well repaid for the long hours of effort that will be necessary to bring about this miracle. I'll keep in touch with you and run up from time to time."

"But, Doctor Gilbert," Deborah began breathlessly. She had been swept along so fast that she was way beyond her depth. "You don't understand. You see, I am not the permanent nurse. I am a Public Health Nurse. My district is or was the North Side in Medford and I am going back there just as soon as another nurse can be brought here."

"What did you say your name is?" the doctor asked, looking at her closely.

"Bradley. Deborah Mary Bradley, Doctor Gilbert, and I——"

"I know you now. Stupid of me, I'm sure. You're the little nurse—the heroine of the Fernald Street tenement fire. Well, well, well, let me shake your hand." He pumped it up and down, smiling benignly at her from his superior height. "So you want to go back there and take some more risks, eh? Can't say that I blame you exactly—ours is a business that's chuck full of risks." He laughed suddenly, crinkling his eyes, throwing back his head and opening his mouth in a great guffaw. "I said that once and a man caught me up with the remark that it was a risky business all right—for the patient, and dammit, Nurse, I think the fellow meant it! But about this case here. Do you really feel right about leaving just now?" He looked keenly at her again, and Deborah nodded her head. "Of course you know your own business better than anyone else, my dear. I'll look over the nurses I know best and send one up to relieve you soon after I get back. We shall be glad to have you in Medford again. They're short-handed at the Center, Hamilton tells me."

The die was cast, now. Deborah felt that she had burned her bridges. She must tell Peter that everything was settled and that Doctor Gilbert was sending up a new nurse to take her place. But somehow she couldn't find the opportune moment for her disclosure that day. Peter appeared to be avoiding her. The rare glimpses she caught of him showed him wrapped in gloom. Yet why should he feel sad when his daughter was definitely out of danger and would some day be well and strong like other girls?

Polly was quite unlike herself, too. She talked about

the new nurse who was to supplant Deborah and wondered if she was going to like her. She hoped she would be pretty for she felt Nancy needed a pretty girl near her, and it must be definitely understood that the new nurse must be young and able to laugh a lot. There had been far too much unhappiness in Nancy's short life as it was. Perhaps they might be able to get one who sang and played some instrument like a guitar or a banjo— something that would make a gay accompaniment. Of course, in the fall, Peter intended hiring a governess and he had promised she, too, should be pretty. Polly laughed excitedly.

"Cliff House'll wake up, Debby. It'll laugh again and all the old ghosts that have haunted the place for the past few years will pack up their duds and skidaddle. By the time Nancy's up and around she won't know the place for the gloomy old barracks it has been. Maybe some time durin' the winter or next spring you can run up to Harmony and visit us and see all the changes that've happened. We'll show you somethin' all right."

It went on that way for two days and Deborah grew more and more unhappy. No new nurse appeared and, perversely, Deborah was glad of it. Toby was the only one in the place who appeared at all normal and even he spoke about the difference new life would make in the place. He showed her the Priscilla Jordan rose bush, flourishing apparently, but without a single blossom.

"What happened to them all, Toby?" Deborah asked, surprised that the blooming was over so early. Other bushes still bore profusely but the rose named for the first mistress of Cliff House was without a bud.

"Blight, Miss," Toby said sadly. "Some pesky worm got into its heart and after the first batch, not a rose was perfect. So I cut 'em all and I'm doctoring it. It did that once before—years ago before my time, Mr. Peter told me. So's I wouldn't feel s'bad, I've a notion," he smiled at her, his blue eyes bright and knowing.

"Oh, I hope it will be all right," Deborah said. "It is such a lovely thing!"

"When you aim on going, Miss?" he asked after a minute in which he snipped off a withered leaf or two. "You're leaving us at the very nicest time o' the year.

September's the prettiest month, I think, unless it's
October when the leaves are turning and the chrysanthemums are at their best—we have late roses, too. Novem-
ber's nice. It's then we put everything to bed for the
winter, but I think I love December most of all, when
the brave old firs are about the only green thing anywhere around and the lake is covered with ice and everything's so clean and white. January's pretty and so's
February when we begin to look for the first flowers
under the snow and listen for the wild geese to come
back and maybe catch a glimpse of an early robin or a
bluebird. March is grand and we have a hard time trying to keep things from dancing away from sheer joy.
April's here before we scarcely know it. The showers
work with me and the sun and we're busy from sunup
to sundown getting our children uncovered and awake
for another year. You been here in May, June, July and
part of August—I wish you could see the other months,
too. You'd get to love Cliff House like the rest of us
do, if you did."

"But I love it now, Toby," Deborah insisted. "Don't
think I'm leaving because I don't like it here. I'm leaving because I must. I—I have a job, you see, and I
must get back to it."

"But you've got a job here, ain't you? I don't see
what's the difference whether it's here or in some other
place. If it's a job and you can do it right, it's your job,
ain't it?"

"Maybe, but—— Oh, you just don't understand,
Toby," the girl cried and turned away.

"Maybe I understand more than you think I do," he
muttered as he watched Deborah's flying feet.

"I'll leave tomorrow," Deborah told herself angrily.
"I—I can't stand it!" She burst into the house and
was halfway up the stairs when Polly called to her.

"Debby, will you go down home and get the Methodist cook book out of the second draw' in the kitchen
cab'net? Peter feels like one o' my choc'let cakes and
for the life of me I can't recall the exact rules. You
better leave your car at Tilden's for a complete goin'
over if you're plannin' on goin' back to Medford in a
day or two. You might sort of cheer Kitchener up a

186

mite, too, if you got time. I guess the poor thing's pretty lonesome with me up here most all day. Mis' Norman's been right neighborly, but Kitchener's sort of partial, you know. I'd go myself only Mis' MacDonald wants me to help her look over the wool blankets. I ain't in no hurry, so take your time, Debby."

"But who is staying with Nancy, Polly?" Deborah asked.

"Peter's got a new picture book, showin' dogs and horses and what-not. Seems Doctor Gilbert sent it up to him this mornin' and he thought Nancy might like it. Evidently she does for I heard her a-squealin' over a cunnin' little pony as I came out a minute ago. So you run along—it'll do you good."

Deborah turned the key and entered the hall of the house where she had spent so many happy hours. Lord Kitchener hurried in from the kitchen and grunted delightedly at seeing her. If it had been possible for him to gambol, Deborah was sure he would have gamboled to show his joy: as it was, he grinned and sniffed her ankles and Deborah sat down on the shining stairs and hugged him to her.

"You dear old thing!" she whispered. "You love me, don't you? You haven't changed. Oh, I wish I had never come here!" She buried her face in the dog's well-padded neck and wept. Gentleman that he was, Lord Kitchener stood perfectly still, undoubtedly understanding her woe and sympathizing with it. But he could not repress a grunt of discomfort as he felt a dampness, not altogether agreeable, in the spot where Deborah's cheek rested. The girl laughed shakily. "Don't mind me, darling," she whispered, wiping her eyes. "I'm just a weak fool, crying for the moon. I'll feel better now. It's been dammed up for days and simply had to break loose."

The dog followed her to the immaculate kitchen where she began a systematic search for the Methodist cook book desired by Polly, for the second drawer of the kitchen cabinet disclosed no cook book either Methodist, Presbyterian or Episcopalian. Nothing but carefully folded dish towels reposed in the second cabinet drawer. The first drawer held wax paper, rubber bands, clips and a box of thumb tacks. The third drawer proved to be a flour bin. On the other side was sugar and below it jars containing staples such as rice, cereals, etc. The small middle drawers contained kitchen cutlery and the one below held a hammer, screw driver, can opener and other like tools. Deborah looked around the kitchen, searching for a likely place for a cook book whether of Methodist or other persuasion. She would examine the cupboards. Now that she was here she intended finding it. Her car would not be done for two hours at least so she had nothing better to do than try to find Polly's cook book.

It was not on any of the lower shelves, that was certain. She set up the small stepladder and mounted a step in order to get a clear view of the fourth shelf.

"Let me get what you need, Deb," a voice said softly. "Peter!" Deborah cried and sat down abruptly.

"You've been crying!" he accused, and Deborah's face flamed, but he went on; "Why have you been avoiding me?"

"I, Peter? I avoid you?" the girl stammered. "But I haven't. It's you—you—I wanted to tell you——"

"What? That you can't stand me or my home any longer? That you are fed up with the whole Jordan tribe and their troubles?"

"You know that's not the reason, Peter. You know I love it here—that I already love Nancy but——"

"But you don't love Nancy's father, is that it, Deb?" he interrupted. "I know I'm not a Galahad, Deb," he went on. "I'm just a slow sort of chap who will never do anything either very heroic or spectacular, but I love you with every ounce of my being, Deborah, and I would spend my life trying to make and keep you happy."

Deborah sat and stared at him with wide-open incredulous gray eyes. Her color came and went as her heart misbehaved alarmingly and in a way that made it impossible for her to either speak or move. What was the matter with her, anyway? Her tongue was paralyzed;

188

only her eyes seemed capable of answering and then even they shamed and betrayed her by brimming over with tears. And she had told Peter that tears were the oldest trick in the world! Her head drooped and she bit her lips to still their sudden trembling.

Peter took a step forward and laid a comforting hand on her shoulder.

"Never mind, darling," he said huskily. "I think I understand. Is it the Doctor, Deb? Your Doctor Brown?"

"He isn't my Doctor Brown, Peter Jordan!" Deborah cried, suddenly finding her tongue. "Don't you call him that, and why haven't you told me this before? Even— even months ago when you asked me to marry you you never mentioned love—I distinctly remember that you never said one word about loving me and—I—I thought ——"

What she thought didn't come to light then nor for some time after for she found herself in Peter's arms, her face buried in his dear comforting shoulder, and thoughts didn't matter—nothing mattered except that they loved each other and all eternity was not long enough in which to prove the depth of that love.

The shadows lengthened in Polly's immaculate kitchen. Lord Kitchener snored contentedly in his corner and still Peter and Deborah sat and murmured of this miracle that had come to them. It was the telephone that brought them back to something like normalcy and Deborah jumped to her feet with an exclamation of surprise.

"That's the garage. My car must be finished." She fled down the hall to the telephone stand. Peter followed more slowly and after a minute she turned a startled face toward him. "Mr. Tilden says that Mrs. Quick—Polly— asked them to send someone out with my car right after I left it there but that if they get it the first thing in the morning I can have it by noon tomorrow. I don't understand, Peter."

"Don't you, darling?" Peter laughed happily. "Can't you see Polly's gentle hand in this? Did you find the Methodist cook book she sent you for?"

Deborah replaced the telephone and laughed back shakily. "I forgot all about it, but it wasn't in the second drawer of the cabinet, Peter."

"I wonder if there is such a book," Peter said. "Polly has always jeered at housekeepers who are slaves to cook books. I never supposed she used one of the things and I bet she doesn't. She sent me for it, too. 'Debby loves eclairs!' she assured me so you must have them before you left. What was the culinary marvel I was supposed to yearn for—chocolate cake, I'll bet a cooky, wasn't it? It was for me you were getting the book, wasn't it? You see, I know Polly's little ways. Of course when I thought you hankered after eclairs, I flew right down here." They laughed joyously.

"The precious old matchmaker!" Deborah said, her gray eyes tender. "Do you realize how she adores you, Peter?"

"And she adores you, too, my dear. I wish you could have heard the dressing down she gave me after you went to bed this morning. 'Yellow,' she called me. 'Jellyfish,' afraid of my shadow, afraid to tell a girl I loved her. Wow!"

"How dared she say such things about you, Peter?" Deborah demanded. "Is that why you came, darling?" she asked demurely.

"That's one of the reasons. You see, I was afraid you didn't care—you never said you did—never hinted that you did, and there was this Brown fellow—such a courageous chap, devoting his life to brave living——"

"Don't, Peter," Deborah whispered. "I know how brave you've been—how chivalrous and dear. Don't rub it in. You reminded me once that brave living wasn't necessarily dangerous living and that 'they also serve who only stand and wait.' I know, darling. It will be a

190

waiting game for us until Nancy is well and strong again. But it won't be hard or tiresome for we'll serve and wait together."

"Together!" repeated Peter, his arms holding her close. "What a blessed word that is!"

THE END

www.ingramcontent.com/pod-product-compliance
Lightning Source LLC
Chambersburg PA
CBHW020635180626
46816CB00003B/982